OWL RIDERS

A Novel of the Clockwork Legion

DAVID LEE SUMMERS

Hadrosaur Productions, Mesilla Park, NM

Owl Riders
Hadrosaur Productions
Second Edition: May 2022.

First date of publication: April 2018

ISBN-13: 979-8-9851120-3-0

Hadrosaur Productions
P.O. Box 2194
Mesilla Park, NM 88047-2194
www.hadrosaur.com

Praise for
THE CLOCKWORK LEGION SERIES

"*Owl Dance* has everything. Airships, owl-ornithopters, a clock-work wolf, a multiple alien entity, a fast-shooting sheriff, a Russian plot to conquer America, and a very sexy, eco-aware, Bahá'í Persian healer-woman – **I mean** *everything!* **Heaps of fun!**" Richard Harland, author of *Worldshaker* and *Liberator*

"David Lee Summers is a talented spinner of pseudo-science adventures with nary a vampire or zombie in sight … it's great fun to read and well worth the time spent doing so. Don't miss it!" Neal Wilgus, *Small Press Review*

"Airships battling! Samurai fomenting war with Russia! Historical characters and powerfully drawn fictional ones mixing it up with political intrigues make David Lee Summers' *The Brazen Shark* a steampunk novel not to be missed. Put it at the top of your reading list. Now!" Robert E. Vardeman, author of *Gateway to Rust and Ruin*

Other Books by David Lee Summers

The Solar Sea
The Astronomer's Crypt

The Space Pirates' Legacy Series
Firebrandt's Legacy
The Pirates of Sufiro
Children of the Old Stars
Heirs of the New Earth

The Clockwork Legion Series
Owl Dance
Lightning Wolves
The Brazen Shark
Owl Riders

The Scarlet Order Vampires Series
Dragon's Fall: Rise of the Scarlet Order Vampires
Vampires of the Scarlet Order

To my brother, Dale Summers.
Turning on *Star Trek* when I was young and impressionable
turned me on to a whole world of speculative fiction.

ACKNOWLEDGEMENTS

Owl Riders sprang from a question by Douglas Empringham, who wanted to know more about the man Fatemeh Karimi had been betrothed to.

Thanks to my brother, Dean Summers, for introducing me to the works of Lafcadio Hearn. I've been a big fan ever since and even made a pilgrimage to his house and the location of his office in New Orleans.

Eric Schumacher has played both Wyatt Earp and Doc Holliday on film. I appreciate his insights into those historical figures, which helped to shape how they're portrayed in this novel.

Many thanks to Marita Woywod Crandle of Boutique du Vampyre in New Orleans who has hosted book signings for me in the French Quarter and who sent me on a pilgrimage to the New Orleans Pharmacy Museum.

Thanks to Jeff Lewis, Kumie Wise, Doug Williams, and Autumn Summers who all read early drafts of this novel and gave me valuable feedback that made it stronger. Autumn also served as a valuable consultant on Japanese culture, and patiently followed me through New Orleans' French Quarter and adjoining neighborhoods as I walked in the steps of Ramon, Fatemeh, and Alethea.

Also, thanks to Manny Frishberg for working with me to polish this manuscript. His keen insights have helped assure that I'm telling the story I want to tell in the most effective way possible.

This book was created with the generous support of my Patreon supporters. Among them are Robert E. Vardeman, John D. Payne, Anthony D. Cardno, the Creative Play and Podcast Network, and Madame Askew and the Grand Arbiter. I'm pleased to have received their support and comments through the process of revisiting and updating the Clockwork Legion Series.

OWL RIDERS

CHAPTER ONE
BATTLE WAGONS

A scout whistled a warning.

Lozen's eyes flew open and she sat up, looking around for Dahteste. She remembered her companion remained behind at Fort Bowie. She tossed the blanket aside, threw on boots, grabbed a pair of binoculars, and scrambled from her wickiup into the chill spring morning air to see warriors already scrambling toward the battle wagons. The wagons rumbled to life like giant beasts as the warriors stoked fires in their boilers. A young chieftain named Naiche called to his riflemen to take positions then tied on a bright, red headband. Lozen lifted binoculars and scanned the horizon.

On her second sweep, she spotted dark forms bobbing near the rising sun. Once again, General Miles sent his mechanical birds to dislodge the Tsokanende—the people the white men called Chiricahua Apache—from the lands they'd claimed in Southern Arizona. She counted three of the so-called ornithopters. Lozen lowered the binoculars, then calmed her mind, preparing for the coming ordeal.

The battle wagons, which resembled small locomotives with cannons on top, coughed up smoke and rumbled forward. Unlike locomotives, these battle wagons required no rail to move. Instead, they rolled along the ground on continuous-track treads. The riflemen opened up a path for the wagons.

The original wagon hadn't been built for battle at all. Instead, it drilled into nearby mountains. Cattle rustlers armed with a gun that threw lightning bolts had stolen the machine hoping to wipe out Geronimo and his warriors at their camp in the nearby Dragoon Mountains.

Fortunately for the Tsokanende, the army had wanted the lightning gun back.

1

The army defeated the rustlers and then left. They had a bigger problem than "Apache troublemakers." Soldiers from a country called Russia had invaded the Pacific Northwest. When the U.S. Army left to fight the Russians, they also left the rugged mining machine behind.

Geronimo used his contacts in Mexico to find machinists willing to build battle wagons based on the mining machine. In exchange, they received rights to mine Tsokanende lands. The Mexican government turned a blind eye to these activities, but Lozen had heard the Rurales—the Mexican rural police force—were glad to see a buffer between the United States and Mexico. Cowboy raids on Mexican ranches had diminished considerably.

The original mining machine had a drill at the front. That had been removed to give the drivers better visibility, and the decreased weight allowed a large cannon to be mounted atop the machine. Because they had treads instead of wheels, they could traverse almost any terrain. This would have put the Tsokanende at a considerable advantage, except the army had an ace in the hole—the flying machines.

Spotters called out targets and the gunners aimed the battle wagons' cannons. A great roar echoed across the landscape as the weapons fired. One of the army's mechanical birds crumpled and tumbled end over end, crashing into the earth just ahead of the battle wagons.

Lightning bolts flew from the two remaining mechanical birds. One scorched the earth near a battle wagon. Another scored a direct hit. Lozen gritted her teeth. If the men inside weren't dead, they would be burned and maybe unconscious. The metal machines conducted the lightning guns' electricity all too well.

Naiche directed two warriors to inspect the stricken battle wagon then shouted an order to his riflemen. They took aim and fired at the remaining mechanical birds as they passed overhead, ripping several holes in the cloth fabric. Both birds flapped harder, attempting to gain altitude as they continued forward. Naiche's men reloaded. The active battle wagon lumbered forward, and turned in a wide arc to face the mechanical birds which had nearly reached the village.

Lozen sent runners to the camp. Bombs dropped from the birds as women and children fled the wickiups. She threw herself to the ground.

A fireball erupted from the building where they stored the munitions and gunpowder. The shock wave leveled several wickiups and hurled rocks and debris into the air. Lozen struggled to her knees and spat out dirt. Several Tsokanende lay on the ground, wounded or dead. She wiped angry tears away as the mechanical bird whirled around for another pass.

Naiche shouted orders to his men, who took aim and fired again. The range had increased but a warrior got lucky and hit a mechanical bird's wing control cable. No matter how hard its pilot tried, he could not keep the craft airborne. It plummeted to the ground, throwing up dust and mesquite. When the dust settled, it lay still, in a broken heap.

The final bird flew on, firing a lightning bolt as it passed the battle wagons. However, from the greater height, its accuracy diminished. It scorched the earth just behind one of the wagons, then continued back the way it came. The battle wagon fired at the retreating bird, but missed. The warriors yelled and whooped, shaking rifles and fists at the ornithopter as it set course for Tucson.

Lozen didn't yell, instead cold fury gripped her heart as she watched the bird retreat. Once convinced it wouldn't turn around for another strike, she turned her attention to the village. She called to Naiche's riflemen, instructing them to douse the flames before they spread.

Although losing the gunpowder and munitions stung, they kept most of their armaments at Fort Bowie to the east and Lozen could always bring more.

Around the village, women and children now stood and moved about, helping to extinguish the fires and picking up debris. It seemed most had escaped and found cover. Nearby, though, a toddler screamed at his mother who didn't move. Shrapnel had punctured her back and blood burbled from the wound. Lozen stepped over, took the toddler into her arms. Uncomfortable with children, she scanned the ruins. She spotted Naiche's wife, Haozinne, and gestured for her. She walked over and took the child, whispering soft words.

Turning around, she saw Naiche hunched over one of the mechanical birds his riflemen downed. She approached. The thing was a heap of cloth and saber-thin steel. Lozen had been told the lightning guns made the machines heavy and they couldn't fly high enough to stay out of rifle range, so their best strategy was to attack with the sun at their backs. As such, the Tsokanende were especially vigilant in the morning and the evening.

A low moan sounded from within the mechanical bird's wreckage. Naiche tore the cloth to reveal a bloodied and broken white man. Enraged, the warrior continued pulling the wreckage from the man until he could yank him clear. The white man screamed as Naiche hefted him upright. The pilot's arm dangled loose, dislocated from the shoulder, but his legs seemed sound enough.

Lozen narrowed her gaze and gestured for Naiche to follow with the captured soldier. She led them to the young mother's body. "Why do you do this?" she asked.

The white man made a noise somewhere between a stifled sob and a snarl. "Why do you Indians steal our land?" He turned his head, despite apparent pain. "You're Natchez, ain't ya?" He addressed Naiche, ignoring Lozen. "Your pa agreed to live on the reservation."

"Reservation." Naiche spat on the ground. "First they give us poor land with little water in the south. Then they move us to San Carlos where we have even less water. Only desert." He gave the white man a shove. The soldier dropped to the ground. To his credit, he didn't cry out, but his face scrunched, betraying pain. "The land is not yours to give."

Lozen knelt down and grabbed the white man's dangling arm. The man's eyes widened. He cried out as she pulled the arm and reset the dislocated joint. The white soldier fell back onto the ground, with a huff, sweating, but his face relaxed.

Lozen then hefted the soldier to his feet and pushed him toward the burnt-out village. Naiche followed close behind. "Where are you taking me?" demanded the soldier.

"You'll be our guest for a time." She would let the soldier rest a while, let his pain argue with him, then come back to see how many birds General Miles still had to throw at them.

Lozen led the soldier to a corral and instructed him to sit.

While Naiche tied him to a post, Lozen returned to the scene of the battle. She located the other downed flying machine. Flames had already ravaged the cloth skin and the metal frame was bent and twisted. Peering into the wreckage, Lozen could just make out charred, bloody chunks of flesh. No one remained in this mechanical bird to question.

She scanned the battlefield. Two men carried bodies from the lightning-struck battle wagon. They had repulsed the attack, but at what cost? They had killed one soldier and took a second captive. Her eyes roved the village. She estimated they'd lost half a dozen people. She reflected for a moment on where they would be if Old Man Clanton and Curly Bill Bresnahan had not attacked the Tsokanende with the original mining machine.

Naiche's father, Cochise had surrendered to the white soldiers in 1872 and agreed to move to the Chiracahua Reservation, which at least had arable land. When the white men decided they wanted that land, they moved the Tsokanende to the San Carlos Reservation out on the barren desert.

Geronimo and his men had continued to resist the white soldiers, but Naiche had foreseen a time when they would be forced onto a reservation as well. Now with the battle wagons, the Tsokanende had carved out their own slice of land in Southern Arizona, but now they had to fight almost every day to keep it.

White men wanted the silver in the mountains and the water in the San Pedro River for farming and ranching. Now that the Russians no longer distracted them, the army seemed willing to keep throwing mechanical birds at them until they signed a new peace treaty—a treaty where Apaches got the worthless land while the whites got everything of value.

Lozen returned to the ruined wickiups. She found Naiche sorting through the remains of his own dwelling. He snorted. "If the white men keep attacking us like this, we could lose everything we've fought for."

Lozen frowned and nodded. "How do we get the white men to stop?"

"We have to take the attack to them."

The woman who had proved herself in battle alongside her brother, Victorio, narrowed her gaze. "Raiding Tucson would be suicide. Starving Tucson might get the soldiers to negotiate."

Naiche nodded slowly. He valued the advice of the woman who was not only a warrior, but had a reputation as a sorceress. "They have airships and trains to supply them. How can we stop them?"

Lozen grinned as she turned her gaze northward. "Airships are like ornithopters. They only carry so much weight. The train is the key."

"I don't care about cotton," grumbled Alethea Morales. "I want to play with my friends."

"You get to play with Francoise and Annette at school. The Cotton Exposition will be fun," countered her mother, Fatemeh. "There'll be music, food, and all kinds of new inventions."

The little girl wrinkled her nose and folded her arms across her chest. "It better be fun."

Her father, Ramon, forced himself not to laugh at the girl's serious expression. He adjusted his spectacles and turned in the seat to look out the window. The family rode on the horse-drawn streetcar along St. Charles Avenue in New Orleans. There'd been talk of converting the cars to chemical reaction steam power, but the Crescent City still suffered the economic woes brought by the Civil War—the War of Northern Aggression, Ramon reminded himself—and Reconstruction.

The streetcar passed palatial houses far grander than the family's humble French Quarter flat as it trundled down the tree-lined avenue. He'd wanted to see the World Cotton Exposition since it opened months earlier, but his busy schedule only now allowed the family outing.

Ramon, Fatemeh and Alethea hopped to their feet and shuffled off the streetcar when it stopped next to the Upper City Park. The driver rang the bell and snapped the reins as the family crossed to the park filled with several huge buildings. At the gate, Ramon paid $1.50 for the family's admission.

"When you enter, go past the main building to get to the

Mexican pavilion," said the ticket seller as he handed Ramon a program book.

Fatemeh sighed as Ramon smiled and extended his hand. "Ramon Morales, Assistant U.S. Attorney for the Eastern District of Louisiana. I'm glad to see you have a keen interest in our neighbors to the south."

The ticket seller took Ramon's proffered hand, but sniffed.

"You're funny, daddy," said Alethea as they passed through the gate into the fairgrounds.

Ramon considered saying something about keeping good humor even when people showed prejudice, but decided that conversation could wait until his daughter was older. Instead, he smiled down at her, then paused just inside the gate and opened the program book to a map. The U.S. and State Exhibits occupied the building to the left and those to the right housed livestock. The centerpiece building beyond these two was perhaps the largest building he had ever seen. It reminded him of the Winter Palace in St. Petersburg. A shiver traveled up his spine as he remembered traveling there aboard a Japanese Airship eight years before.

"It'll take us days to see everything," remarked Fatemeh.

"We don't have to do everything today." Ramon shrugged. "We can always come back."

"If your schedule permits, Mr. Assistant U.S. Attorney." Fatemeh's tone held a razor edge, but when he looked up, she beamed a proud smile.

"Let's go to the biggest building," urged Alethea.

Ramon nodded. "It's the one labeled 'A' on the map, might as well start there." They strode through the park on the mild spring day. Growing up in the desert Southwest, Ramon thought he had experienced harsh summer heat, but in New Orleans, the humidity was a palpable force in its own right. What's more, when he served as a sheriff in New Mexico territory, no one expected him to wear a jacket unless the air grew chill. As an attorney in New Orleans, his peers expected him to wear a jacket, cravat, and waistcoat almost all the time.

The World Cotton Exposition's Main Building reminded him of a warehouse, completely unlike the Russian Winter Palace and its cavernous, white and gold entryway. Having resided in New Orleans for almost a year, he'd been to Mardi Gras, but the noise levels paled when compared to a vast space filled with people speaking, machines running, and music from a steam calliope competing with a Wurlitzer Band Organ.

"Wow!" gasped Alethea as she ran ahead to the first display. Ramon and Fatemeh bolted after her. Before them stood a sleek, shiny, brass automaton on continuous track treads. Piston-like arms pointed forward and a maw dominated the machine's "head." The word "Jackalope" had been painted in handwritten script on its side.

Fatemeh whistled. "That looks like no Jackalope harvester I've ever seen."

A man in a bowler hat, pinstripe suit, and bow tie stepped around the harvester. "That's right, ma'am. This is a brand-spanking new and improved Jackalope harvester. It's designed for maximum efficiency in any conditions." He winked at Alethea. "Would you like to see it work, little lady?"

"Sure," said the girl.

The man opened a panel on the machine's side, threw a switch and turned a dial, reminding Ramon of Katsu Kaishu's automaton rickshaw driver in Japan. The brass harvester rumbled to life, spewing a cloud of smoke toward the high ceiling. It spun around toward a bed of sod, dotted with cabbages. Its piston-like arms shot out, grabbed the vegetables, and shoved them into its mouth, as though it were a ravenous beast.

The man nodded. "If you're familiar with the early Jackalope harvesters, you know they were modeled on rabbits and hopped. They worked in a lot of terrain, but they could get stuck and burned lots of fuel. These new harvesters are much faster and the tracks keep them from bogging down in muddy fields."

"It's monstrous," breathed Fatemeh, though her eyes betrayed a degree of admiration.

Ramon nodded to the man and they continued down the aisle, passing clusters of people who watched new farm equipment demonstrations. Besides harvesters, they passed tillers, planting machines, new-fangled mills, gins, and presses. After a few displays, Alethea's eyes began to glaze over and her attention wandered.

She pointed up to the rafters. "There's a bird in here."

Ramon adjusted his glasses. "That's no bird. It's a little ornithopter."

"What's an ornithopter?" Alethea's brow creased.

Fatemeh knelt down next to her daughter. "A machine that flaps its wings to fly, Alethea joon." She poked the little girl in the nose, setting off a round of giggles.

A man wearing a boater hat and a string tie stepped away from his display. "I see you've taken an interest in our new toy." He held up a box, similar to the ones used to control the Jackalope harvesters. "It's a remotely controlled ornithopter. Both the ornithopter and the control box use electromagnetic coherer units to send signals to one another. It's technology developed by Heinrich Hertz in Germany."

"That's the same principle as the clackers we use in my office." Ramon retrieved a device the size of a pocket watch from his belt. "I thought M.K. Maravilla here in America developed electromagnetism for remote communication."

"Scientists around the world are working to grasp the power of the electron." The man with the control box grasped the joystick and brought the ornithopter down from the rafters. "This flying machine can be used to spray insecticide or the new liquid fertilizers coming onto the market."

"I wish I had one." Alethea clapped her hands. "It would make a grand toy."

The man controlling the small ornithopter ticked up an indulgent smile. "I'm afraid these are much too expensive to be playthings for little girls."

Fatemeh frowned. Before Ramon could ask what bothered her, she pointed to a tall display near the pavilion's center. "Let's go over there."

Ramon followed her gaze to a two-story tall banner displaying a book cover with the title *Le Cuisine Creole*. The author was a local newspaperman named Lafcadio Hearn. Fatemeh led Alethea toward the booth and Ramon scrambled to catch up.

"I wonder if that salesman would tell a boy ornithopters were too precious to be toys," grumbled Fatemeh as they walked.

"It did look expensive." Ramon shrugged.

Fatemeh narrowed her gaze. "Yeah, and we'll find cheaper stuff in the Mexican Pavilion, I'm sure."

Ramon let the jab slide off. He understood her annoyance and had no argument with it.

Several people hovered around Lafcadio Hearn's booth. Ladies passed around serving trays with cakes and small sandwiches. Ramon's stomach growled and he understood the booth's popularity. He took a sandwich and offered it to Fatemeh, who waved it away, so he offered it to his daughter. She sought out the cake lady instead, so Ramon swallowed the sandwich.

A thin Irishman with a bushy mustache and sad eyes sat at a table in the booth surrounded by stacks of books. He perked up when he caught sight of Ramon and Fatemeh. "Mr. and Mrs. Morales." He waved them over. "So good to see you here!"

Ramon, Fatemeh and Alethea approached the Irishman.

Hearn reached under the table and retrieved a book, different from the cookbooks stacked around him. "I just received the first copies yesterday. They should go on sale within the week." He passed the book to Fatemeh while Ramon looked over her shoulder. The title on the cover read *Owl Riders*.

Over the last year, Hearn had interviewed Ramon and Fatemeh about their adventures out west and in the Far East. He wrote about the Russian invasion of the United States and how Fatemeh had organized a ragtag band of pirates and gunslingers to drive them out when the Army had failed. He then told how Ramon had stopped samurai air pirates to prevent war between Japan and Russia. When telling their story, Ramon and Fatemeh had left out the part about an invisible creature from the stars called Legion.

Eight years after last hearing Legion's voice, Ramon began to doubt his own memories of communicating with the spirit-like creature.

Fatemeh flipped through the book.

Alethea tugged on her skirts. Fatemeh knelt down so the girl could see.

"No pictures?" The girl frowned

Fatemeh smiled and shook her head. "Nope, he paints

pictures in your mind with his words."

Alethea snorted and looked to see where the cake lady had gone.

A tall, thin man with a waxed mustache and a dark suit approached. "Excuse me," he said in a drawl more Georgia than Louisiana. "Do I understand that y'all are none other than Ramon and Fatemeh Morales from New Mexico?"

Ramon narrowed his gaze. The man's breath reeked of alcohol and it wasn't even ten in the morning.

The stranger pulled out a handkerchief as a racking cough surged through him. Ramon thought he saw blood specks as the stranger folded the handkerchief and put it away. "Pardon my manners. I'm Dr. John Henry Holliday. Mr. Morales, could we have a word?"

Ramon followed Dr. Holliday outside the exposition hall, relieved to exit the building's din. While they walked, Ramon wracked his brain, trying to remember where he'd heard the name "Doc Holliday" before. A booth sold beignets and café au lait. After ordering, they sat at an open-air table under an umbrella.

"It's been a long time since I've been here in the south." The doctor retrieved a flask from his coat pocket and added amber liquid to his coffee. He offered the flask to Ramon who held up his hand. The doctor shrugged and recapped the flask. "I live out in Arizona, working with some business associates who want to develop Eastern Pima County."

With that, Ramon remembered where he'd heard of Doc Holliday. "You're an associate of Wyatt Earp, the Tucson businessman." Ramon could tell he was becoming a politician. Earp and his brothers were gamblers, saloon operators, and occasional lawmen—when it paid.

"That's right," said Holliday. "My associate has become acquainted with Albert and Edward Schieffelin…"

Ramon narrowed his gaze while he sipped his café au lait, not recognizing the names.

"I believe you and the Schieffelin brothers have a mutual acquaintance." Holliday gulped the doctored coffee. "I believe he goes by the nom de plume, Professor Maravilla?"

The light dawned. "Now I know who you're talking about.

They're prospectors. The professor built the mining machine based on javelina research for them." Ramon bit into a beignet, conscious of how much his girth stressed his waistcoat's buttons. He ate much better as an attorney in New Orleans than he had as a small town sheriff in New Mexico Territory.

"That's right." Ramon couldn't help but notice how skinny the doctor was as he swallowed the last of a beignet. "They know there's a lot of, shall we say, mineral wealth in the Mule Mountains of Southeastern Arizona…"

"But the Apaches have claimed that land for their own…"

Holliday smiled. "That's exactly the problem." A rattling cough shattered the doctor's smile. He lifted the handkerchief to his mouth again and Ramon waited for it to subside.

"Why come to me? How did you even know where to find me?"

Holliday drank his coffee and smiled again. "You see, I'm here on family business. My father wants me to return home to Georgia. He says there are doctors researching my—" he shrugged "—condition at Emory University out in Oxford. I think goin' back to Georgia would kill me before they could cure me. Much as I love New Orleans, it hasn't done my lungs much good."

"You're a doctor," Ramon leaned forward, gaze narrowed. "Surely you'd be one of the first to embrace new hope. You have tuberculosis?"

"I'm a lunger, yes. My doctorate is in dentistry, not medicine. My views on the subject, are, shall we say, jaded."

Ramon frowned, then sipped his coffee. "That still doesn't tell me what you want."

Holliday nodded slowly, as though trying to recapture his train of thought. "On the airship over here, I read about your exploits in the *Times-Democrat*." He referred to the newspaper that employed Lafcadio Hearn. "You're a man who's negotiated with the Emperor of Japan and the Czar of Russia. I thought you might be the man to negotiate with Natchez and the army. I was approachin' Mr. Hearn to ask him how I might find you when lo and behold he hands your wife the very book he wrote about you."

Ramon tapped his fingers on the table. "Dr. Holliday, I'm

the Assistant U.S. Attorney for the Eastern District of Louisiana. I can't just up and leave my job to help you with a land dispute."

"My associates could make it worth your while if you'd help out. They have holdings in several business interests and if they succeeded I'm sure you could be given an interest in the mine, perhaps a parcel of land. Can't be easy havin' your ... skin hue here in the South."

Ramon's fingers stopped their dance. The statement held more truth than he wanted to admit. He loved New Orleans and the French Quarter, but he often grew homesick for the Southwest. Although he made good money as an Assistant U.S. Attorney, he wished he had more time to spend with his wife and daughter.

"May I take your silence to mean my offer tempts you?" Holliday leaned on one elbow and took another gulp of his coffee.

"Let me do a little research and think about it." Ramon picked up another beignet and swallowed it down, followed by more coffee. "How can I reach you if I want to discuss this further?"

Holliday retrieved a card and a pen from his pocket. He wrote down a name and passed it to Ramon—the Commercial Hotel, a respectable establishment—but not too far from Bourbon Street, Ramon thought with a snort. "I'll be here a week more, then I'll head west again," said the dentist.

Ramon finished his coffee, then stood and shook Holliday's hand. "I can't promise anything. Not even sure if I want to get involved, but I'll do some homework."

"That's all I ask," said Holliday.

Ramon brushed confectioner's sugar from his waistcoat and returned to the main building. He found Fatemeh and Alethea still talking to Hearn at the cookbook display.

"There you are," said Fatemeh. "I was worried you'd gotten lost. Who was that man?"

"A dentist from Arizona named Holliday." Ramon shrugged and glanced over to Hearn. "Seems he read your articles in the *Times-Democrat*."

"I hope I've given him a favorable impression." Hearn

bowed in a way that almost reminded him of the Japanese.

A clacking sounded from the device hanging from Ramon's belt. He lifted it and tapped an acknowledgment in Morse code, then held the device to his ear to listen. His shoulders slumped. "I'm needed at the office. There've been some new developments in the lightning gun case I'm working on."

Fatemeh put her hands on her hips. "I wish they'd never invented those clackers. It's Saturday, for God's sake."

"I know. I'm sorry." He stepped forward and embraced his wife's shoulders. "You stay here and enjoy the fair. You'll be able to get home okay?"

"As though I need you to be my escort." Good natured sarcasm coated her words.

He kissed her. "I'll see you soon, Corazón."

She handed him the copy of the book, *Owl Riders*. "Take this. Maybe it'll remind you of your family."

He laughed then picked up Alethea and gave her a big hug. "Have fun, listen to your mom, and be good." Setting her down, he took the book from Fatemeh. He was honestly curious what Hearn had written about them and how it had attracted Holliday's attention.

"You be good, too," said Alethea.

Ramon waved. "I'm afraid, being good is why I have to go to work. See you as soon as I can."

CHAPTER TWO
BETROTHED

Ramon hopped off the streetcar at the edge of the French Quarter on Canal Street and strode past clothing stores, a tobacconist, a grocery, and more. A decade ago, as a small-town sheriff in New Mexico Territory, such a busy street filled with a mix of day laborers, businessmen, and even bums would have unnerved him. Since then, he'd visited Tokyo and St. Petersburg before moving to Boston for seven years to get his Bachelor's Degree followed by a Juris Doctorate. Afterward, his doctoral adviser wrote a stellar recommendation to several attorneys.

He soon reached the U.S. Custom House and Post Office Building. The building housed the U.S. District Court as well as the U.S. Attorney's offices. Though newer than much of the Quarter, it seemed somehow more drab with its imposing granite construction.

At first Ramon didn't want to move to New Orleans. The city had a seedy reputation. People said it was a hub of Caribbean crime. Hard times in the wake of Reconstruction meant poverty ran rampant. Then again, the reputation wasn't much different than places out west. People in Boston imagined everyone in New Mexico ran around with six-guns and fights broke out at a moment's notice.

While Ramon pursued a law degree, Fatemeh applied to the Massachusetts College of Pharmacy. They denied her application. Using resources available at Harvard, Ramon had discovered the New York and Philadelphia Colleges of Pharmacy had already admitted women. He filed a law suit, but the school's administrators admitted Fatemeh before the case went to trial.

Fatemeh discovered she could not open a pharmacy in New Orleans under her own name since she was both a woman and "colored." After six months in New Orleans, Fatemeh partnered with a surly man from the bayou named Picou who knew local plants well, but did not have a pharmacy degree. They rented a small shop on Royal Street, near their flat on St. Ann. Though grumpy, Picou proved reliable, which allowed her to make excursions like the one to the Cotton Exposition.

Ramon wished he could have that much free time.

He unlocked the back door of the Custom House, then climbed the stairs to the U.S. Attorney's offices on the fourth floor. There he found a law clerk with folders containing briefs and depositions ready for review. "Sorry to call you in, Mr. Morales, but the judge scheduled a hearing first thing Monday morning. Mr. Leonard wanted you ready." The clerk referred to Albert H. Leonard, the U.S. Attorney for the Eastern District of Louisiana.

"Thanks, Jacob," said Ramon.

"Do you need anything else?" The clerk shot nervous glances at the ticking clock, betraying his desire for an afternoon away from the office.

Ramon thumbed through the stack, then shook his head. "No, I think I have everything I need. Have a good afternoon."

"Thank you, Mr. Morales." With that, the clerk made a hasty retreat, the glass in the wooden door rattling as it shut.

Ramon entered his office and sat down behind the desk. The folders contained receipts and affidavits showing the purchase history of a supply of thermionic tubes and conductors slated for a lightning gun manufacturer in New Orleans but never arrived. Instead, they were found being offloaded from a barge across Lake Pontchartrain. The men who had them worked for a competing firm in Biloxi, Mississippi who also bought parts that never arrived. The crime being tried was theft, but accusations of fraud and uncertainties about who actually did own the parts complicated the matter.

As he read the documents, he wondered how he went from solving disputes between world leaders to solving disputes between gun manufacturers. His mind drifted to the Apache situation in Arizona. He thought about going to the library, checking newspapers, perhaps requesting more information.

Each time his mind wandered, he forced himself back on track until at last he constructed a chain of events in the case and had drafted an opening statement for Monday's court hearing. By the time he finished, the outside light had faded to twilight gray.

He lit the lantern on his desk and looked at his pocket watch. His stomach rumbled. It had been a long time since he ate those beignets at the Cotton Exposition. He sorted the folders and put them away, then found the book *Owl Riders* and flipped it open to a scene where Fatemeh sat next to him during their Hawaiian honeymoon. Ramon chuckled to himself as he remembered the ridiculous swimsuit Fatemeh coaxed him into wearing.

The next line mentioned her concerns about the man she had been betrothed to, a Persian merchant named Hamid.

Wait! What?

Ramon read the line over again to be sure.

Fatemeh had never mentioned a betrothal before they met. He didn't remember reading about Hamid in the original newspaper articles. He turned to look at the French Quarter through the window. Lights were just coming on in the buildings around the neighborhood.

He shook his head. Hearn must have made this up to give the book interest, like the stuff in those dime novels. While a student in Boston, an upperclassman handed him one about his "famous" shootout with Randolph Dalton. Ramon read the whole thing wide eyed. It made Dalton out to be a gun-slinging desperado, not a rich mine owner who hired some men to make him disappear.

Ramon guessed if he kept reading Hearn's book, he'd find a chapter where he had to duel this Hamid with sabers in order to rescue his lady love.

Much as he tried to dismiss his concerns with good humor, something didn't ring true. Lafcadio Hearn didn't strike him as the kind of newspaper man to invent material to sensationalize a story. Yes, he had a flowery prose style, but he endeavored to be accurate.

Ramon closed the book, blew out the lantern, and left the office. On the way home, he stopped off for a quiet supper at a café in Pirate's Alley, a small thoroughfare near his flat, behind the towering St. Louis Cathedral. A fiddler played a quiet tune while Ramon tried to imagine the little cobblestone street outside filled with pirates selling their goods. The New Orleans black market was alive and well, but no longer operated out in the open.

Once home, he found Alethea already in bed. Fatemeh sat before a mirror, brushing out her hair. He considered raising the subject of Hamid, but decided to wait. Instead he undressed, climbed between the sheets and fell into a restless slumber.

Ramon awoke a few hours later to the smell of coffee and baking bread. He climbed from between the sheets and went to the kitchen where Fatemeh pulled a fresh loaf from the oven. He kissed her, then poured a cup of coffee and sat at the table.

"Alethea joon, you should get out of bed, sleepy head," called Fatemeh.

Ramon watched his wife while she tossed some more wood into the oven, then he reached over and sliced the fresh bread. On the table, a small crock held a soft cheese alongside three jars of jam. He spread some cheese and added jam, then took a bite. Delicious.

Over the years, he'd grown to love Fatemeh's traditional Persian breakfasts. Some days, though, he still made bacon and eggs. Although not a strict vegetarian, she preferred to avoid meat.

Alethea padded from her room and plunked down at the table, groggy.

Fatemeh looked at Ramon. "You've been awfully quiet since you got home last night. Something on your mind?"

Ramon sipped his coffee, then snorted a self-conscious laugh. "It's nothing really. Just something strange Mr. Hearn said in the *Owl Riders* book."

"Oh, what's that?" Fatemeh poured coffee for herself, then joined her husband and daughter at the table.

"He said you'd been betrothed to someone named Hamid. Where do you suppose he got that from?"

"What's betrothed mean?" asked Alethea as she spread some peach jam on her bread.

"Betrothed means my mother and father entered in a

business deal with a man. Part of the deal was for me to marry him." Fatemeh looked up into Ramon's eyes. "I barely knew Hamid Farzan. He was a merchant who owned a few ships. My father was in love with Hamid's money."

"Will I ever meet my grandfather?" Alethea asked the question around a mouthful of bread.

Fatemeh frowned for just a moment. "I don't know. We'll see one day."

"My friend Annette says her grand-père loves her and buys her toys." Alethea looked up at Fatemeh. "Doesn't my grandfather love me?"

Fatemeh sniffed. "I'm sure he does, sweetheart." She coughed to hide the catch in her voice.

Ramon pushed his glasses up his nose and looked into his daughter's brown eyes. "I was thinking about going to mass at the St. Louis Cathedral this morning. Would you like to come along?"

Alethea brightened. "The big church? Sure!"

"Then finish your breakfast and get ready. We'll need to leave soon."

Alethea nodded, smiled, and dove into her breakfast. Ramon finished his bread and turned his attention to Fatemeh. "I'm just a little surprised you didn't tell me."

Fatemeh gave a sad smile and shrugged. "Things were such a whirlwind when we first met, I never found the time. If anything, he represented what I hoped to escape. I never loved him. Never had any feelings for him. By the time we reached Boston, you were busy with your studies and I was trying to get into school. Once we got here, I practically forgot about him."

"But you remembered him well enough to mention him to Mr. Hearn." Ramon cringed at his own words, hearing the attorney within, cross-examining Fatemeh.

"Mr. Hearn badgered me for details. You didn't." She reached out and took his hand. "That's one reason I love you and not Mr. Hearn."

The St. Louis Cathedral's bells chimed. Ramon pointed to his daughter. "Go get dressed."

She pointed back at him. "You too, daddy." She hopped up from the table and went to her room.

Ramon and Fatemeh stood together and embraced. "Do you want to come with us to the cathedral? You used to like coming with me to church."

"Picou is picking me up soon. He's going to take me out to one of the bayous near Chalmette where some herbs grow that are especially good at soothing an upset stomach. After that, we'll make a circuit of the countryside to get some other herbs for the shop."

"It's Sunday, do you really have to work today?" Ramon shook his head.

"It's the only day the shop's closed and both Picou and I can be away." She led Ramon into the bedroom and pointed to the closet. "Now you need to get dressed or you won't hear the end of it from your daughter."

She kissed him, then pulled the door closed as she left the room.

Ramon doffed his nightshirt and put on the suit he wore the day before. He looked at his hair in the mirror and frowned. He poured some water into a basin, and splashed it over his head, crying out as it chilled him. A brief, stifled laugh escaped from the other room before he ran the comb through his hair. Although the results displeased him, a quick glance at his pocket watch while he wound it confirmed they didn't have much time.

At the kitchen table, Fatemeh wound Alethea's long hair into a braid. She wore a pink, frilly dress and white shoes. Ramon smiled and took his daughter's hand. The two waved at Fatemeh and walked down the wooden steps to the courtyard below. The church was just two blocks away.

"Why didn't grandma and grandpa ask you to marry mamma?"

Ramon considered the best way to answer. "Because I didn't know your mamma when they decided to make a betrothal."

"Will you and momma find someone for me to marry?"

Ramon shook his head. "Nope, you get to do it the hard way, just like your mom and me. You get to find someone you love all on your own."

"Will we live happily ever after, like a storybook?"

Ramon took a moment to consider his imperfect life with Fatemeh. Often busier than he liked, it made him happy and he couldn't imagine anything coming between them. "If you find the right person, it'll be better than a storybook."

They entered the cathedral right as the priest stood to deliver the Confiteor.

A battle wagon rumbled alongside the San Pedro River toward the Dragoon Mountains under a star-filled sky. Two warriors steered the machine while Naiche and Lozen sat behind them contemplating what they'd learned from the soldier they'd taken captive.

The soldier had been trained well. At first, he revealed nothing but his name and rank. Letting him sit in the sun all day with nothing for company but the pain of his swollen arm and the smell of horse piss brought him to the point that a sharp knife thrust into the ground near his crotch loosened his tongue. The army only had three flying machines besides those destroyed by the Tsokanende. More had been commissioned, but building them took time.

"How close can your flying machines approach the mountains?" asked Lozen.

The soldier clamped his cracked and split lips tight. Naiche pushed on the man's swollen shoulder until he cried out.

"They can't get real close. Unless you've practiced around a particular range, it's best to avoid the mountains altogether."

Lozen folded her arms. "Why is that?"

"Winds get tricky around mountains." The soldier's rapid nodding betrayed his eagerness to please. "If you don't know what to expect, it's easy for the winds to carry you too high. Sometimes they carry you right into the mountainside."

"And have you practiced near the Dragoon Mountains?"

The soldier shook his head. "No, we haven't."

Lozen, who had shown mercy by resetting the soldier's arm showed more mercy with a swift death from a single bullet to the brain.

Naiche asked Lozen to join him for a brief war council with

the elder Kas-tziden, also known by the Spanish nickname, Nana. They decided to leave one battle wagon to defend the village while another battle wagon would blockade the railroad at a narrow pass in the Dragoon Mountains. Most of the riflemen would stay at the village, but the six best would ride along with Naiche and Lozen.

The battle wagon rattled and thumped onto the train tracks at the appointed place. Tsokanende scouts had watched the area for weeks. A train would come from the east in the morning.

The warriors removed supplies from the wagon, then set up camp beside the rails. They ate a sparse meal, then Lozen instructed the men to take crowbars from the wagon and pull up the adjoining sections of track.

"Why do that?" Naiche narrowed his gaze. "The battle wagon itself will cause the train to stop."

Lozen glanced at the large machine. "Do we want the locomotive to collide with the battle wagon? What if the battle wagon has to leave to defend the village?"

Naiche considered that, then nodded. "You are wise. Didn't General Sherman make something he called neckties from the track in his march through Georgia during the Civil War."

Lozen grinned at him. "He did indeed, but that can wait until after we deal with the approaching train.

The warriors set to work pulling spikes, hefting ties and moving the ties, so they could be used to light fires under the metal. This would allow them to bend and twist the rail so it couldn't easily be reused.

After the hard night's work, they found places to sleep. Lozen slept inside the battle wagon—a spurious luxury granted her as a woman and a "sorceress." She longed for the company of her companion Dahteste, but that would wait for her return to Fort Bowie. The machine's metal floor was colder and somehow harder than the sand-covered rocks outside. At least inside, the odds of a scorpion or snake sharing her blankets was negligible.

In the original mining machine, the place Lozen occupied had been used for storing and sorting minerals. In the Mexican-built battle wagons, the space could be used for cargo or troops. That could be useful if Lozen and Naiche's ally, Geronimo, succeeded in his mission. He'd gone to Mexico to negotiate for more battle wagons and to get military help.

At present, they had three battle wagons. Naiche had one of the war machines. Lozen commanded the second and used it along with the third to capture Fort Bowie near the New Mexico territorial border. That third battle wagon remained at Fort Bowie under Dahteste's care.

These thoughts and more occupied Lozen as she fell into an uneasy slumber. A freight train would not hold many armed men, so she didn't anticipate battle, but she worried about whether they had pulled enough rail for the lumbering locomotive to stop before inertia carried it into the battle wagon.

Lozen awoke in the dark when Naiche pounded on the wagon's side. She opened the heavy door and blinked at the sun, already above the Dragoon Mountains' bare, yellow rocks. She exited the wagon and ate venison and chigustai for breakfast. As she finished, a train whistle sounded in the distance, earlier than expected.

Naiche ordered the riflemen to their places. He sent his most trusted warrior, Itza-cha up into the battle wagon's cannon turret. He took a position beside the rails where he could watch the action through binoculars.

He handed the binoculars to Lozen.

A man ran along the tops of the train's boxcars. He dropped down onto the tender car and shouted at the engineer and fireman. A man in the cab leaned far out, and soon brakes squealed. The man who had run along the boxcars almost lost his footing before he stumbled into the caboose.

The locomotive ground to a stop, dropping off the end of the rails. "What's the meaning of this?" called the engineer.

Lozen handed the binoculars back to Naiche. "You are encroaching on our land."

"This ain't Apache land," called the engineer. "You ceded it to the U.S. government years ago."

"We're taking it back!" Naiche folded his arms.

The fireman joined the engineer. "Apaches never had a problem with the railroad before."

"That was before the white man started attacking our

settlements with flapping mechanical birds."

A bullet struck the rock outcropping next to Lozen's head and ricocheted with a whistle.

She ducked and glanced back toward the caboose. The conductor sat in the cupola with a rifle pointed out the window. Naiche called to a riflemen high in the rocks. A shot shattered the cupola's nearest window. A moment later, the conductor returned fire. A second Tsokanende rifle shot followed suit, rendering the caboose silent.

Lozen stood and pointed to the engineer. "You! I want you to go to Tucson and tell them no trains will pass this way until President Arthur sends a representative to negotiate with us in good faith."

The engineer shook his head. "Chester A. Arthur isn't president anymore. Grover Cleveland is the white father now."

"Don't use that childish phrase with me," growled Lozen, "and I don't care who your leader is. He will send an emissary to negotiate with us in good faith, or we will use our battle wagons to starve Tucson and then raze it to the ground."

"How am I supposed to get there?" The engineer's lower lip protruded like a spoiled child.

"Walk." Naiche planted his hands on his hips.

"It's almost forty miles to Tucson. That'll take me all day, maybe two!"

Lozen looked from the engineer over her shoulder toward Tucson. "Then you'd better get started."

The engineer looked around at the rifles aimed at him, then turned to the fireman. "Make sure they don't steal anything." He hopped from the cab.

"Don't leave me here!" The fireman ran after the engineer. "They can have the train as far as I'm concerned."

Lozen sneered. "Stop squabbling and run, or you'll never get there!"

The two men blinked like stupid cattle. Naiche pointed to a rifleman, who fired a shot between the two and they ran past the battle wagon, following the rails to Tucson.

CHAPTER THREE
SABOTAGED

"Has anyone told you the loa of an owl hovers near you?"

Fatemeh reached for a jar of herbs and brought it to Marie Lalande, the slim woman with elegant, aquiline features who stood at the counter. "No, but it pleases me to hear that."

Marie raised an eyebrow in a smooth, fluid motion. "I would not be so sanguine. The loa Marinette is dangerous indeed. She is vicious and cruel. She possesses the power to send people into slavery or free them from bondage at her pleasure. Marinette killed many French slaveholders in Haiti."

Fatemeh quirked a smile, but fought to suppress it.

Marie pointed a long finger at her. "My story amuses you, I can tell."

Fatemeh poured some herbs onto a scale, weighed them, then shook a few back in the jar before pouring the rest into a small paper bag. Marie operated a small, unmarked shop for Voodoo practitioners. She sold candles, herbs, and made gris-gris bags. Despite that, she claimed to be a devout Catholic.

"I've also heard the story of the young girl courted by the shy owl who never showed his face." Fatemeh passed the bag across the counter.

"That is merely a bedtime story, and I suspect the owl you married was never so shy." Marie smiled and her dark brown eyes twinkled.

Fatemeh tried to remember if she ever told her Ramon's nickname from New Mexico. His family called him Búho because he resembled an owl with his round glasses. "Do you think he's also a vengeful spirit?"

Marie considered that. "I believe he could be, if unleashed."

The bell over the shop door jangled and Marie's daughter Francoise burst in with Alethea on her heels. The girls attended the Ursuline day school near the Quarter. Fatemeh suspected that contributed to Marie's decision to present herself as Catholic. Of course, the nuns would teach any girl with money for tuition. Fatemeh wanted Alethea to attend one of the free, secular McDonough schools, but the ones in the Quarter only accepted white students.

"How was school today, Alethea joon?" asked Fatemeh.

Alethea shrugged and tossed her book bag on the counter, nearly upsetting the herb jar. Fatemeh caught it just in time. A book with a tattered paper cover slipped partway out. "The nuns are making us read the Psalms, so we can learn about poetry. There's lots of hard words I don't understand."

"We'll look at them together tonight." Fatemeh retrieved the book that had slipped part way out of the bag. "And what is this?"

"I loaned that to her," said Francoise. "I hope it's okay, Madame Morales."

Fatemeh glanced at the title: *The Authentic Life of Cowboy Charlie* by Pat Garrett. She opened the book and read the first paragraph. The book detailed Charlie Bowdre's life and tragic death. Flipping through the pages, she came across lurid woodcuts of the most dramatic scenes and smiled to herself, remembering her daughter's complaint about *Owl Riders*. Fatemeh closed the book and creased her brow, trying to recall where she'd heard the name Charlie Bowdre.

"Alethea told me about the real cowboy you met at the Cotton Exposition." Francoise breathed the words, as though her friend had made a rare find. "I know you and Monsieur Morales are from New Mexico territory and I thought she would enjoy the story."

That's where she knew the name Charlie Bowdre from! He was Billy McCarty's old friend. She looked at the book again, grateful McCarty had left Lincoln County and hired on with the chile farmer Masuda Hoshi in Las Cruces. If he'd remained in Lincoln, Pat Garrett might have written a book about him! Cowboy Billy just didn't have the same ring as Cowboy Charlie, but then Fatemeh remembered Billy used to call himself

"Kid Antrim."

"So, where exactly did *you* get this book young lady?" asked Marie, eyes narrowed at her daughter.

"Monsieur Boudreaux at the bookshop had copies." Francoise turned her toe on the floor.

"I think I will have a talk with Monsieur Boudreaux about appropriate books for young ladies," said Marie.

Fatemeh held up her hand. "It's all right. If you want, I'll pay for the book."

Marie blinked and then gave a light, almost musical laugh. "If you're not careful, your daughter won't fit in with proper society."

"Do you and I really fit in with *proper* society?" Fatemeh winked and smiled. Despite her good humor, it rankled that women shunned her at social affairs around New Orleans even though she was a business owner and the Assistant U.S. Attorney's wife. Then again, most people didn't know she really owned Blessed Life Apothecary.

"No, I suppose you're right." Marie pulled a coin from her purse and paid for the herbs. "Come by the shop and have tea, soon. You are always good company."

"I will." Fatemeh waved as Marie and Francoise left the shop. Rumors floated around the Quarter that Marie was the granddaughter of none other than Marie Laveau, New Orleans' so-called Voodoo Queen who had died just a few years before. It seemed ironic such a woman would be so free to lecture her about propriety. Despite that, she liked Marie Lalande and enjoyed learning about Voodoo. She preferred her company to those society ladies who shunned her.

As a Bahá'í, Fatemeh believed all religions held truth. Voodoo practice both fascinated and scared her. Still, she'd learned long ago that people reacted to the unknown with fear.

"Will we ever travel to New Mexico?" Alethea's question shattered Fatemeh's revelry.

Fatemeh didn't know the answer to that. She missed her friends there, but bad memories lingered as well. "Perhaps, some day."

"Are there lots of men like Dr. Holliday there with big sombreros?"

Fatemeh laughed as she retrieved the herb jar and returned it to the shelf. "There are many men in big hats, but few are as slick as Dr. Holliday."

"What do you mean by slick?" The girl narrowed her gaze.

Fatemeh leaned on the counter across from her daughter. "It means he's slippery. You can never quite get a handle on him."

"Ewww."

"That about sums up men like Dr. Holliday, Alethea joon." Fatemeh thought back to the brief encounter with the doctor. "There's also an air of sickness around him. Consumption, I think…"

"Did daddy wear a big sombrero?" Alethea gazed out the shop window at the passers-by and played with her braid.

Fatemeh reached across and poked her daughter's nose as she remembered the lurid woodcuts. "Yes, he did, and he wore guns like the men in your book."

"Why doesn't he wear guns anymore?"

"Because men of peace don't need to wear guns." Fatemeh stood upright and put her hands on her hips. "Now, go to the back room and start your homework. I still have an hour before I close the shop and then we'll go look at those difficult psalms the nuns assigned you."

Late at night, Lozen sat by the campfire while Naiche paced next to the battle wagon, restless. The young chief worried that the soldiers hadn't attacked yet. He expected them to be so desperate to retrieve the stranded train they would throw soldiers and flying machines at him until they exhausted their resources. Lozen thought he underestimated his opponents.

She looked across to the Dragoon Mountains stretching up toward the starlit sky as though the mountains were pillars and the sky a vast ceiling. "Do you remember the story of how Coyote trapped Lizard on a tree? Lizard convinced Coyote the tree held up the sky and it would topple over if Coyote removed Lizard. To avoid that fate, they agreed to exchange places. Coyote agreed and Lizard ran away."

Naiche frowned and followed her gaze. "You wonder if I've been 'clever' like Coyote and sit in place holding up the sky while the white men laugh at me from afar."

Lozen shook her head. "The white men need their goods and they will be back for them, but white men do resemble Coyote sometimes and we must be cautious even as we're patient."

Naiche nodded, grunted, and resumed pacing.

The wind picked up, howling through the rocks. Lozen turned toward the fire and watched the embers drift upward on the breeze. She remembered another story, about a mountain spirit dance. Two strangers came and joined the tribe's spirit dance night after night. On the fourth night, the tribe grew curious about the strangers who only appeared for the dancing and chased them. The strangers hopped on horses and rode straight for the mountain. A portal opened up and the strangers disappeared inside. The strangers were mountain spirits.

Lozen may be called a sorceress, but she wasn't certain she believed in mountain spirits. She hoped if they did exist, they blessed this endeavor. The Apaches didn't deserve to have their homeland stripped away just so white men could gain wealth.

She excused herself, went inside the battle wagon and soon drifted off to sleep.

A loud bang startled her awake. She opened the door. Naiche looked skyward. She followed his gaze. Bright, sparkling lights appeared in the sky. A whistle sounded and then more bright lights appeared followed by another loud bang. She jumped from the battle wagon. The white men were firing rockets.

Naiche shouted orders. The Apache warriors fanned out into the rocks surrounding the pass. Naiche and Lozen crept forward, each of them grasping rifles.

A ghoulish howl warbled through the rocks, making the hair on Lozen's neck stand on end. It reminded her of the mountain spirits. She gestured to Naiche and they continued forward. Something popped up from behind a rock, then disappeared. Lozen studied the apparition.

From their left, a warrior named Bodaway ran away screaming. Lozen blinked. Bodaway was no coward. She turned forward. The figure behind the rock popped up again.

A dead man—a skeleton.

Naiche dropped his rifle and took several steps backward, his breath short.

Itza-cha and two other warriors screamed and fled into the night.

Lozen calmed her mind, setting aside years of stories about the dangers of approaching the dead and forced herself to watch.

The skeleton popped up again, then disappeared behind the rock. A couple of minutes later, it did the same thing all over again. She ground her teeth. This was no spiritual manifestation.

She scanned the ridge line where other skeletons sprang up from behind rocks.

A bang echoed through the canyon as the white men launched another rocket.

Unlike his men, Naiche didn't flee. He reached down and grabbed the rifle while Lozen crept around the skeleton's rock. The old bones had been mounted on a piston. A motor turned and every time it reached a certain point, the skeleton bobbed upward. Lozen studied the skeleton even more. Not even real, just plaster, like the calacas Mexicans make when they celebrate the Day of the Dead.

Naiche continued forward to a view of the downslope to the San Pedro River valley. Lozen joined him. Tucked in behind some rocks, a man loaded a rocket into a mortar, then fired. The rocket exploded, illuminating the sky.

Naiche lifted his rifle, aimed, and fired. The man behind the rock flinched and looked up. When Naiche aimed again, the man ducked behind the rock.

Lozen considered the wisdom of pursuing this quarry, then turned her attention to the battle wagon. This was no military maneuver. This reminded her of Lizard trying to get Coyote to change places with him. She turned and ran back to the camp, hoping other warriors had already overcome their fear.

She cursed when she found the battle wagon abandoned, its door open. Had she left it so? As she approached, a lone figure with a long beard hopped out. Lozen aimed and fired, but missed. The man in buckskin hit the ground, rolled and drew a pair of six guns. He fired from where he lay on the ground, forcing Lozen to take cover.

She waited a moment, then peered around the rock. The white man had retreated. Lozen spat a curse, then followed the man's trail onto the rocks, where it disappeared. A scuffling sounded ahead. She ran forward and found Naiche tying the man's hands behind his back. She studied his face, but the beard obscured all but his eyes.

Lozen crouched down near the man and asked him a question in English. "Who are you and what did you hope to achieve?"

Hidden behind the beard, she found it difficult to read the man's facial expression, but his shoulder's slumped, more cowed than angry. "Just doing a job ma'am," he said.

"And what kind of job is that?" spat Naiche.

"We're here to scare you off," said the bearded man. "That's all. You see, back about eight years ago, my brother and I found a silver vein down in the Mule Mountains. There were just the two of us plus a partner, not enough people to work the claim and guard it as well. Even so, we found some stuff to help out. We found an old skeleton, and we found an old camel walking around. My brother knows something about clockworks..."

At that moment, Lozen remembered the story. "You're Ed Shieffelin, the miner who created the 'ghost camel' that haunted the Land of the Tombstone. Your brother is named Al."

"That's right ma'am."

Naiche shook his head. "But you and your brother tried to help Geronimo and his warriors. You tried to stop the first battle wagon from destroying our camp. Why are you attacking us now?"

"We're not attacking you." Ed shook his head. "We're just trying to run you off. We knew you Apaches were spooked by skeletons. We didn't have any more real ones, so we just rigged up something with some plaster skeletons."

Lozen unsheathed her knife and held it in plain view. "You still haven't told us who hired you to do this job."

Ed Shieffelin swallowed. "A businessman by the name o' Wyatt Earp. He wants to set up a town near our old claim and mine the silver."

"That's our land," growled Naiche.

"He's willing to work with you," suggested Ed, "unlike the army that just wants to blast you out."

Lozen narrowed her gaze and considered what the miner said. "So, he's not allied with the army."

Ed shrugged as best as he could with his hands tied. "He's allied with whoever'll get him the land."

Lozen heard a scuffling nearby and then realized she'd not heard any explosions for a while. She leapt to her feet and whirled around brandishing her knife. She found herself facing another white man. This one wore a shorter beard than their captive, but his eyes looked similar. "You must be Al Shieffelin."

The new arrival gave a curt nod. "I'll be going with my brother now."

Lozen looked to Naiche, who still held his rifle on Ed. She saw no advantage in starting a fight with the new Shieffelin and perhaps letting Ed go would make this Wyatt Earp, who-ever he was, more cooperative. She nodded to Naiche, who lowered his rifle.

"You may go," she said to Ed.

He rose unsteadily to his feet, hands still bound behind his back. She stepped back next to Naiche while Ed joined his brother. The Tsokanende warriors watched the two miners walk away down the hillside.

Once they were out of sight, Lozen returned to the bat-tle wagon, climbed inside and inspected the machinery. All the knobs were in place and the machine appeared to be in good order. Perhaps they'd caught Shieffelin before he'd had a chance to do harm. She ground her teeth, unconvinced. She'd have the warriors make a thorough check.

Once the warriors regrouped, Bodaway and Itza-cha in-spected the wagon. They fired up the boiler and found they could move the wagon. Lozen then had the men inspect the top-mounted cannon. They soon noticed the striker mechanism had been removed, leaving the battle wagon's cannon nothing more than a useless tube. The Shieffelin brothers' pranks had not been so innocent.

Naiche instructed the warriors to stack the rail ties they'd removed into a pile and light a bonfire. They placed the rails over the fire and heated them. At that point, several warriors working together turned and twisted the rail.

Once the job was complete, Naiche established a watch, then ordered the rest of the warriors to get some sleep. Lozen decided to remain outside and allowed the bonfire to warm her as she dozed.

Dawn seemed to come too soon. Over breakfast, Naiche and Lozen discussed plans. They only had so many warriors and that limited how much rail they could destroy using General Sherman's method. Lozen suggested another approach to increase the damage to the rails, though it meant a terrible sacrifice. If she was right, they could reduce the number of soldiers pursuing them as well.

Naiche sent all of his warriors except Bodaway and It-za-cha back along the San Pedro River to the encampment. Afterwards, Lozen worked with Bodaway and Itza-cha to learn about the valves inside the battle wagon. Once satisfied, she sat near the entrance, keeping the fire stoked under the machine's boiler while the warriors disappeared into the rocks to hide. A lizard sunned itself on a rock nearby.

As the sun settled on the horizon, a bird call sounded three times. Lozen scanned the horizon north of the sun, toward Tucson. On her third pass, she spotted three dots. The last three ornithopters approached. Lozen hopped from the wagon and ran into the rocks to watch. As though understanding what was about to happen, the lizard scurried off the rock to find shelter.

While still about a mile distant, the ornithopters fired into the pass, then whirled away. The blast threw up a shower of gravel which cut Lozen's arm when she threw it up to protect her eyes. The ornithopters circled back toward the pass and fired again. One hit the ground near the battle wagon. Lozen gritted her teeth, glad she wasn't actually in the wagon.

The ornithopters whirled around and fired once more. This time when they turned away, they continued flapping back to Tucson. Lozen watched them for a time. They'd hoped to draw the battle wagon out. She hoped they'd respond as she expected when nothing happened.

She returned to the battle wagon, built the fire back up,

then made herself as comfortable as possible while she waited. In the warm battle wagon, she again dozed.

After midnight, more bird calls caught her attention. Two sharp calls followed by a warble indicated movement on the ground. A small force approached. Naiche made sure his rifle stood nearby. Lozen revived the fire and began shutting off valves. She watched with grim satisfaction as pressure within the lines began to build. She added one more shovelful of coal to the firebox, closed it up, then ran from the wagon.

Soon afterward, a half dozen soldiers approached. They fanned out, alert. Not meeting any resistance, two of them entered the war machine. Lozen hoped they weren't sufficiently expert on steam engines to release the building pressure.

One of the soldiers screamed a warning. A moment later, the battle wagon exploded. Even though Lozen and Naiche hid some fifty yards away, shrapnel flew by overhead.

Lozen lifted her head. The battle wagon and the rails underneath it had been destroyed. All the soldiers nearby were down or blown to bits. Nearby, Naiche gave a short sharp whistle, ordering his men to retreat.

Lozen ran for her horse. The animal, though brave and well trained, trembled in the explosion's wake. She gave the animal a reassuring pat, then hopped on. The horse needed little urging to run as far away from the loud noise as possible.

Naiche and Lozen reached the encampment along the San Pedro soon after dawn. The warriors had fallen back and camped around the adobe remains of an old Spanish presidio. The crumbling walls provided some shelter and the site gave the warriors a good view of the surrounding landscape. The lone surviving battle wagon stood as a sentinel.

The chief and Lozen dismounted and handed their horses' reins to a young warrior. The two then sought out Nana. The elder had taken up residence in the office that once housed the presidio's commandant. No roof remained and the walls no longer rose above anyone's head. Nana wore a straw hat with an upturned brim. A campfire burned in the center of the space and Lozen warmed her hands.

"The soldiers will come, and soon, I'm afraid," said Naiche, "seeking revenge for sabotaged rails."

Nana shook his head. "They will be more worried about re-pairing the track right now and getting the train moving again than attacking us. That gives us time." He turned to Lozen. "We need a man who understands us and speaks the white man's language. I would like you to go seek him out."

"I am fluent in their English." Naiche patted his chest. "I can speak to them."

The old man's cavernous wrinkles extended and empha-sized his frown. "I know, but we need someone they respect and will listen to. We have shown we can cause them grief and we are not afraid to continue. I suspect it will take them a while to regroup for an attack. It will also take our Mexican allies a while to build us another battle wagon. We should use that time to talk."

Naiche ground his teeth. "More useless treaties."

"Treaties are only useless if we have no teeth to back them up." Lozen grinned wide and dangerous. "We have shown we have the teeth."

"Very well." Naiche looked from Lozen to Nana. "Who is this man you trust so much? Another lying white man?"

"He is a friend of Geronimo, a warrior from Japan named Masuda Hoshi."

CHAPTER FOUR
HEIRS OF POWER

Lozen's skin crawled as she rode up to a field on the Rio Grande's banks in the New Mexico Territory. Machines, like skeletal rabbits, hopped along furrowed rows. In perfect synchronization, they stopped, dug holes with their front claws, then spat something into the ground. They each made a quick pivot, covered the holes with their back feet, then moved a little further along. She could imagine such hungry-looking beasts turning their unfeeling gazes upon her. No human farmer appeared to be around to call them off should they set upon her.

She swallowed and controlled her nerves. Although she'd seen the white man's Jackalope Harvesters before, this was the most she'd seen in one place. She surveyed the farm. There were numerous places the farmer could be, observing and controlling the planting, but unseen from the road.

Lozen sat up straight and squeezed the horse's flank with her knees. The animal walked down the dirt road to the simple house. Dried red chile peppers hung on either side of the door and paper lanterns hung from the porch's ceiling, swaying in the breeze.

Just as she reached the house, the hairs on the back of her neck rose as she sensed movement out of sync with the harvesters. She reached for the knife at her belt.

"That is unwise if you wish to retain your fingers."

Lozen held up her hands and eased her head around to face the speaker. He was bald, Asian, and wore a long mustache that framed his mouth. She attempted the most charming, coy smile she could. She hated herself for doing it, but such a tactic often disarmed men better than force. She expected to see a gun aimed from a distance. Instead, the man stood close by

36

with a sword all too near her hip. "I am but a woman," she said.

"That is apparent, but the most dangerous warrior I know is a woman." Lines around the eyes and some loose skin at the man's neck were the only things that betrayed his age. He wore loose-fitting trousers tied around the waist instead of belted and a blue pin-striped shirt. He looked like the Chinese railroad workers she'd seen, but something about him wasn't quite the same, in much the same way she could tell when other Indians weren't Tsokanende. "What is your business here?"

"I seek Masuda Hoshi. A mutual friend requires assistance."

The man grunted, but didn't lower his sword. "What friend would this be?"

"He is called Nana."

Hoshi shook his head. "I know no Nana."

"He is Geronimo's brother-in-law."

"You mean Kas-tziden."

She was impressed that he knew Nana's Tsokanende name.

The sword wavered just a bit. Few others would have detected the slight movement. "I hear the Apaches have captured territory in Southern Arizona. The newspapers say their battle wagons terrify the soldiers in Tucson. They even used one to stop the train. What could a lone, old swordsman do to help your cause?"

"May I dismount? This conversation would be easier if I weren't on horseback with my hands in the air."

Again, the man grunted. "You may, but do not reach for the knife at your belt or the rifle near your thigh."

Lozen nodded and then eased to the ground. She turned and faced the warrior who proved to be shorter than she expected.

"We … Apaches have fought a good fight, but we have suffered many casualties and taken damage. At the moment, the Americans and the Apaches are at an impasse. However, if the Americans decide it's necessary, they can bring much greater force to bear on our holdings. Our war chief, Naiche, believes the time has come to parlay."

The man barked out a laugh barely discernible from his snorts. "I have never met this Naiche."

"Kas-tziden has said you're the best man to speak for us." Lozen gazed into Hoshi's eyes. "He says you have worked for the American soldiers and they respect you."

Masuda Hoshi frowned. "It depends on the soldier. Last I knew, General Johnson was in St. Louis. Who leads the American troops?"

"General Nelson Miles in Tucson."

Hoshi shook his head. "I don't know him." He narrowed his gaze and looked her up and down. After a moment, he took a step backward and sheathed his sword. He adjusted his footing, more at ease, but still ready to grab his sword.

Lozen folded her arms. "You have decided to trust me?"

Hoshi shook his head. "No, I have decided you are not here to rob me or do me harm." He looked out over the Jackalopes, going about their work. "I am no diplomat. What's more, I have no hired hands at this time."

Lozen looked at her saddlebags. "We have some gold and silver. We can help you hire someone to tend your field."

"I respect the Apaches, and Geronimo is my friend," said Hoshi, "but I'm uncertain this is wise. I know someone who is a better negotiator than I am, but he is far away. I think it would be prudent to ask if he could help."

"Who is this?"

"A man named Ramon Morales. He has faced Japan's Emperor and the Russian Czar and moved them with his words." Hoshi turned his head to face Lozen again, though she believed he was always aware of her movements.

"Do you think he will help us?"

"He owes me a favor. He took me from my farm eight years ago to help with a ... situation. I have no qualms asking if he will help me in return now."

"What if he turns you down?"

"Let me consider that as I ride into town to send him a telegram."

"I will go with you." Lozen prepared to mount the horse.

Hoshi held up his hand. "I attract enough unwanted attention in Las Cruces. I do not need the great Lozen along with me."

"I think you will find most white men cannot discern one

'Apache squaw' from another."

Hoshi barked out another laugh. "That may be true, but I need someone to watch the Jackalopes. They will be finished in about an hour and need to be commanded to stop, or they will keep going until they hop into the river and rust." He removed a metal box with several buttons and tiny levers from his belt and held it out to her. He pointed to a red button in the center. "When they reach the end of the row, press the red button."

Lozen took the control box. "How did you recognize me?"

"Your exploits with your brother and Geronimo are well known. It was not hard to guess who you were." Hoshi went to the barn. Fifteen minutes later, he emerged riding a small horse. He wore a straw hat, similar to a Mexican sombrero and sat astride a beautiful lacquered wooden saddle. "I will return soon, then I will prepare dinner and we can discuss plans. Don't forget … the red button." With that he rode off.

Lozen blinked, then turned to face the Jackalopes. She looked at the box, trying to figure out how it commanded the machines. The battle wagons moved through steam-powered linkages. No cables ran from the small box to the automata.

When they reached the end of the row, she pressed the button, half expecting the box to make a sound. Nothing happened. She shook the box, thinking she had done something wrong. Then she looked up. The Jackalope army stood dead still gazing at her. She watched them for a moment to make sure they made no move toward her.

Satisfied the machines had stopped, she eyed the box with new appreciation. She earned her reputation as a sorceress because she could predict their enemy's movement in battle, but this box held powerful magic indeed. She set it on the porch, then grabbed her saddlebags and went inside the house to await the strange wizard-warrior's return.

Ramon returned to his office after a tedious day in court. His fingers twitched as he placed folders on the desk. A criminal case about stolen lightning guns should be intrinsically interesting, but this one proved more a case of following a paper trail of who owed what to whom. His job was to prove beyond a reasonable doubt that men committed a crime, but the defense did a damn good job of raising doubts to the jury.

A knock at the door interrupted his thoughts. "Come in," he called.

The law clerk, Jacob Darrant, entered. "This just came in for you." He handed Ramon a telegram.

Ramon thanked the clerk, who ducked out of the office. Ramon's fingers relaxed as he read the telegram from Masuda Hoshi. It asked if he could travel to Tucson and serve as an intermediary between the Apaches and Southern Arizona's white settlers. He snorted a laugh and tossed the telegram to the corner of his desk.

He opened up a folder and started to review another affidavit, but again his fingers twitched and his mind wandered to the conversation he had the other day with Dr. Holliday. He forced himself to read another paragraph, but Hoshi's request kept returning to the forefront of his mind. Finally, he placed the paper in the folder, crossed the hall to another office, and knocked.

U.S. Attorney Albert H. Leonard cleared his throat and invited Ramon to enter. The attorney had wavy hair and a thick walrus-like mustache hid his mouth. "How is the case going?"

"It goes well," said Ramon. "I suspect we'll make closing arguments tomorrow."

"Good, good." If Leonard showed pleasure, the mustache hid it. "How can I help you?"

"I know I've only been here about a year, sir, but I wondered if I could take a month's leave of absence once this case is wrapped up."

The senior attorney's eyes widened just a little. "What in the world for?"

"A former associate in Arizona has asked me to consult with him on the Apache crisis."

Leonard's eyes narrowed. "I don't see why that should be any concern of yours."

"The situation is reminiscent of Louisiana's secession." Ramon folded his hands and leaned forward, knowing he trod on sensitive territory. "I thought perhaps insight into the Apache claims might help give me better insights into the legal challenges facing Louisiana twenty years after the … war of Northern Aggression."

Leonard shook his head. "Completely different situations, Morales. Louisiana's secession was a legal action by a recognized government. The Apaches are not a state within the Union. They are more like invaders. That's a job for diplomats, not government attorneys."

Ramon took a moment to compose his thoughts. "I respectfully suggest that the United States has been dealing with the Indian tribes as sovereign states and therefore they are entitled to the same rights as the states of the Union."

"I don't agree with your argument, but even if I did, this is still well outside the purview of your job and I see no reason to grant you this leave of absence."

Ramon took a deep breath and blew it out. He knew Leonard was correct about his responsibilities. He needed his boss to see the bigger picture. "Sir, may I respectfully remind you that in the long run, I would like a position with the State Department? Investigating this case would be beneficial to that goal."

The ends of Leonard's mustache lifted a little. "Your long-term goals are commendable, Mr. Morales, but I still must decline your request." He leaned forward. "I appreciate your enthusiasm, son, but we've got plenty of work here to keep you busy."

Ramon's fingers twitched again as he struggled to keep his face neutral. He understood his request being declined, but the "son" rankled. It might have been okay, if Leonard had said it in a way that implied true paternal feeling, but to Ramon, it sounded like a superior white man speaking down to his brown employee. At last, he met his boss's gaze. "I understand. Thank you for your time and I'm sorry to have interrupted you."

"Not at all." Leonard sat back. "I'm glad you have such a keen interest in national affairs."

Ramon stood and excused himself. He returned to his office, but couldn't bring himself to open the case files again. He realized he knew the folder's contents by heart and further study wouldn't help. He picked up Hoshi's telegram, folded it, and put it in his coat pocket.

He left the office and told Jacob to send him a message by clacker if anyone needed him. The Commercial Hotel where Dr. Holliday stayed was only two blocks away. It was an imposing structure of stark, white blocks offset by elaborate scrollwork around the window over the front door. Entering the lobby, he approached the clerk in a fine suit behind the gleaming wooden front desk and asked where he could find the doctor.

Information in hand, Ramon walked up the stairs and knocked on Holliday's door. Receiving no response, Ramon thought it would have been nice if the clerk had told him that Holliday had gone out. For good measure, he knocked again. This time a thump sounded from within. A moment later, the door opened. Doc Holliday stood in the doorway unshaven, in a nightshirt with rumpled hair, seeming at odds with the fine establishment where he stayed.

"Well, well, well, if it isn't Mr. Morales. I'd about given up on you."

Ramon fought a reflex to wave aside the man's breath which reeked of alcohol and rotten meat—no doubt that latter a result of the man's tuberculosis. "You said your associates out west might be willing to pay for my time should I help with the Apache problem. I hoped you could tell me more about how much they offered to pay and for how long."

Holliday nodded. "Please come in and we'll discuss it while I make myself more presentable."

Ramon wondered if he made a mistake pursuing the Apache affair at all, but even if he decided to turn down Hoshi and Holliday, he knew he would always regret the decision if he made it without having all the facts.

Buzzing cicadas serenaded Fatemeh and Alethea as they strolled down St. Ann Street in the early evening. The sun had set and the three and four-story structures surrounding them cast deep shadows. Overhead hung pink-tinged clouds threatening an evening shower. Fatemeh appreciated the longer days. At least she didn't have to walk Alethea home in the full winter dark.

A man lighting gas lamps tipped his hat as they passed. In the next block, Fatemeh stopped and listened. "Do you hear that, Alethea joon?"

"All I hear are cicadas."

"Listen closely." Fatemeh pointed up into a skinny tree planted beside the street. In its branches a reddish owl peered down at them. Its throat vibrated and it made a soft trilling. Fatemeh furrowed her brow.

"I think I hear it." Alethea's eyes widened with wonder. "Daddy says you sometimes talk to owls."

Fatemeh would have laughed, if not for the hollow feeling in the pit of her stomach. She did manage an indulgent smile. "Owls don't talk … at least not the way people talk. The secret is understanding what owls care about."

"And what do owls care about?"

Fatemeh stood upright and continued down the street. "They care about their territory, the wind, and their prey." She considered the rats hiding in the buildings surrounding her.

"Do they ever care about people?"

Fatemeh paused and gazed down into her daughter's brown eyes, so much like her father's. If she wore spectacles, she could almost be him in miniature. "They do, especially if people's actions affect them."

"So, what was this owl saying?"

Fatemeh sighed. "They don't speak in words, but screech owls usually trill like that in fall, not in the spring. They trill to alert invaders that they've entered an owl's territory."

Alethea frowned. "Was the owl talking about us?"

Fatemeh shook her head. "We did enter the owl's territory, but I don't think she trilled about us. Something else approaches."

They walked another block and reached the three-story tall pink building containing their flat. Lights illuminated the windows. Fatemeh breathed a relieved sigh, glad Ramon was already home. She opened the courtyard gate, walked Alethea up the stairs, and opened the door. "Ramon, are you here?"

"In here, Corazón," he called from the bedroom.

She followed his voice and found him hanging his

waistcoat. He turned around and kissed her. "I heard from an old friend today."

Fatemeh smiled and put her finger on his lips. "Can you tell me when I get back? I need to run a short errand."

"An errand? What for?"

"One of my customers left something on the counter." Fatemeh chuckled, hoping her nervousness didn't show. "She lives just up the street. Would you be a dear and start the fire in the stove for supper?"

"If it's just a short walk, I could come with you?" Ramon's brow furrowed.

"And leave Alethea alone?"

"She could come with us."

"She has homework."

Ramon's fingers twitched. "You're right."

Fatemeh leaned in and kissed Ramon's cheek. "I want to hear your news, but I don't want to be too late. I'll be right back."

With that, Fatemeh left the house, scurried down the steps and strode toward Bourbon Street. The neighborhood was becoming home to many of New Orleans' bars and saloons. Still early on a weekday, the drunks hadn't emerged. Even so, the hairs on the back of her neck stood up as she turned down the street and passed each alley and shadow. The owl hadn't been in distress, but it sensed something and she should prepare. She jumped as a bottle crashed followed by raucous laughter

Fatemeh breathed a relieved sigh when she turned on to St. Peter Street and caught Marie Lalande just as she locked her shop's door. "I hear you can make a gris-gris for protection."

Marie narrowed her gaze. "There are different kinds. We can discuss it tomorrow when I come over to await Francoise."

Fatemeh's mouth went dry. "I'd rather not wait."

Marie unlocked the door and invited Fatemeh inside. "Is this a gris-gris for you? Is something wrong?"

"It's for Alethea," said Fatemeh.

Marie gazed into Fatemeh's eyes for a long time before she nodded. "Gris-gris of this kind are expensive. Not only do they need to protect the daughter, but they need to protect the mother as well."

"I don't care about myself."

"I know, cher." Marie put her hand on Fatemeh's arm. "We mothers don't care enough for ourselves, but where will our daughters be if harm befalls us?"

Fatemeh frowned but gave a reluctant nod. "Cost is no object to me. Do what you can." She knew Ramon wouldn't necessarily agree, but they had saved considerable money while in New Orleans. She would do anything necessary.

Marie squeezed Fatemeh's arm and disappeared through a curtain into a back room. Fatemeh debated whether or not she should follow. Something in Marie's demeanor told her she should stay put, so she glanced around the room. Alligator skulls lined a shelf and candles lined the one below. Even though she worked around herbs, the heavy scents in Marie's shop threatened to overwhelm her. A painting of a stunning Creole woman hung on the wall. She wore a stern expression, her hands folded in her lap. Fatemeh stared at the painting and could swear the woman stared back at her.

A clock's ticking grew palpable. She looked at it and gasped, surprised how much time had passed. Ramon would be worried. She eased toward the curtain when Marie thrust it aside, holding a small, cloth bag on a string.

"Is that the gris-gris?"

"I have begun preparations. Have your daughter wear this. All will be in place by the time Francoise and Alethea come home from school."

"Thank you, my friend." Fatemeh still felt a hollow in the pit of her stomach, but it had lightened somewhat. She took the gris-gris from Marie, then went home to make dinner and hear Ramon's news.

Ramon added fire to the wood stove as she entered the flat. He looked up. "I was afraid I needed to send a search party out for you?"

Fatemeh flashed a nervous smile as she hung her coat on the rack beside the door. "I wasn't that long, was I?"

"No, not really. I'm just anxious to tell you my news."

"Tell me while you scoop out some rice from the bin." Fatemeh grabbed a pot from the cupboard, added water, and placed it on the stove.

"Hoshi wrote to me. He wants me to be an intermediary between the army and the Apache forces in Southern Arizona." He added the rice to the pot.

She grabbed three chayote squash—a variety the man at the farmer's market called mirliton—diced them, then chopped some onion. "It's flattering they want you there. Would Mr. Leonard grant you a leave of absence? Would the Apaches be able to pay you?"

Ramon narrowed his gaze and thought for a moment before responding. "I've spoken to Dr. Holliday. He's working with some men whose primary interest is getting access to the silver veins the Shieffelin brothers discovered. If I help them, he promises to pay a great deal."

Fatemeh shook the frying pan with the squash and onions, perhaps a little harder than necessary. The water for the rice boiled and Ramon moved the pot to a cooler part of the stove and covered it. "So, who would you be working for, the Apaches or Dr. Holliday's friends?"

"A good diplomat works for everyone's best interests." Ramon sat down at the table. "I thought this might be a good opportunity to go out west and have some time together as a family."

Fatemeh's stomach clenched. Part of her liked the idea of running as far away as possible, but she sensed something coming she must face. "Picou is a good man, but I don't want to leave the shop in his care that long without help and we can't pull Alethea out of school."

Ramon frowned, betraying disappointment. "When we first met, you would drop everything to help someone in need."

She turned around and folded her arms. "I won't stop you if you feel you must do this." Her expression softened and she approached him and lifted his chin. "If this takes until summer, maybe we can come out and join you then."

Ramon pursed his lips. "I don't think Mr. Leonard will give me time off," he admitted. "I'll be taking a chance on getting paid."

"If you think it's the right thing to do, you should do it regardless, but I can't help you decide beyond that." She hoped her words sounded genuine. Her fingers on his chin trembled despite her best efforts to calm them. He took her hand in his and she drew on his quiet strength.

"Is something wrong? If you think I should stay, I will."

She smiled and the trembling finally ceased. "I don't want you to go, Ramon. I love you and want to be with you. But, if you must go, I won't stop you. I know you're not content to remain a lawyer." She returned her attention to the meal.

"It could be a futile gesture. After all, we have the first Democratic president of my adult lifetime." Ramon shrugged. "He may not be as sympathetic to the Apaches' plight as his Republican predecessors."

Fatemeh snorted a derisive laugh. "Just because the Republicans ended slavery doesn't mean they liked Indians better than the Democrats. Washington politics won't be your biggest challenge, I think."

Ramon looked up. "You sound as though I've made up my mind."

"You'll do the right thing … whatever it is," said Fatemeh.

Alethea emerged from her room. "Is dinner ready? I'm hungry and it smells good."

"Help me set the table, Alethea joon," instructed Fatemeh.

"What are we having?" The girl looked at the pans. "Squash again?" She wrinkled her nose. "Can't we have beef like the cowboys out west?"

Ramon shook his head. "Those vaqueros out west would kill for fresh spring vegetables like this. And if they ate beef all the time, they'd be eating their profits. Be grateful for what you've got. How do you know about cowboys anyway?"

"Francoise gave me a book about a bad hombre called Cowboy Charlie."

Ramon chuckled. "Don't believe everything you read."

Alethea scowled at him as she set the silverware on the table. "Are you going out west?"

Ramon pointed at his daughter. "You were listening in, weren't you?"

Alethea stuck her tongue out at Ramon. "Of course I was."

Fatemeh served a plate and handed it to her. "Your father has been asked to do a very important job. He'll decide if he can help."

Alethea set the plate in front of Ramon. "You're a hero, daddy. If someone asks for help, I know you'll be there for them … even if they're slick."

Fatemeh's eyes widened as her daughter repeated her words. "Alethea!"

"Slick?" asked Ramon. "Who are you talking about? Dr. Holliday?"

"How'd ya' guess?" Alethea grinned, proud of herself.

Ramon laughed. "Dr. Holliday does have some hidden agendas, yes, but he's right that the territorial fight in Arizona needs to come to an end. If I don't go, they'll turn to someone else, and I'm not sure they'd have the Indians' best interest at heart."

Fatemeh brought her plate to the table and sat across from Ramon. "You see, I knew you'd make the right decision."

"I didn't say I'd made a decision, Corazón." Ramon took a bite of squash.

"You didn't have to." She winked then brushed her hair back. Ramon's eyes twinkled and she knew his thoughts moved closer to home.

Later that evening, Ramon, Fatemeh, and Alethea sat in their flat's small common room. On the couch, Ramon read *Owl Riders* while Alethea played with her clothespin dolls. Fatemeh watched Ramon's expressions as he read and she could imagine him reliving their past adventures. Their last few years in Massachusetts and Louisiana had been an adventure as great as any in the book, but she knew Ramon grew restless.

Fatemeh looked up at the clock. "Alethea, it's time for bed. It's a school night."

The girl frowned, but stood. She came over and gave Fatemeh a hug, then hugged Ramon and started for her room.

"Don't leave your toys in the middle of the floor."

Alethea pouted, but collected her dolls and took them to the room.

"I'll be in shortly to tuck you in," said Fatemeh.

Ramon closed the book and set it on the table beside the couch. "So, do you ever wonder what's become of this Hamid?"

"He was a successful businessman," said Fatemeh. "I can only imagine he's continued to grow his business."

"Do you suppose he ever wonders what happened to you?"

She snorted. "In our culture I would have been a possession to him." She stood from the chair and sat down next to Ramon. "You're worried about leaving Alethea and me for what? A few weeks at most? As a trader Hamid would have been gone nine or ten months out of the year and he wouldn't have bothered to be concerned about my feelings." She leaned against Ramon and he gathered her into his arms. She loved the security and wished she could stay there forever, but she knew she had to share him with the world. "I want you to be a diplomat so you can heal the world much as I hope to heal bodies and spirits. I know you'll need to be gone sometimes and take chances. Thank you for being concerned about your family."

"You're my heart and my soul. Of course, I love you." Ramon looked up at the clock. "I need to go to bed as well. I have a court date in the morning, then I'll find out when I can catch an airship west." He gave her a tender kiss on the cheek, then lingered a little longer on her lips. "Hopefully, I can find some way to do this and keep my job." Ramon gave her another squeeze, eased his arms from around her, and went to the bedroom.

Fatemeh listened to cloth rustling and drawers sliding in and out as Ramon changed into his nightclothes and turned back the blankets. Once he'd settled in, she stood and entered Alethea's room. "I have something for you." Fatemeh removed a pouch from around her neck and put it around Alethea's.

Alethea looked at the small, red fabric pouch, then sniffed it. "It smells like the herbs in your shop."

"Madame Lalande's shop, actually. And yes, you smell herbs." Fatemeh gave her daughter a reassuring smile. "If you ever feel scared or confused and you can't find me while your dad is away, promise me you'll look for Madame Lalande or one of her friends. If you show her friends the gris-gris, they'll do everything they can to help you."

"Why wouldn't I be able to find you?"

Fatemeh shrugged. "We all get lost sometimes."

Alethea turned the gris-gris around in her hands and nodded. "I promise."

With that, they recited a prayer together and then Fatemeh

tucked her daughter in. "Does the gris-gris really contain Voodoo magic?"

Fatemeh considered that for a bit. "I believe it does, but you have to understand something. People often expect magic to be flashy and miraculous. In fact, magic is often quiet and subtle. Sometimes it's even easy to understand, if you take time to listen and pay attention."

"Like listening and paying attention to owls?"

"Precisely." Fatemeh kissed her daughter, then blew out the lamp and left the room, closing the door behind her. She extinguished the lamps in the sitting room and kitchen as well. From the kitchen, she could hear Ramon snoring, already asleep.

Fatemeh stepped out to the landing in front of their flat. She walked over to the end of the porch overlooking St. Ann's. Across the way stood a two-story brick building with wrought iron railings. To her left, the spires of St. Louis Cathedral projected skyward, like sentinels guarding the city. She could just make out a few strains of music, the occasional laugh, and a few raised voices from Bourbon Street. Despite that, the flat's surroundings were peaceful and the air still. She rubbed her arms to stave off the moist chill and stared out into the street.

She considered the owl and its warning about an intruder. Marie Lalande's gris-gris would keep Alethea safe whatever happened. Ramon would fly off to Arizona, where he would be safe. Fatemeh said a short prayer of thanksgiving. Now, she had the freedom to do anything necessary to confront this mysterious invader.

CHAPTER FIVE
PLAYING TO WIN

"You are pleasantly quiet company for a man." Lozen cast a glance at Hoshi.

The former samurai arched an eyebrow. The two crossed the border from New Mexico to Arizona territories under cover of darkness. Despite the barren desert terrain, they had no shortage of food or water. Lozen knew just where and how to obtain both while keeping them on schedule. "You have told me what I need to know. I understand what the Apaches want and what they'll settle for. I understand your strengths and weaknesses and have a sense of those the American force commands. What more should I ask?"

"Many men are curious about my brother Victorio. Some want to know why I never married. Others ask if I really am a sorceress." Lozen glanced over at Hoshi, his face illuminated by the quarter moon's pale light. He appeared just a little older than her with eyes that roved over the countryside as he carefully evaluated the surroundings. Lozen could see how Geronimo and Kas-Tziden could respect this man.

"I have read about Victorio's battles and I'm sorry for your loss." She sensed his words contained genuine remorse at not being able to meet her brother.

"He allowed his passions too much control." Her voice quavered with a mixture of anger and sadness. "I might have counseled restraint had I been with him at the final battle."

"The book I read on the subject did not say whether or not you were there."

"I'm surprised the white men's books mention me at all."

Hoshi snorted. "They don't. I know of you because the newspapers have written about you since you took Fort Bowie."

"Yes, that battle made the white men take notice." Lozen was proud of her warriors. She glanced around the countryside and turned her horse southward.

Hoshi changed the subject. "Do you still have a telegraph at the fort?"

Lozen shook her head. "No, the army cut the lines soon after we occupied it."

"Before we proceed, I should go to the San Simon Butterfield Stage Station and follow up on the messages I sent from Las Cruces."

"I don't want to delay this close to Fort Bowie." Lozen narrowed her gaze and evaluated Hoshi. Soldiers were stationed at San Simon. If he meant to betray the Tsokanende cause, it would be an easy place to do so.

"Once we enter Apache Territory, I will be cut off from all communication until I get to Tucson. I would like to know what is happening before we get that far." His argument made sense.

Lozen remained silent for a moment as though weighing options, then gave a sharp nod and pointed to the north. "We're about five miles due south of San Simon. It's on the rail line. I will take you there."

"Aren't you worried the soldiers will recognize you?"

She considered that. Whether the soldiers recognized her or not, they could make trouble for her. "I'll stop before we reach the station. The soldiers will be suspicious of anyone in this area, Indian or not. You must take care and make sure they do not follow you when you leave."

Hoshi nodded. They turned their horses and Lozen led them slightly east of due north. When they reached the railroad tracks, they pulled out their bedrolls and took a short nap while waiting for the sun to rise.

Hoshi concealed his sword among the saddle blankets, then mounted the horse and rode along the railroad tracks. Lozen watched him for a time, then climbed on her horse and made a circuit to the north of Hoshi's path. She came to a wash lined with trees, dismounted, and made her way along the tree line using the morning shadows as cover. She reached a point where she could see the station.

She raised her binoculars. Hoshi had already arrived. He bowed low to the soldier at the door. The soldiers glanced at one another, then shook as though they laughed at him. She failed to see the humor, but nonetheless, they let him pass.

Hoshi entered the station and the soldiers huddled together as though planning something. Lozen licked her lips and prepared herself, in case she needed to intervene. A few minutes later, Hoshi left the building. One of the soldiers tripped him. Hoshi recovered quickly and came up in a fighting stance. Two of the soldiers backed away in mock fear. The third soldier approached Hoshi closely. Again, the samurai bowed low and backed away from the soldier. The angry soldier made as if to follow, but his partners said something to him. Hoshi mounted his horse and rode to the south.

Lozen returned to her horse and rode back to the place where she and Hoshi had camped the night before, arriving at nearly the same time.

"I presume you were watching me," said Hoshi.

"Of course." She looked to the south. "We should ride on. There is water a short distance away and we can refresh our mounts." As they continued their ride, she glanced over to him. "Were you able to get your telegrams relayed?"

"I only received two of the responses I expected, but they give me hope." Hoshi stared straight ahead, his gaze narrowed, as though considering the information he received. "Ramon Morales says he will come on the next available airship after he finishes the trial he's prosecuting. I suspect we'll reach Tucson before him, but that's hardly certain."

"And the second telegram?"

"General Johnson in St. Louis has instructed General Miles to agree to parlay." He pursed his lips. "On the surface that is good news and it is what I desired, but I'm concerned about how well General Miles will listen to those orders."

"As you say, this is hopeful news so far." She considered what he said. "You expected a third telegram?"

"I wrote to a fellow former samurai in Japan," explained Hoshi. "Ramon Morales and his wife helped her secure an influential position in the Meiji government."

"Her?" Lozen wondered if she'd heard that correctly. "I

know very little of Japanese samurai. Can women achieve such a position?"

"Not often." A smile flitted across his features for just a moment. "I suspect few Japanese would guess that Apache women could be warriors."

When Hoshi said nothing further, she pressed on with her next question. "Do you think she can help?"

Hoshi considered that. "She could help if she chose. Whether or not she will choose is … uncertain."

Lozen thought about pressing the matter, but decided it would do no good. This mysterious woman samurai would help or she wouldn't. In the meantime, she would take Hoshi to General Miles and see if they could reach an agreement.

They reached Fort Bowie around noon. The warriors at the gate recognized Lozen and admitted them unchallenged. Dahteste—a sight for sore eyes—waited near the commander's office. As Lozen dismounted, Dahteste, heedless of the men around them, rushed up and caught her in an embrace. She demanded all the latest news. Lozen patted her back and asked if they'd had any trouble with the white men. They walked into the commandant's office. Once inside, Lozen realized she'd forgotten Hoshi.

She whirled around and stepped back out into the sunlight. He had dismounted and chatted with one of the warriors. She called out orders to find him food and a bed for the night, then turned her attention back to Dahteste.

Ramon grinned as the judge's gavel pounded and the bailiff called for all in the courtroom to rise. After all was said and done, the jury had agreed with the state that the men on trial had stolen the lightning gun parts.

Ramon's boss would be pleased. He hoped, under the circumstances, Mr. Leonard would rather give him a month off than lose him altogether. If he gambled wrong, at least the victory might dull the shock of his impending resignation. Ramon reached over and shook hands with the defense attorneys. They'd put up a good fight.

As Ramon gathered his papers, the clacker on his belt chattered to life. He listened to Jacob's urgent request to come upstairs. Mr. Leonard wanted to see him as soon as possible. Ramon's brow furrowed. Word of the victory couldn't have traveled upstairs that fast. Something else must have arisen. Ramon packed his papers, then hustled upstairs to the U.S. Attorney's offices.

Jacob Darrant looked sheepish as he pointed toward Leonard's door. Ramon nodded as he approached his boss's office. He knocked, then entered when Leonard barked out, "Come in!"

The senior attorney leaned across his desk. "It seems you are a popular man, Mr. Morales. I've received two telegrams this morning. The first is from the Japanese Ambassador. He wants you to assist a Mr. Masuda in Arizona."

Ramon's heart raced and he dropped into a chair, even though Leonard had not invited him to. "I'm sure that's to do with the business I spoke to you about. Sir, we won the lightning gun case."

Leonard waved the words aside and sat back. "That was open and shut, really, I had every confidence in you." He picked up the other telegram. "This second one is far more disturbing. Something about a theft eight years ago..."

The pounding in Ramon's chest intensified. He couldn't help but associate the query from the Japanese ambassador with the second telegram and assumed Hoshi's request had triggered a long-forgotten inquiry into an incident where he "borrowed" a Japanese automaton and revealed its existence to the Russian Czar. No one pressed the matter at the time in the interests of peace and because Ramon hadn't revealed any secrets. He struggled to focus on Leonard's words.

"Mr. Morales, I can't have controversy in this office. I want you to take leave without pay until this matter is resolved."

Ramon blinked. Although he hated to lose pay, this was just what he wanted. Again, he couldn't read Leonard's expression behind the damned mustache. "I understand, sir, and thank you." Ramon reached out to shake Leonard's hand, but reconsidered when the attorney sat back and folded his arms.

Ramon crossed to his office and dropped off the case folders, then decided he could use some fresh air. As he passed Darrant's desk, the clerk held up his hand. "Mr. Morales, I'm supposed to collect your keys."

Ramon pursed his lips. That seemed like overkill for the kind of inquiry he faced. Still, he didn't want to cause trouble when it looked as though he would have time to go west just as he wanted. He handed over the keys, then turned toward the door.

Darrant stood. "I don't think Mr. Leonard wants you to leave."

Ramon shrugged. "I just need to make some arrangements, I have my clacker if anything pressing comes up."

The clerk shot a glance at Mr. Leonard's door, but made no move when Ramon left the office. He walked downstairs trying to put the pieces together. He should have asked more about the theft inquiry. He shrugged, figuring details would emerge soon enough. He exited the building through the back door and made the short walk to the Canal Street Dock, where airships exchanged cargo with Mississippi riverboats. A cool breeze blew off the Mississippi and Ramon took a deep breath. The air refreshed him. The Quarter may be colorful, but an odor of waste clung about its walls.

A grand, silver aircraft chugged in from the west, trailing smoke. Ramon entered the building and glanced at a timetable beside the ticket counter. An airship bound for Tucson departed that afternoon. If he missed the flight, it would be a week before he could catch another.

Ramon chewed his lip in indecision. Delaying the journey would give him time to clear up this odd matter of a theft and do more research into the Apache situation. Then again, if the charges were cleared, Leonard might change his mind and terminate Ramon's leave of absence. Figuring it was often easier to be forgiven than ask permission, he bought a ticket for that afternoon's flight.

From there, Ramon walked back to the flat. Although strange to be home in the middle of the day, he opened the closet and retrieved an old carpet bag. He smiled when he realized Fatemeh used to carry her herbs and healing supplies in it. He packed for a two-week trip, then locked the door and went to Fatemeh's shop.

She stood behind the counter tending a customer. Once the customer left, Fatemeh smiled at him. "What brings you around so early?"

"It would seem Hoshi's pulled some strings. There's been a formal request for me to go out west." He lifted the carpet bag. "The next airship leaves today, so I figured I better be ready."

"Good for you." She gave him a proud smile and Ramon felt better about his decision.

The clacker at Ramon's belt erupted with urgent clicks and clacks. "The sheriff?"

"What's the message?" asked Fatemeh.

Ramon shook his head. "It was something about the sheriff of Orleans Parish being in the office to question me."

"Why would the sheriff want to question you?"

Ramon shrugged. "Mr. Leonard mentioned a theft in addition to the telegram from the Japanese Ambassador. The only thing that comes to mind is the incident with Katsu Kaishu's mechanical servant in Russia."

Ramon grabbed the clacker to respond, but Fatemeh put her hand on his wrist. "I think it might be best if you pretended you hadn't received the message. You should get to the airship."

Ramon shook his head. "What in the world do you mean? This sounds more serious than I thought."

"Exactly." Fatemeh's grip on his wrist tightened. "Call it intuition, but I think someone is trying to keep you here. This feels like a delay tactic from someone who doesn't want peace."

Sometimes Fatemeh's voice assumed an almost hypnotic tone and Ramon had a difficult time finding arguments. He reached down, took off the clacker and handed it to Fatemeh. "I'll miss you," he said.

"You'll do an extraordinary job." Fatemeh pulled Ramon into her embrace. He gazed down into her eyes. "Go make peace in Arizona."

A short time later, Ramon dropped his carpet bag onto the upper bunk in his cabin aboard the *City of New Orleans*. It seemed smaller than the cabins aboard Japanese airships, but these were crammed with more furniture. The cabin held a bunk bed and a small writing desk. Open curtains revealed a small port hole. A suitcase already lay on the lower bunk. Ramon had agreed to share a cabin with another passenger in order to save a little money.

Ready to get underway, he walked forward to the lounge area. John Henry Holliday sat at a table, nursing a clear drink. "Well, fancy seeing you on this flight."

"Indeed." Ramon adjusted his glasses. "This is fortuitous. It gives us a chance to discuss the situation a little more as we travel."

A steward approached the table to take Ramon's drink order. Ramon considered ordering a beer to settle his nerves, but decided on a coffee instead. The waiter gave a curt bow and left the men alone.

The airship's engines rumbled to life sending a shudder through the floor. Ramon excused himself and joined several other passengers at a bank of windows. He leaned over the railing and his stomach fluttered as he watched the Mississippi and New Orleans grow smaller. Soon the ship turned and the calm, blue expanse of Lake Pontchartrain spread out beneath them. The Japanese airships had external catwalks and Ramon remembered wind blowing through his hair. He wondered how those ships had evolved over the last eight years.

He turned around and his coffee steamed on the table next to the doctor. Ramon returned and took a sip. The coffee hit his stomach and soured as he considered his rapid departure. He sat down and wondered if he should have stayed behind to sort things out with the sheriff.

"Would you care for a game of faro to take your mind off your troubles?" asked Holliday.

"Do I look troubled?" Ramon's brow furrowed.

Holliday nodded. "Trust me, when you've worked in as many saloons as I have, you begin to recognize it. I have a faro set in my cabin. I'll be just a minute."

The doctor sauntered through the lounge and tipped his hat at a lady sitting alone at a table. Once he'd left the lounge, Ramon grabbed Holliday's drink and sniffed. The alcohol scent almost overpowered him. Despite that, Holliday had shown no sign of staggering.

Ramon returned the glass and sipped his coffee. Holliday returned after a moment and set down the faro set. "So, what cabin are you in?" asked the doctor as he worked.

"Cabin 12."

"Ah, so we're roommates!" The doctor sat and shuffled cards.

Ramon's stomach churned again, but he ignored it as he watched Holliday discard the soda card—the eight of hearts—and move a bead on the abacus that marked which cards had been played.

"Place your bet," said Holliday.

"Do you have any chips?"

"It ain't fun unless we play for real money."

Ramon dug in his trousers for change. He placed nickels on three of the cards. He then placed a penny on one of those, coppering the bet.

Holliday turned over two cards.

Ramon won a little money and he placed another bet. "I understand you and your associates want access to the Mule Mountains to exercise your mining claims, but I'm still not clear what you'll give the Apaches in return."

"Well, the army is offering them a one-way trip to Florida and they'll hang the leaders." Holliday turned over two more cards. "That seems a right powerful disincentive to negotiation."

Ramon lost his coppered bet. He placed another bet and coppered another card. "That's true. Now as I understand it, the Apaches' primary complaint is that they don't have arable land on their reservations. Why not let them keep land along the San Pedro? That way you'd still have access to the silver in the Mule Mountains."

"We need the water for ore extraction." Holliday spoke in a matter-of-fact tone. "And we need it for any settlers who help work the mines. Now I see no problem with allowin' the Apaches to buy into that land and havin' jobs in the mines."

"And where exactly would they get the money to buy in?"

"That's not my problem to solve." Holliday turned over two more cards.

This time Ramon had money on both winning and losing

cards, splitting the stake. As Holliday adjusted the abacus, Ramon thought he moved one too many beads. "I believe we've only played one king so far, Dr. Holliday."

Holliday grinned and moved a bead back. "I believe you're right." He waited for Ramon to place another bet. "I should warn you, I do play to win."

Ramon gave a curt nod. "Of that, I have no doubt."

Fatemeh compounded a stomach remedy for Mr. Gautreaux. She measured chemicals and herbs, adding them to a pestle. As she worked, she wondered whether it had been such a good idea to encourage Ramon to return to the west. If Alethea faced danger from an intruder, Ramon would do everything in his power to keep her safe like a vengeful owl loa. Then again, that could be construed as a problem in its own right. He would destroy himself to keep them safe and she didn't want to see that happen.

For that matter, the owl's warning might not apply to her family at all. That was the problem with owls, they weren't always precise, especially when the danger didn't concern them.

She poured the stomach remedy into a bottle, then wrote out a label with instructions. Just as she stoppered the bottle, the bell over the shop door jangled. She expected Marie Lalande. Fatemeh breathed a relieved sigh and turned, but the breath stopped dead as she saw not Marie, but a Persian man with graying hair in a business suit and a kolāh—a pillbox-like hat—on his head.

A cold chill caused her to shiver as she understood the owl's warning.

"It's been a long time, Fatemeh joon."

The endearment caused her jaw to tighten, even though she sensed no malice or ill will. "Mr. Farzan, what brings you here?"

He took no apparent offense at the formality. Then again, as Fatemeh searched her memory, she couldn't recall ever referring to him as anything other than "Mr. Farzan."

"My company has been doing business in America for five

years now." He waved his hand as though it should be a given. At that moment, Fatemeh realized he held a book in his other hand. He smiled. "I gather you've been here about eight years."

Fatemeh swallowed, but nodded. "It's a country where I could put my skills as a healer to use."

He shrugged. "Your skills as a healer have many uses." He glanced at the bottles on the shelves. "What I remember most is how much you wanted to travel." He waved his free hand at the bottles. "It seems as though you've settled down."

"The world has a way of coming to New Orleans." She narrowed her gaze at the man she'd once been betrothed to. "Apparently."

Hamid gave a lighthearted chuckle. "You know, it hurt me when you ran away." He held up his hand to stop her before she could interject. "But I forgave you. I loved you precisely because you were not some bird to be caged, but because of your sense of adventure. I figured you would fly for a time and eventually return home." He shook his head and looked down at his feet.

"The problem is, the place I grew up never felt like home," said Fatemeh. "I was caged there and the further I flew, the more I needed to escape."

He gave a non-committal grunt, then held up the book—a copy of *Owl Riders* as she suspected. "Don't misunderstand me, I admire your wanderlust. I love to travel the world myself. There's so much to see and experience. Have you ever been to New York?"

"For a week or so, a long time ago…"

"The Italian immigrants have a wonderful flat bread called pizza. I'll have to take you there sometime." He caught himself and stopped. Again, his face fell into a frown. "Wandering I could forgive, but zina?" He shook his head. "Did this reporter, this Lafcadio Hearn speak the truth when he said you'd married?"

"I fell in love." Fatemeh made the statement as simply and truthfully as she could. She had nothing to justify and she never loved Hamid Farzan.

"I gave no permission to break our engagement and neither did your father."

"That's only true under a particular interpretation of Islamic law." She shook her head. "I am no longer Muslim."

He sighed. "Apostasy and heresy as well?"

Hamid leapt forward and grabbed her wrist. The book hit the ground with a thud. "The time has come for you to return home and face your family for what you've done to them," growled Hamid.

The shop bell jangled again. "Let her go." Marie Lalande stood in the doorway, a .22 caliber derringer pointed at him.

A struggle played across Hamid's face, but after a moment he let go.

He backed away. "Our discussion has not ended."

Marie kept the derringer aimed at Hamid. He lifted his hat and left the shop. Marie kept her eye on him until he rounded the corner. She bent down and picked up the book Hamid dropped. "I just saw these in Mr. Boudreaux's bookshop on my way over. I almost bought a copy."

Fatemeh rubbed her wrist. "You're welcome to that one."

"Now I understand why you wanted the gris-gris." Marie placed the derringer in her purse.

"Now I do as well," said Fatemeh.

CHAPTER SIX
ABDUCTION

Hamid Farzan waited in the shadows and watched the apothecary shop. In its window stood bottles of bright liquids in a variety of colors from orange and red to green and blue. He stopped a passerby. "What do all the colors mean?"

"When there's only one color, it means there's an epidemic in progress and the pharmacy has plenty of the remedy in stock. Multiple colors means it's safe to be out on the street." The passerby looked Farzan up and down, then continued on his way.

Soon, two young girls strolled down the street, one with chocolate-brown skin like the woman who'd aimed a derringer at him and one with lighter brown skin, like a Persian. The book *Owl Riders* ended with Fatemeh and her husband leaving New Mexico Territory for Massachusetts. It mentioned no children. The thought churned Hamid's stomach.

The book.

He left the book behind in Fatemeh's shop.

He shook his head. It didn't matter. The book had already served its purpose.

He'd discovered the book in New York City. He'd concluded business at his American import agent's office and decided to walk to the Little Italy neighborhood where vendors sold flatbread covered in tomato sauce and herbs from metal washtubs they carried around on their heads. They called the flatbread "pizza."

He first saw the book at a newsstand while eating the pizza. He wasn't sure what drew him to the book. Perhaps it was the title, *Owl Riders*. He remembered Fatemeh had an infatuation with owls. The family even kept one as a pet. What was

63

its name? Sah-bum?

Motion from the shop brought his attention back to the present. The black woman and girl left together. Curious, Hamid followed at a discreet distance. The woman walked tall, and never glanced over her shoulder. She entered a building and closed the door.

He looked around and noted a dressmaker, a haberdashery, and a cobbler. Hamid thought it strange so many businesses should surround a dwelling. If it was a business, why weren't there signs? New Orleans seemed so unlike other American cities with its ramshackle assortment of multicolored, vine-covered buildings. It seemed more like a Mediterranean or even Caribbean port city. He tugged at his collar. The heat and humidity definitely reminded him he wasn't far from the Caribbean.

"Two for two."

"What?" Hamid looked around. A black man with stark white hair stood right behind him.

"Two for two." He pointed down at Hamid's shoes. "Two shoes, two dollars."

"That's an expensive shoe shine."

"You visit the Quarter, you want to look your best."

"No thanks." Hamid waved his hand.

"Might cost you more if I leave."

Hamid's brow furrowed. He shrugged and dug out two dollar coins and handed them to the man. The man took polish and a cloth from his pocket, then knelt down.

"Whatcha doin' watchin' that building?" asked the man as he set to work.

"Just curious." Hamid tried to sound conversational.

"About what?" The man buffed Hamid's shoe.

"The door straight across looks like it should be a storefront, but there's no sign. Is it someone's dwelling?"

The man didn't bother to look up. He just kept working on Hamid's shoes. "Curiosity of that kind is dangerous. Don't be askin' questions about that place."

"Why not?"

"There's magic in there. Voodoo magic."

Hamid frowned. He'd heard a little about the strange religion practiced in parts of the Caribbean and brought to New

Orleans by black slaves. As the man continued to buff his shoe, his foot grew warm and memories surfaced. In New York, he'd walked to a café and ordered a cup of their strongest coffee. He'd found an empty table and scanned the book as fast as he could.

He'd flipped through pages searching for references to Fatemeh. According to the book, she formed the owl rider corps who fought the Russian airships over Denver. She led the sheriff who was the book's hero to the Russian commanders in California. Once there, he somehow convinced them to pull back to Alaska. At that point in the book, a cold sensation settled in his gut.

He'd finished his coffee, but it hadn't warmed him, so he'd ordered more.

Fatemeh married Ramon Morales.

Then they went to Hawaii.

In an all too intimate scene, Fatemeh remembered the man she'd been betrothed to. Hamid read his own name right there on the page.

He remembered Fatemeh's father coming to him, to apologize. She had run away ten years ago, never to be seen again.

He loved her and would have made her a queen. He built his shipping empire so he could buy her anything. Every night, he prayed he would find Fatemeh.

And his prayer had been answered at a newsstand in New York.

And still tears ran down his cheeks.

He'd continued thumbing through the book, learning what he could. Ramon had gone on to smooth over a diplomatic incident between Russia and Japan. He'd been instrumental in making peace between Russia and the United States.

Hamid had heard the Persian Consul General to India had traveled to Washington D.C. on a diplomatic mission. No doubt he could make inquiries about this Ramon Morales.

Warmth from his foot brought him back to the present. He wasn't in New York, but New Orleans, having his shoes shined. The more the man buffed, the warmer it got until it grew downright hot. Hamid tried to jump back, but found his foot rooted to the spot.

The man looked up at him and smiled. Unlike the buffing,

the smile held no warmth. "You look as though there's some-thin' wrong."

Hamid yanked his foot upward and stumbled backward. The black man stood upright and leapt forward, taking Hamid's elbow. "You be careful there. It's easy to get lost in time around these parts."

"Lost? In time?"

"You know … nostalgia, memories, that sort of thing." The man winked at Hamid.

The merchant looked down at his shoes, which had been polished to an impeccable shine. "Thank you."

"My pleasure." The man laughed as he faded into the shadows. For just a moment, all Hamid could see was the man's bright smile, then even that winked out as though the man had never been there.

Hamid glanced around. The street was neither empty nor crowded. No one appeared to have taken notice of the strange scene, so he moved on. He strolled toward the river and located the grand building which held both the post office and the federal courthouse. Inside the post office, he found a bulletin board with a handful of wanted posters. One showed a dapper man with short hair and round spectacles. The poster promised a modest reward for Ramon Morales. The merchant smiled.

After leaving New York, Hamid's ship had stopped in Washington D.C. where Haji Hossein-Gholi Khan had granted him an audience. Over the past decade, Russia's might in Asia increased and many feared the empire would attempt to expand its borders. The Consul General to British India hoped the Americans would help contain the Russians.

"Have you heard of Ramon Morales?" Hamid had asked the question, uncertain how important Morales really was in American politics.

Hossein-Gholi's answer had surprised him. "You could say Morales is the man responsible for the situation in Asia." The diplomat stood and retrieved a scrapbook from the shelf behind him. He'd opened it to a page of clippings about the Russo-American war. "He helped broker a peace between the United States, Russia, and Japan, but the peace left Russia with disproportionate power. That was frightening enough with Alexander II. Now that his son has the throne..."

Hamid had held up his hand. "I know. I do considerable business with both British India and the United States. That could be jeopardized if the Russian Empire expanded its holdings."

"That explains your interest, but not why you're interrupting my work."

Hamid had pointed to the scrapbook. "Do those articles mention a woman named Fatemeh Karimi?"

Hossein-Gholi nodded. "She's quite prominent in these stories."

"We were engaged," Hamid had explained. "She and Morales have committed zina. It's a crime punishable by death."

"Only if the shah agrees." Hossein-Gholi had shaken his head. "You know as well as I do that most people convicted of illegal intercourse are sentenced to a flogging, not death. I doubt I could get an extradition order for such an offense."

Hamid had forced a good-natured chuckle. "I don't want them extradited. I just want Morales detained. Send a telegram to New Orleans and have them arrest him and ask some questions. Once he's given answers, give him a couple of days, then have him released." Hamid had nodded to himself. "Yes, that should be sufficient."

"You want me to help you with a personal vendetta?" Hossein-Gholi had folded his hands on the desk.

"I know powerful businessmen around the United States and Europe who could put pressure on their governments to help you." Hamid had tapped the side of his nose. "Consider this a way to help your mission succeed."

"All right, why do you want me to do this?"

"I want to talk to the girl. She ran away from her father, left him heartbroken." Hamid had put on a sad face, which hadn't all been show. Fatemeh's departure really had hurt her father. "I want to give her the opportunity to return to Persia and set things right. However, I fear Morales could cause trouble if he's around."

Hossein-Gholi had agreed to the request. Soon after Hamid arrived in New Orleans, Ramon had disappeared. In custody or on the run from the law, he wasn't certain. It didn't matter.

Hamid walked to St. Ann Street. Convenient that the

Quarter was laid out like a grid. It made it easy to find one's way around even though the buildings were tall and similar enough to afford few landmarks. He found a restaurant which gave him a view of a nearby flat. Entering, he requested a table by the window.

"It'll be a little while," said the waiter.

The merchant checked his pocket watch and nodded. "That's fine, I'm in no hurry." He scanned the restaurant and noticed a couple taking their time with their meal while they eyed one another.

Hamid remembered going to Shiraz to make arrangements for the wedding. Fatemeh's father said she'd abandoned God to join the Bábis. The sect now called itself Bahá'í. Hamid stared at the young couple by the window and thought that could have been Fatemeh and him. He wondered what about the strange religion could have steered a curious innocent onto such a dangerous path.

The couple finished their meal and the waiter led Hamid to a seat.

The restaurant specialized in creole food. When the waiter came for his order, Hamid shrugged. "Bring me the house specialty." As the waiter wrote on a notepad, Hamid grabbed his sleeve. "It must contain no shellfish other than shrimp, and no pork."

The waiter lifted an eyebrow, but nodded. "I think I know just the thing."

A short time later, the waiter brought a dish of shrimp and vegetables in a tomato sauce over rice. Hamid tasted the dish and smiled as the spices danced on his tongue. Whatever this was, it might surpass New York's pizza as a favorite dish.

As he finished the meal, Fatemeh and the little girl in a braid approached the pink-walled building he watched. They disappeared through a gate, but soon appeared on an upstairs landing. They entered the flat and light appeared from within.

The waiter checked on him and he ordered dessert. He took his time with a slice of pecan pie and a cup of coffee. By this time, the waiter made frequent visits to his table, anxious for him to vacate. Hamid paid the bill, satisfied Ramon Morales would not return home that night.

Hamid returned to his ship. The ship he named for the woman he loved.

The *Fatemeh.*

He crossed the gangplank to the main deck where Captain Darrius Turan waited for him, arms folded, tapping his foot.

"Why are we lingering here?" asked the captain. "The crew is paid out of the voyage's profits. We picked up no cargo in Washington. We've picked up no cargo here. The longer we stay here, the less they get per day."

Hamid waved his hand. "Don't worry, Captain. We'll be ready to depart as soon as we collect a passenger. I need at least four volunteers to report to my cabin in an hour. There will be a generous bonus in it for anyone who volunteers."

The captain narrowed his gaze. "You aren't planning anything illegal are you? American and Spanish warships in these waters take a dim view of piracy."

The ship's owner folded his arms. "I do not condone piracy at all, Captain Turan. How dare you think I would put one of my own ships in jeopardy?"

"Forgive me, Mr. Farzan, but your actions on this voyage have been … puzzling."

"What if I told you a young woman from Shiraz had been lured away from God's path by Caribbean Voodoo?"

The captain considered the question for a moment before he nodded. "I'd hate to see that happen."

"As would I," said Hamid. "Make sure those volunteers report on time. If you do, there will be a double bonus in it for you."

Turan perked up a little at the mention of a bonus. "Yes, sir. I'm on it."

A thump, a bang, and a scream cut short yanked Alethea Morales from her sleep.

"Saket Bash!"

Alethea thought she recognized the phrase as one her mother used when she wanted her to be quiet, but instead of her mom, it was an angry man. She rubbed her eyes, climbed out of bed, and peeked through the bedroom door. The door to the outside hung open and four men held her mother's limp body between them. They spoke among themselves but she couldn't understand their whispers. A man in a striped shirt seemed to be the leader.

Alethea dropped back into the bedroom and pressed herself against the wall behind the door, her heart pounding like she'd just run on the playground. A moment later, her door creaked open a little and a man in a stocking cap peered into the room. The man in the striped shirt asked a question and the man at her door answered in their strange language. Striped shirt issued a harsh command and stocking cap tromped back toward the others.

Alethea eased away from the wall and looked through the gap by the hinges. A big man missing a tooth hoisted her mother over his shoulder and made for the door. She wanted to run out, scream and pound on these scary men for hurting her mom, but fear rooted her to the spot. When the men's footsteps disappeared outside, Alethea's thoughts crystallized. A little girl could do nothing against four big men. They would hurt her and either leave her in the flat or take her with them.

If only her dad were here. He wouldn't let the men take her mom!

Then again, she never thought her mom could be captured so easily. They must have hurt her to keep her from struggling.

Alethea swallowed hard and ran to her parents' bedroom, which faced the street below. No lamps illuminated the house, but just enough moonlight filtered in from outside that she could see where she went without stumbling. The gap-toothed man still held her mom over his shoulder and they stalked down the quiet street toward St. Louis Cathedral—and the river.

She clenched her fists and tried to think what to do. The gris-gris rubbed against her chest, distracting her. She reached up to remove it, then remembered her mom told her to seek out Marie Lalande if something happened. Francoise and her mother lived just up the street. She needed help and soon.

She returned to her room and donned shoes, then grabbed a warm coat. As she left the flat, she pulled the door closed, making sure not to lock herself out. She crept to the landing's edge and looked around. The men had disappeared from view.

Alethea ran down the stairs, through the courtyard, and up the street. By the time she reached the Lalande's house she had a stitch in her side and she wanted to pause. Francoise's mom scared her a little and she feared she'd be angry if she knocked so late at night, but fear of what would happen to her own mom spurred her on. She banged on the door.

Neighborhood dogs barked and a few voices, some speaking English, some French, shouted in response. Alethea knocked again and she began to shiver more from fear than rain-chilled air.

The door creaked open and a big man in a nightshirt peered down at her. "Wha'chu want child?" He growled out the words like a bear and Alethea fell back two steps. "Chil'ren should be asleep at this hour."

"Monsieur Lalande, bad men broke into our house and took my mom!"

His eyes went wide. "Where's your pa?"

"He left yesterday on a business trip out west. He's on an airship far away."

"Come in child." The growling voice seemed less intimidating now and sounded more like an enormous cat's purr. He stepped aside and she entered the dark room. "Wait here."

He disappeared into the darkness.

Alethea rubbed her hands together as her heart continued to pound. It seemed like the adults took forever and the stitch in her side began to ease. She resisted the temptation to open the door and peer outside. Her mom's kidnappers would be far away by now.

At last Marie Lalande materialized. "Alethea, cher, what are you doing here? It's three in the morning."

"Men broke into our house and took my mom!"

Marie knelt down and put her hands on Alethea's shoulders. "Slow down, cher. Who were the men? Where did they take your mamá?"

Alethea shook her head and tears leaked from her eyes. She struggled to get the words out. "I don't know the men. They were big with dirty shirts and hairy arms. One wore a stocking cap, another a striped shirt. They hurt my mom. She wasn't moving."

"Where did they go?" Marie's voice took on a deep resonance and Alethea breathed easier. The woman smelled of sandalwood and smoke.

"Toward St. Louis Cathedral. Toward the river."

Marie nodded and stood. "Jacques." Although she spoke in soft tones, her voice carried. Soon the man who's opened the door appeared. Now he wore a work shirt and trousers held up by suspenders. She spoke to him in Creole French. He nodded and departed through the front door.

"You come with me." Marie led Alethea into a bedroom with a big, curtained bed. Marie pulled back the blankets and Alethea climbed in. The sheets were still warm and fragrant with sweat from the bodies which had been there just moments before.

In the dark, Marie went to the armoire, picked a dress, and took it behind a screen. A moment later, she emerged in the dress, bent over the bed, and kissed the girl on the forehead. "Don't you worry, cher. We'll do everything we can to get your mamá back."

"I wanna help!" Alethea's words came out louder and more desperate than she intended.

Marie held her finger to her lips. "I know you do, and you have. Rest now and let Madame Lalande take care of the rest."

With that, the creole woman left the room. Alethea lay in the warm blankets, swearing she wouldn't go to sleep until her mother came home. She tried to remember the prayer of protection her mother taught her, but she only remembered a few phrases. She said them anyway, then drifted into an uneasy slumber.

A pounding in Fatemeh's head throbbed each time her head bounced. She opened her eyes and tried to move her hands at the same time. She found herself in a carriage seat, her hands bound with rope. She remembered waking up and seeing strangers in her bedroom. She'd called out, hoping Alethea would run and stay safe, then darkness.

Where was Alethea? She looked around, and struggled against her bindings.

"Aroom bash," grumbled a man in a striped shirt. The words were Persian for "calm down."

She had no intention of calming down. She tried to sit up straighter, but found it almost impossible with her hands behind her back and her feet tied. Four men occupied the carriage with her and Alethea was nowhere to be seen. She tried to roll and knock herself into the man next to her, but he just laughed, and put one hand on her shoulder, holding her in place.

The carriage creaked to a stop and two of the men hopped out. A burly man with a missing front tooth grabbed her feet and a man in a stocking cap grabbed her shoulders and they hefted her from the carriage. She did her best to get her bearings. A freighter swayed nearby at the riverfront docks. She gasped as she read the name written on its bow. Her name.

As the men carried her toward the ship, other men emerged from the shadows. A tall bear of a man approached, slapping a blackjack in his palm. "Put her down now," growled Jacques Lalande.

Her abductors dropped her and she clamped her jaw shut on a scream of pain as her tail bone hit the wooden dock. Jacques swung the blackjack, connecting with stocking cap's head. The others backed away from her. As they did, Jacques knelt down. "Are you all right?"

"I think so. Where's Alethea?"

"Safe." He just got the word out when the stripe-shirted sailor leapt in and kicked Jacques in the shoulder, sending him sprawling and the blackjack flying. It disappeared among some cargo crates on the dock. Jacques' friends jumped into the fray. In the cloudy moonlight, Fatemeh couldn't tell who struck who, but her fuzzy thoughts finally coalesced and she realized the men who abducted her were sailors from the ship that bore her name—Hamid's men.

She did her best to shimmy toward the cargo crates. Perhaps she could retrieve Jacques' blackjack. At least she would be out of the fight's path.

Jacques leapt to his feet and tackled the man with the

missing tooth. When the man lifted his head, Jacques landed a punch into his jaw, but another sailor grabbed his shoulders and threw him backward. More sailors ran off the ship and joined the fray. One of the sailors made a feint toward a creole man, then sucker-punched him in the stomach.

At last Fatemeh reached the crates. She could just see the blackjack, but she couldn't reach it with her hands trussed up. A rusty nail protruded from one of the boxes. She backed up against it and thought she could use it to help break her bonds. The rope snagged on the nail and she found herself held fast. "Damn it!"

She looked up again. Three sailors and all of the creoles, except Jacques, lay on the dock. A sailor and Jacques circled each other, looking for an opening. Jacques feinted and the sailor lunged forward, but Jacques sidestepped, grabbed his arm and hurled him further along. He turned to deliver a blow when a shot rang out.

Blood sprayed from Jacques' back and he fell face-forward onto the dock. Birds shrieked a sudden protest and flapped away.

The sound gave way to an eerie silence that lasted an indefinite moment before several dogs started barking.

Footsteps sounded on the pier and Hamid Farzan strolled toward Fatemeh. He dropped a revolver into a hip holster, then knelt down next to her. He unsnagged her bound hands from the nail, then called orders to more men who followed behind.

"Why are you doing this?"

Hamid didn't answer. Instead, he turned and strolled back toward the ship.

Sailors came forward. One grabbed Fatemeh's feet, the other her shoulders as before and they carried her across the docks and toward the ship. She looked around. Jacques still lay face down on the dock, blood pooling around him.

A tear fell as guilt welled within her. She hated the thought of Francoise growing up without a daddy and all because he tried to save her. The men holding her chattered with each other, as though they performed a routine chore. She wanted to shout at them to shut up, to pay respects to the fallen man, but she knew they would only laugh.

The sailors carried her aboard the ship, and took her below decks where they placed her on a bed in a cabin. They cut her bonds, then left, closing the door behind them. She rubbed her wrists for a moment to get the feeling back. As the pins-and-needles sensation faded, she stood and went to the door, which was locked from the outside. No surprise there.

She stomped over to the porthole and looked out. She was on the ship's river side. Distant engines rumbled to life. She tried to open the porthole but found it sealed shut. Even if she could open it, she didn't think she could squeeze through.

She dropped back on the bed to think. At least Jacques had reassured her Alethea was safe.

CHAPTER SEVEN
PREPARING FOR NEGOTIATIONS

"I have four men on the injured list, Mr. Farzan. Now you tell me to have men stationed at the guns?" Captain Turan tugged on his beard with meaty hands. "We are no cowards aboard the *Fatemeh*, and I'm prepared to fight pirates when needed, but I never expected to do so in America."

"For all intents and purposes, New Orleans is the Caribbean's northern most port." Hamid waved the captain's concerns aside as he walked to the bridge's window and looked out at the city lights rolling past as they steamed toward the Gulf of Mexico.

"Yes, but it's been seventy years since Jean Lafitte sailed these waters." The captain put his big hands behind his back and walked up beside Hamid. "Your 'cargo' better be worth it." Hamid detected an edge to the captain's voice.

"May I remind you, Captain, that you work for me?"

The captain pursed his lips. "And you should remember it as well. I am a good captain who moves cargo reliably from point to point. To attract a good crew, I must maintain a reputation for good sense. If the owner sends my crew on foolish—personal—errands, I can resign and go to work for another owner."

Hamid sighed. True, he had taken the ship on a personal errand, but he thought it served a greater good. "Trust me, it won't become a habit."

"It better not." The captain turned to examine buoy markers and check the ship's compass.

Hamid straightened and strode from the bridge to Fatemeh's quarters. He unlocked the door and his cheeks flushed hot as he entered a lady's chambers uninvited. He clenched his jaw and saw the harlot who committed zina with another man.

She faced away from him, staring out the porthole, hands behind her back. "What do you want with me, Mr. Farzan?" Her voice was cold and dry.

He blinked. "How did you know it was me?"

She snorted. "I can see your reflection in the glass." At last she turned. The youthful innocence had vanished. Her green eyes shone cold and hard, but her face remained smooth and unblemished, framed by uncovered dark tresses. She wore only a nightgown. It revealed little but tantalizing hints of the curves beneath. The vision of a wedding night that could have been tugged at Hamid's heart.

"Why are you taking me away from my home?" She took a step toward him and Hamid's heart rate increased.

"I'm taking you back home," he choked out. "We were betrothed and you ran away."

"I never loved you, Mr. Farzan." The formality caused his gut to clench as though she had driven in a knife. "My father promised me to you because you promised him riches."

"And the riches I promised him were nothing compared to those I would have given you."

"And they're nothing compared to the riches I have found in America." Her voice held contempt. "Let me go."

"Or what?" Hamid shook his head. "You converted to a heathen religion that won't let you fight and what's worse is your hypocrisy. You will not fight, but you let others fight for you."

She planted her hands on her hips. "I did not ask those men to fight for me." She took another step forward and he stopped her, grabbing her shoulders. "If I find out your men tried to harm my daughter..." She shoved his hands away, then attempted to push past him. He shoved her toward the bed and she tumbled backwards onto the mattress.

"It seems you have some fight in you after all where your brat is concerned." He shook his head. A plinking and clanging against the ship's hull drew his attention before he could say more. Someone fired on the *Fatemeh*. "And once again, it seems others fight for you. Marie Lalande, the black creole man, and now river pirates. How many will you let die for your sake?"

She jumped to her feet, but before she could approach,

Hamid backed from the cabin and slammed the door, locking it.

He strode forward to the bridge where Captain Turan shouted orders. "Status, Captain?"

The captain ignored him and gave a new course heading to the helmsman. At last he turned. "Two cutters came alongside. We repelled one with rifle fire. We've just put men on the port side swivel gun."

Hamid went to the window. A small boat ran alongside the *Fatemeh*. The swivel gun crew fired. Splinters and smoke erupted from the small boat. A man in the cutter's bow attempted to throw a line, but a sharpshooter aboard the *Fatemeh* killed him. Meanwhile, the swivel gun crew took their time loading another round, even though the small cannon was a breech loader. They weren't military and drills weren't a regular part of ship routine.

At last, the swivel gun fired again, blowing another hole into the cutter. This time, it veered away and fell into the *Fatemeh's* wake.

"Any other stops in the Americas, Mr. Farzan?" The captain stood beside him, his thick arms folded, tapping his foot.

Hamid rubbed the bridge of his nose. "No, Captain. Let's go home."

A raging headache blossomed and Hamid wondered if this errand had been worth the effort, after all.

Alethea Morales woke screaming in a dark, strange room. Francoise bolted through the door. "Alethea, what are you doing in my mamá's bed?"

Alethea heaved deep sobs, oblivious to Francoise climbing in next to her. In one night, Alethea's entire world had collapsed. Her mom had been taken and she didn't know if she'd ever see her again. Her dad was far away. Even if they could get a message to him, could he return in time?

Marie Lalande entered the room. The single gas lamp cast deep shadows and exaggerated the lines in her drawn and haggard face. She sat down and held her arms open.

"Come here, cher."

Alethea hopped off the bed and settled into Marie's lap. She breathed in her spicy scent, different from her mother, but she still felt like a mom and the woman's presence quieted her. She sniffed and looked up into Marie's face. Up close, she could tell the woman's eyes had turned red, as though she'd shed her own tears this night. "Did you get my momma back?" Alethea asked the question, even though she feared she already knew the answer.

Marie gave a tiny head shake. "But we have not given up, cher. We will chase her across the wide Atlantic if we need to."

Francoise had shown her the boats her family and their friends used. She didn't think such small boats could make it all the way across the Atlantic Ocean. She also knew adults sometimes said things to children just to make them feel better in troubled times.

"Now listen, cher. Can you tell me where your papá has gone? It would help if we could talk to him."

Alethea sniffed and Marie handed her a handkerchief, which she used to blow her nose. "He went to Arizona. He had important work to do."

Marie nodded. "Can you tell me what kind of work?"

"He wanted to talk sense into the Army and the Apaches fighting near Tucson."

Marie choked out a strange laugh, as though she were sad and didn't want to laugh, but couldn't help it. "That will take much skill and patience, but if there's anyone who could do it, it would be your papá." She held Alethea for a moment and rocked. The motion comforted her and she sensed it comforted Marie as well. "He didn't tell you anything else, like where he would stay, did he?"

Alethea shook her head. "I don't think he knew."

"All right, cher, we'll do our best to get a message to him." She sat up, and eased Alethea to the floor. "Now, you should get some sleep and let the grown-ups tend to business."

"Will Monsieur Lalande be able to catch the bad guys who hightailed it with my momma?" Somehow, funny words like "hightailed" which she'd read in Pat Garrett's book made her feel a little better and made the bad situation seem a little less dire.

Marie's throat constricted and she shot a brief glance at Francoise, as though she thought she should say something, but didn't believe the time had arrived.

"I won't lie, child. It will be difficult once the bad men get to the Atlantic, but I promise, we won't give up." She stood. "Now you and Francoise need to get some sleep. We'll talk more in the morning."

Marie didn't mention school like her momma would. School didn't feel like a high priority right now, but somehow the omission bothered her. "It is a school day tomorrow," she said.

Marie stood and gave Francoise a kiss and a fleeting smile. She looked up. "Yes, it is, but we'll cross that bridge when we come to it. You two can stay in here to sleep."

As Marie went to the door, Alethea climbed into the big bed next to Francoise, who wept softly. "What's wrong?"

"I don't know, but mamá isn't telling me something. I'm scared."

"If your momma can get a message to my daddy, I'm sure he can help us." Alethea spoke with more than a little pride.

"Your papá is all the way in Arizona. How can he help?"

Alethea thought of Pat Garrett's book and all the people out west with their six-guns. She imagined her daddy riding one of Professor Maravilla's mechanical owls, facing down the bad guys. She tried to reconcile that picture with her daddy as she knew him—a man in owl-like glasses who wore fancy clothes and talked in a courtroom. Despite the disconnect, she knew her daddy would come running if he knew momma was in trouble. She also knew he had important business in Arizona. With that thought, she saw a way she could help her daddy do his important work and a way she could help her momma too, but it scared her because it involved Voodoo magic.

"Does your momma have a potion that would make people do what my daddy says?"

"If my mamá had a potion like that, we'd be living in a big mansion on St. Charles Street and not in a cottage in the Quarter." Francoise's voice had grown sleepy. Then her eyes widened. "But you know, she does have some herbs that make people want to be helpful."

Francoise slipped out of bed and peered around the door. She motioned for Alethea to follow. They padded through the kitchen in bare feet and out the back door into a courtyard. "Give me a hand." Together, Francoise and Alethea opened the heavy door to the root cellar.

Francoise lit a candle and they descended into the darkness. She found a small paper bag, then went over to a jar on the bottom shelf. She poured a few ground leaves into the bag and handed it to Alethea.

"Is that enough?"

Francoise shrugged. "I don't know, but if I pour out too much more, mamá will know we poked around down here. Better be safe than sorry." She screwed the lid back on the jar and replaced it on the shelf. "How will you get that to your papá?"

"I have an idea," said Alethea.

As the sun rose, the *City of New Orleans* descended over San Antonio, Texas. Ramon watched from the gallery as the ground crew grabbed landing lines and pulled the airship down toward the earth. He couldn't see the crew at the mooring tower, but he thought a faint shudder ran through the vessel as they connected the line.

Doctor Holliday had still been snoring away in their cabin when Ramon left. When Ramon had gone to bed the night before, the doctor had just started a poker game with a few other passengers and had ordered a glass of the finest whiskey the airship had to offer.

Ramon's own sleep had been fitful. He tossed and turned, sensing something amiss back in New Orleans, but he didn't know what it could be. He vowed to send a telegram and check on Fatemeh and Alethea as soon as he reached Arizona.

The whirring of hydraulic pumps brought him back to the present and he realized the ladders descended. He decided to step out and take a brief stroll. As he walked down the ladder, the porter admonished him to be back within an hour. Ramon checked his pocket watch and nodded. He couldn't help but

think the airship's progress would be faster if they didn't stop
so often to pick up passengers and cargo.

Solid ground underfoot pleased him. He took a deep
breath. The air in San Antonio was dryer than New Orleans,
but still humid. A boy sold newspapers nearby. Ramon bought
one, folded it and carried it back aboard the airship. He found
a comfortable chair in the lounge, ordered coffee and unfolded
the paper.

The lead story described the damage the Apaches' did on
the railroad line near Tucson. Repairs were underway, but it
meant Southern Arizona and California had lost a major supply
artery for several weeks, if not months. Ramon frowned. The
army had sent soldiers from Missouri to Fort Lowell to aid in
a retaliatory strike. He folded the paper and hoped he didn't
make this journey in vain.

Doc Holliday emerged from the cabin a little after noon.
Although well dressed, red eyes and haggard features betrayed
his late night. He took a table in the lounge and ordered coffee.
Ramon asked for a refill, then joined the doctor. "Sleep well?"
asked Ramon.

"Indeed, I did, thank you, Counselor." Holliday forced a
smile.

Ramon passed the newspaper across the table. "So, what
do you make of this?"

Holliday scanned the paper and sighed. "I never thought
the Apaches would attack the railroad. General Miles won't
take this news lyin' down, that's for damn sure."

"What can you tell me about this General Miles?"

"Tough old Union dog." Holliday snorted. "He fought in
almost every major battle in the War of Northern Aggression
and even won the Congressional Medal of Honor. Apparently,
those battles didn't take the fight out of him, though. He went
out west to fight Indians. He did well in the plains. He took
on the Comanche, Kiowa, and Cheyenne along the Red River.
Then after General Custer's foul up at Little Big Horn, he came
in like the hand o' God with both lightning wolves and ornithopters. Liked to damn near wipe out the Lakota."

"So, what's held him back in Arizona?" Ramon could guess,
but he wanted Holliday's opinion.

"Two things, the Apache battle wagons and the mountains. Miles knows how to kill Indians on the plains when they're armed with nothing but rifles. It's a different story when they have war machines and can hide in the rocks."

"They only have war machines because some damn fool cattle rustlers stole a mining machine, turned it into the first battle wagon, and tried to wipe out the Apaches with it." Ramon sipped his coffee. "It also helps that the Apaches have allies in Mexico who were able to help them rebuild it when it looked like it was destroyed."

"I saw the illustrations of the original mining machine. Thing looked like a cobbled together wreck when it worked. No wonder no one went back to get the thing."

Ramon set the coffee cup on the table and returned to the conversation's topic. "How long has this General Miles been in Arizona?"

Holliday unscrewed a flask and added some of the contents to the coffee which had been sitting in front of him. He took a sip, and his eyes brightened. "Much better. Now, where were we?" His eyes drifted around the luxurious lounge. "Ah yes, General Miles." He took another sip of coffee. "He's only been in command for about six months. Took over when General Crook managed to lose Fort Bowie to the Apaches."

"Are the battle wagons that strong? I've never heard of Indians taking a fort before."

Holliday shrugged. "Crook is said to have had an over-reliance on Apache scouts." The doctor began coughing. After a moment, Ramon wondered if he could stop. At last the cough subsided little by little. The doctor folded a blood-soaked handkerchief and set it aside, then took a much deeper gulp of his coffee. He sat back, much paler than usual.

"Are you okay?" Ramon leaned forward.

Holliday just smiled. "What do you think?" He held up his hand before Ramon could answer. "There's a good chance the Apache scouts were double agents, leading Crook's men astray and feeding them false information, but that's never been proven. Miles relies on white scouts, who don't know all the Apache's hideouts." Holliday tapped the newspaper, leaving a bloody fingerprint. "Miles got this posting because Crook lost the fort. The Indians blowin' up the tracks gives Miles the excuse to call in as much manpower as he wants."

Ramon cleaned his glasses as he considered what Holliday had told him. "So, why bring me in at all?" He replaced the spectacles and leaned forward. "It seems like you and your friend…"

"Wyatt Earp…"

"Yes, Mr. Earp would benefit just as much if General Miles executes his campaign against the Apaches as planned."

Again, Holliday smiled and gulped whiskey-laced coffee. "The problem with military force is the general's campaign could take years and leave the land in no shape for settlers." His eyes darted down to the folded, blood-soaked handkerchief beside his plate. "Some of us don't have years before we want to see the benefits of Southern Arizona's mines."

Ramon nodded, then excused himself. He walked over to the lounge windows and considered the rolling Texas hill country below them, not so different than Southern New Mexico's or Arizona's terrain, and considered how he could convince a general to slow the machineries of war.

Fatemeh awoke with a start. She looked around and tried to remember where she was, then she struggled to remember where Alethea and Ramon were. She'd fallen asleep on top of the cot. Sweat drenched her nightgown and her head throbbed from where she'd been struck. Red and chafed, her wrists still burned from the rope.

She sat up and looked around. The cabin where Hamid held her captive had a washroom attached. She entered and studied her reflection in the mirror. A bump shone on her temple where she'd been struck and her hair stuck out at all angles. The small washroom had running water and she washed her face. A well-used comb sat on the sink's edge. She did her best to straighten her hair. Not because she cared what her captives thought of her appearance, but because the uncomfortable, tangled hair distracted her. She needed to think.

She returned to the main cabin and gazed out through

the porthole. Three cutters followed at a distance with lowered masts. The white wake behind the craft indicated motors propelled them. They were, perhaps, newer craft than those which attacked before sunrise.

One cutter increased speed and she thought she could make out two men in the bow. A muffled thump sounded from the deck above and a shell just missed the boat. It veered off, but not too far. She wondered how long the small boats would follow. Could they even pursue Hamid's freighter from the Gulf of Mexico into the Atlantic?

Fatemeh tried to understand Hamid's motives for capturing her. He'd mentioned her father's disappointment and anger. No surprise there. He said she'd committed zina. All this sounded as though he wanted her punished. She rubbed her head near the bump and scowled.

Despite his need for vengeance, Hamid had named his ship for her. When Fatemeh left Persia, it never occurred to her that Hamid actually loved her. Not that it mattered, she didn't return any such affection.

She tried to deduce the ship's size from the cabin and what she remembered of Hamid. He'd already built a strong trading business, but she remembered him speaking late into the night with her father about how he wanted to extend it around the world. He wanted to become the most important trader the Middle East had ever seen.

She remembered the copy of *Owl Riders* dropped in her shop with its finger-darkened pages. Like so many petty men, he wanted to control life's every aspect. When he discovered the book, he realized something had slipped from his control.

An almost timid knock interrupted her thoughts. "Come in," said Fatemeh.

A key rattled in the lock and it seemed to take some work for the person outside. At last, a boy Fatemeh guessed to be around fourteen pushed open the door. His hair was cut short and a light fuzz darkened his upper lip. He picked up a tray from the ground and brought it in. The key ring still hung in the door. She considered pushing past the boy and bolting out the door but she knew running out barefoot in a nightgown would be foolish without more information.

Then she noticed the boy trembled.

The deck gun above thumped again. The boy almost dropped the tray, but regained control and sat it down on a table. "I brought your breakfast," he said in Persian, eyes averted.

"Why are you scared?" When he didn't respond, she realized she'd spoken English. She asked again in Persian.

He straightened up and put on a brave face, then blushed and looked away when their eyes met. "I'm not scared." Then the gun fired again and his shoulders slumped as his eyes turned toward the upper deck and he fell back trembling.

"It's okay." She patted the cot next to her. "Come here."

He shook his head. "I can't, ma'am. You're the owner's betrothed."

"I'm more a mom than a ma'am." She smiled. "Come here."

The boy looked over his shoulder, but no one stood in the corridor. Almost as an afterthought, he grabbed the keys and put them in the pocket of his baggy zir-jameh pants, then closed the door. He came over and sat next to Fatemeh.

"I'm scared what the pirates will do to us if they capture us."

She put her arm around his shoulder and glanced back toward the porthole.

"Somehow, I don't think those little boats will do us much harm."

"More of them have turned up. There were only two sailing boats last night. The captain drove one off and sank the other, but there are three today." He gulped and fought to control himself. "The captain thinks the pirates may try to cut us off when we reach the Florida Keys or maybe the Bahamas."

Fatemeh wondered about that. Did Marie Lalande's family connections reach so far? She decided not to share her doubts with the boy. "The cargo aboard must be quite valuable for the captain to risk so many pirates."

"Yes, mom, er, ma'am, er..." The boy's cheeks reddened again as he grew more flustered. With a gulp, he pulled away, as though her embrace embarrassed him more than anything else and looked at her. "I mean no disrespect, ma'am, but the captain thinks you're the reason pirates chase us and he'd be just as happy if we gave you to them."

"Then Hamid Farzan isn't the captain?" Fatemeh narrowed her gaze.

"No ma'am. He's the ship's owner. Captain Turan is the ship's master."

"Would it be possible for me to speak with Captain Turan?"

The boy shrugged. "I don't know."

"Please ask him, though you should probably make sure Mr. Farzan isn't around." She smiled and the boy's cheeks reddened again.

The gun from the deck thumped again.

The boy nodded. "I'll do what I can." He hopped up from the cot and darted through the door. After a moment, the key rattled in the lock. Fatemeh sighed and decided to see what Hamid had sent down for breakfast.

Ramon packed his carpet bag and entered the airship's observation lounge before dawn, his mind turning over the problem of how to bring both General Miles and Naiche to the negotiating table. Holliday claimed Wyatt Earp would help if he could, but Ramon had no reason to trust that assessment. He fought to keep an open mind and not judge Earp before he met him.

Ramon desperately wanted coffee, but arrived before the wait staff. At least the empty gallery meant the ship's fancy electric lights weren't on, so he could see a few features out the window.

He soon grew bored with the unfamiliar, twilit desert landscape with clumps of grass and brush scattered about. He dropped into one of the overstuffed armchairs and peaked his hands.

A waiter came on duty, turned on the electric lights, and wiped down the counter at the back of the lounge. Ramon glanced over his shoulder and watched him make coffee. He sighed and looked out the windows again. They passed over the Dragoon Mountains' yellow rocks. The railroad line disappeared into the rocks, but an encampment on the west side told him repair work was well underway.

A voice with a southern drawl attracted his attention back to the counter. Doc Holliday placed an order. Soon, the doctor approached with two coffee cups. He sat one down next to Ramon.

"I'm surprised to see you out of bed this early," said Ramon.

Holliday snorted. "You didn't expect me to sleep through our arrival did you?" He sipped his coffee. Ramon noticed he didn't add anything to it this morning. "Besides you made quite the racket packin' up this mornin'."

Ramon tilted his head. "I do apologize."

The airship reached Tucson an hour later and the lounge filled up as the ship descended. Ramon had visited the town some eight years earlier. Back then, it had been a thriving, but small town tucked along the Santa Cruz River. Ramon could tell the city had grown. Given that Ramon could see the city from the port-side windows, he knew they approached from the northwest. Holliday told him the airship field sat roughly halfway between Tucson and Fort Lowell.

"So, what should we do first?" asked Ramon.

"I thought we'd hire a coach into town, get you set up in a hotel, then arrange a meetin' with my associates. Then, we can also contact General Miles and arrange a meetin' with him."

Ramon finished his coffee, then nodded.

The airship dropped mooring lines and ground crews rushed to secure the vessel. Ramon and Holliday retrieved their luggage, and arrived at the doors just as the ladders descended.

A half dozen soldiers marched out from the airship terminal and approached Ramon and the doctor. The sergeant who led them looked Ramon up and down. "Are you Ramon Morales?"

Ramon pushed his glasses up on his nose. "That's me."

"Please accompany us to the fort."

"Well, this may be easier than I thought," said the doctor. He turned to the sergeant. "May I come along as well?"

"If you're headed that way, by all means."

The soldiers led Ramon and Holliday through the lavish airship terminal to a small horse-drawn coach. A private stood by holding the reins of five saddled horses. A corporal with bushy muttonchops accompanied Ramon and Holliday into the coach, while another soldier took the driver's seat. The rest mounted their own horses and they rode toward the fort.

"How did the general know to expect me?" asked Ramon.

The corporal shrugged. "All I know is the general ordered us to meet you and bring you to the fort."

"Do you know anything about the negotiations with the Apaches?"

"No, I don't." He reached up and ran his thumb along his sideburns, as though they interested him more than anything.

Ramon frowned but contented himself with watching the scenery go by. The towering saguaro cactus in the Sonoran Desert never ceased to amaze him. They soon rolled through the fort's gate and the corporal stepped out. Ramon started to grab his carpet bag, but the corporal stopped him. "We'll take care of your luggage."

"Why thank you." Out of habit, Ramon almost tipped the young man, but realized that might be perceived as an insult. The sergeant dismounted and led Ramon into an adobe structure, dark after the bright morning sunshine. A private barely glanced up from his work at the desk as the soldiers ushered them through to a back office where three men already occupied chairs. Doctor Holliday smiled and strode over to a stern man in a black suit and shook his hand. That must be Wyatt Earp, thought Ramon.

The general himself sat behind a large wooden desk wearing an elaborate uniform. The man's eyes seemed sad, but his firm jaw offset the impression and Ramon thought the general just seemed bored and impatient. He didn't rise when they entered the room. Masuda Hoshi occupied the third chair in the room. He wore a gray kimono over black hakama. Ramon noted the absence of his katana.

After Doctor Holliday took his seat, there were none left. Ramon shifted uncomfortably under the general's gaze.

"Well this has been quite a morning," said Miles. "A lawman from Kansas and a Japanese samurai warrior have both come to tell me that I should invite Naiche and his band of renegade Apaches to the negotiating table when I have orders to blow them to kingdom come for destroying the rail line outside of Tucson. Mr. Masuda here tells me you can convince me of this. General Johnson has ordered me to listen." Miles leaned forward. "Well, Mr. Morales. I'm listening."

Ramon swallowed and tried to think how to begin.

CHAPTER EIGHT
ELUSIVE FREEDOM

A knock sounded at the door of the Lalande's home. Marie's sister, Nicole answered. Alethea peered around the door, curious what was going on. Francoise's Aunt Nicole, who looked almost identical to her sister, audibly gasped, then ran off, calling for her sister, leaving a tall, lanky man standing slack-jawed at the door.

A moment later, Nicole returned with Marie. "Are you certain, Henri? He's going to recover?"

"He's in a lot of pain, ma'am, but he'd like to see you and the children as soon as you can." The man called Henri rubbed the stubble on his chin.

Marie spoke quietly to her sister and soon Nicole gathered Francoise, her two older sisters, and Alethea in the house's living room and gave them the news that Jacques Lalande had awakened and would make a full recovery. Alethea grabbed Francoise's hands and the two danced around in a circle, then fell down laughing.

"Go get your coats, children and we'll go see your father."

The three Lalande girls ran to their room as instructed, leaving Alethea standing by herself, uncertain about what to do.

"You should get your coat as well, cher," said Nicole.

Alethea sniffed. "Why? We're not going to see my daddy."

Aunt Nicole knelt down and held Alethea's hands. "We can't leave you here all alone. The fresh air will do you good."

Alethea wasn't sure if she believed Nicole, but she ran off and grabbed her coat as instructed. Soon the girls followed Henri, Marie, and Nicole through the streets of the Quarter to the more modern downtown neighborhood nearby. They entered an imposing white building that reminded Alethea a little

91

of the Ursuline convent where she went to school, except that funny smells pervaded the air.

Marie went up to the counter and spoke to a woman in a white dress and hat. The woman looked Marie up and down, then pointed to a stairway. Marie gestured for the rest to follow and she led them upstairs into a room lined with beds.

Most were empty, except for the one closest to the door. Jacques Lalande sat propped up on a pillow, a bandage wrapped around his shoulder and another around his body. He seemed frail compared to what Alethea remembered when she knocked on the Lalande's door looking for help. Standing next to him was a short, tubby man in a striped shirt with beady eyes. Alethea thought he looked like a pirate.

Jacques Lalande tried to sit up taller, but yelped in pain.

"You behave yourself." Marie stepped up to him and kissed him on the forehead. Francoise and her sisters seemed to take that as a cue and ran up, surrounding their father. He reached out and touched each of their heads. It was as though he wanted to bring them into a hug, but couldn't find the strength.

Alethea hung back. She noticed Henri and Pierre had moved off by themselves and spoke in hushed tones. She crept closer so she could hear.

"I thought he was a goner," said the tubby man, Pierre. "Doctors had to sew him back together like a goddamned rag doll."

"I hear Madame Marie made a bargain with the loa to protect the mother and the child." Henri shook his head. "She should have made a bargain to keep her husband safe."

"Bargains with the loa are not made lightly or in vain." Pierre spoke in a scolding tone. "If we fail, there could be ripples throughout the area, maybe even throughout the world."

Alethea didn't understand what they were talking about, but somehow the words reminded her of what her momma said about magic being quiet and simple and that a person could understand if they paid attention.

A shadow fell across her. She shivered and looked back to see Aunt Nicole smiling down at her. The woman guided her back over to the other girls. They must be getting ready to go. Jacques gestured for Pierre to come over as Nicole made sure the girls all had their jackets.

"Do you know the Cisneros Global warehouse near the airship terminal?" asked Jacques

"Of course I do. I have a good contact there. He helps me all the time."

Wincing, Jacques retrieved a pad and pencil from the bedside table. It looked like both of his arms really hurt. He scrawled a note on the paper, folded it, and handed it to Pierre.

"Have your contact get that message to his boss, Onofre Cisneros."

Alethea thought she recognized that name. Her parents knew him. Another owl rider from the Battle of Denver.

Once they returned to the Lalande's home, Francoise and her sisters went to the kitchen for a snack. To Alethea, it seemed as though all their pain and worry had just vanished. Although Alethea was happy for her friends, her chest ached and her limbs grew heavy. She worried the Lalandes had forgotten the reason Jacques had been hurt. Her mother had been kidnapped, taken farther away from home by the minute. Her daddy had gone west and no one had heard from him. She dropped onto the floor and cried.

Aunt Nicole scooped her up into a big hug and said, "There, there, that does no good." As though reading her thoughts, Aunt Nicole sat back and lifted the girl's chin. "Jacques' recovery is good news. We will find a way to bring your mamá home."

Alethea sniffed and nodded. Aunt Nicole handed her a handkerchief to blow her nose, then set her on the floor. Alethea watched the woman stride into another room, tall and proud. Alethea agreed with Aunt Nicole, crying did no good. She also worried that so much seemed to ride on Jacques' recovery. Could no one else help her?

Then she remembered Lafcadio Hearn, the newspaper man. Her mom said Hearn had come all the way from Ireland to Cincinnati, before he moved to New Orleans. Reporters ranged the world looking for stories and feared nothing. They wrote stories like the one Mr. Hearn wrote about her parents. Mr. Hearn might not look like a brave lawman, but she knew he cared and would find a way to help.

She went to the bedroom she now shared with Francoise and gathered up all her spare change and put it into a little handbag. Then she went to the window and looked out. Francoise sometimes sneaked out to play in the small courtyard adjoining the house. Alethea knew Aunt Nicole wouldn't let her go out all alone.

Alethea hesitated and wondered if she should wait for Marie and discuss her plan. However, Alethea thought Marie would try to dissuade her and convince her they would succeed using Voodoo magic. Voodoo always made her tremble. When her mother spoke of healing herbs and even speaking to owls, she always understood why it worked. Voodoo relied on mystical spirits called loa, who she couldn't see.

Was that any different than relying on the God the priests talked about at St. Louis Cathedral?

Alethea swallowed, realizing she still stared at the window. That wouldn't get her momma back any better than waiting for Marie to return. She pushed the window open and climbed outside then pulled it shut behind her. It wouldn't do for people to know she'd gone too soon. She then opened the heavy courtyard gate and exited onto the street. Once there, she realized she didn't know how to latch the gate behind her.

Well, nothing to be done for that now. She closed the gate as best as she could, then walked down the street. At that point, surrounded by imposing walls broken only by solid gates and shuttered windows she realized how small and alone she was. She'd never walked anywhere without at least Francoise with her, and her friend was a whole year older.

Alethea tried to remember how to get to the streetcar. She knew she had to get to St. Charles Avenue. But the most direct route took her along Bourbon Street. Her mother told her to never ever walk there alone. Alethea wasn't sure why, because the few times they walked down Bourbon Street together the men seemed very friendly to her mother.

Still, she had no time for questions and she remembered streets in her neighborhood all ran in straight lines. She could follow the next street after Bourbon and end up where she wanted to be. She stared up at the big houses as she walked, wondering if people watched her. When she reached Bourbon

Street, she hurried across and continued on. At this point, she was close to her own home and the buildings looked more familiar. She shuddered though, remembering what happened when the strange men abducted her mom. She turned onto the next street, called Royal, according to the tiles in the sidewalk.

A woman at a fruit stand stopped her. "Why you're Fatemeh and Ramon's daughter aren't you? What are you doing out here all alone?"

Alethea struggled to put on a brave smile. "I'm a big girl now. Momma sent me on an errand."

"And what would that be?"

Alethea then realized she should have a good cover story in case adults asked her where she went. She pointed to the bakery across the street. "She sent me for some bread."

"Well, isn't that nice." The woman waved as Alethea went on her way. She considered going into the bakery, to give credence to her story, but that would just delay her even more. She ran the rest of the way to Canal Street, which bustled with horses and noise.

She hurried across to the streetcar stop that would take her to the Cotton Exposition and tried to catch her breath. As she started to feel better, the horse-drawn streetcar came around the corner. She climbed in and counted out money to the driver.

"Where are you going all by yourself young lady?" asked the driver.

"I'm going to the Cotton Exposition," she declared.

The driver smiled at her and pointed to the empty seat behind him. "Sit right behind me and I'll make sure you get there safe and sound."

"Thank you." Alethea was proud of herself for remembering to be polite. She sat down and folded her hands, hoping she wasn't too late.

Fatemeh stared out the porthole. The cutters had fallen behind. She saw no land, at least on this side of the ship. The sun lay near the horizon, making the ocean uncomfortably bright.

Although she knew the Lalandes protected Alethea, she worried about her daughter. She also worried about Ramon, hoping she hadn't sent him into worse danger than if he stayed in New Orleans. She knew he could find a peaceful solution to the Apache conflict.

Keys rattled in the doorway. Fatemeh expected the cabin boy with supper. Instead, a tall, thin man with thick arms, salt-and-pepper hair, and a scraggly beard entered with a rolled up paper. He tipped his hat. "I'm Captain Turan," he said in Persian. "Ahmad said you wanted to see me."

Fatemeh nodded, realizing Ahmad must be the cabin boy's name. She sat down at the cabin's small table and invited the captain to take the other seat. He glanced out into the corridor. Satisfied no one watched, he closed the door. "Hamid Farzan tells me you are betrothed to him."

"Our parents arranged a marriage when we both lived in Shiraz. I left, never planning to return. Since then, I married another—a good man named Ramon Morales."

"So I've heard," said the captain. "Though Mr. Farzan doesn't tell it that way." He sat back and folded his arms. "I don't approve of what you did, but I believe Mr. Farzan is going too far in his quest for justice. I think he jeopardizes my ship for a foolish girl's impetuous actions."

Fatemeh bristled at the captain's words, but knew enough to keep quiet. She didn't want to drive away even a faint chance of help. "So, if I'm a danger to your ship and crew, why not hand me to the pirates who follow us?"

"Pirates are rarely so altruistic as to rescue a fair maiden and leave the ship she's aboard unscathed."

Fatemeh shot the captain a wicked grin. "I am no maiden, sir."

The captain scowled. "Be that as it may. Even if the pirates took you, I'm sure they also expect a share of my cargo as reimbursement for their troubles. I'm not happy with Mr. Farzan and to be frank, I may leave his employ, but arriving home with no cargo could end my career forever."

"Then what do you want to do?"

The captain unrolled the paper he'd brought along, which proved to be a map. He pointed to a spot between Florida and

Cuba. "We're here. Later tonight, we will be among the Bahamas." He pointed to a line of long, stringy islands. "I propose to put you on a lifeboat with this chart and a compass. It will be dangerous, but you should be able to find your way to land. There are many settlements, so you should be able to find help."

Fatemeh leaned forward and studied the map. "Why risk helping me escape? Once you pass the Bahamas, you'll be in open ocean. If the pirates fall behind, why does this present a problem for the voyage home?"

The captain sighed and folded his arms. "Perhaps I'm just a superstitious old sailor, but I think you've brought bad luck to this ship. My gut tells me the pirates are just the beginning and the worst is yet to come."

"What if someone catches you and finds I'm not aboard?"

"Are you trying to talk me out of helping?"

Fatemeh shook her head. "I just don't want you to get in trouble for setting me free."

The captain snorted. "I see why a man like Hamid Farzan could fall in love with you."

Fatemeh smiled.

The captain leaned forward again. "What do you say? Will you take a chance on your freedom?"

"I have been taking chances to gain my freedom for more years than you know," she said. "I'm not about to stop."

The captain nodded. "I'll leave the map here so you can study it. I'll send Ahmad down with your supper along with rain gear, which will be more … appropriate than what you're wearing."

Fatemeh looked down at her nightgown and though she didn't embarrass easily, her cheeks warmed.

The captain continued. "I'll be back around midnight. Be ready to go. If I knock and there's no answer. I'll leave you here."

"I understand."

The captain stood, cracked the door and peered out, then left without another word. Fatemeh looked out at the ocean, hoping the waters would remain calm.

Alethea climbed off the streetcar and walked to the Cotton Exposition's front gate. Her palms grew damp as she wondered whether the man would sell her a ticket. She was just a child all alone. A family got off the streetcar behind her. Passing her, the father went to the gate and paid. She followed behind the family as they entered and no one challenged her.

On this weekday afternoon, the Cotton Exposition proved much quieter than when she'd visited before. Heart thumping, she continued forward to the great hall, trying to think what she would say to Mr. Hearn when she reached his table. Would he even remember her or care? She knew Mr. Hearn liked travel. She could promise a grand Wild West adventure like the one in Pat Garrett's *Authentic Life of Cowboy Charlie*. Maybe her daddy could even introduce Mr. Hearn to the real Cowboy Charlie!

Although there were fewer people outside, she still found the main exhibit hall a forest of trousers, skirts, and bustles. She followed the exhibits to keep her bearings. Despite her mission, she stopped and watched the Jackalope demonstration again and she stood slack-jawed as miniature ornithopters whirled and danced overhead. She couldn't believe her momma had flown a full-sized version at the Battle of Denver. Tears threatened to flow as she wondered whether or not she'd see her momma again.

She sniffed and reminded herself she had a job to do. If the ornithopters whirled overhead, she must be near Mr. Hearn's booth. The forest of legs parted for just a moment and the booth for *La Cuisine Creole* stood before her. She ran for the table, but no one sat behind it.

The cake lady stepped out of the crowd. "Where are your mama and papa?"

"We were separated." Alethea grinned to herself, thinking that wasn't even a lie. "Mr. Hearn is their friend. I hoped he could help me find them."

"Ah, I remember you now. You were here a few days ago and you liked the chocolate cake best of all." She set the sample tray down on the table and allowed Alethea to take a piece.

"Do you know where Mr. Hearn is?" Alethea took a bite.

"Mr. Hearn is a busy man. He's an editor for the *Times-Democrat* and can't be here as much as he'd like." She stood upright and thought. "You wait right here just one minute, and I'll take you someplace where you can wait for your mama and papa." The cake lady disappeared behind the display, then returned a moment later without the tray. She held out her hand and led Alethea through the forest of legs, back outside.

They walked around the Furniture Pavilion to a small building labeled "Administration" huddled beside a huge cypress tree. Inside, the cake lady told the man behind the desk about Alethea, explaining she'd been separated from her parents.

"Thanks, I'll take care of it, Simone," said the man.

The cake lady left and the man smiled down at Alethea. "Now who are your mom and dad?"

"Their names are Ramon and Fatemeh Morales." It seemed strange and forbidden to speak their names. "My daddy is the assistant U.S. Attorney, and my momma owns the Blessed Life Apothecary in the French Quarter."

The man smiled and nodded while taking notes. He told her to take a seat over in the office's corner. "This is the lost and found. Once your parents have noticed you're missing, I'm sure they'll come here looking for you."

Alethea's brow furrowed. "But I'm not the one who's missing. They are."

The man chuckled and reiterated she should sit down. He opened his desk drawer and retrieved a clacker, similar to the one her dad used at work. He clacked out a message. A few minutes later, he received a reply. When he turned to face Alethea, he frowned. "Are you sure your father's Ramon Morales, the Assistant U.S. Attorney?"

Alethea nodded. "Yes, sir, he is."

"I just contacted his office, and they think he left town."

"He did. He's out west. That's why I wanted to find Mr. Hearn."

The man brightened as though he now understood. "Ah, so you're here with your mother?"

Alethea shook her head.

The man frowned again, then turned around to send another message on the clacker. When he received the response, he sat back and pinched his nose between his fingers in a way her daddy sometimes did when he got a headache. With a sigh, he turned around and placed his hands on his knees. "Stay right there. I need to talk to my boss."

The man stood up and walked into a back room.

Alethea folded her arms and looked around. Sitting in the office didn't help her mom and dad. No one stood between her and the door. Maybe the nice cake lady, Simone, could tell her how to get to Mr. Hearn's office.

She left the administration building and returned to the main exhibit hall, where she moved through the swarming adults who didn't always notice her. When she reached the booth, she looked around, but couldn't see Simone. As she walked toward the booth, a gruff voice called out, "There you are."

She looked up. Pierre, the pudgy creole man from the hospital pointed at her. "Little girl, come with me. Madame Marie has been worried sick and she sent me to fetch you."

Alethea shook her head and turned to run, but before she could get anywhere, she found herself scooped up in strong arms. She opened her mouth to scream, but his hand clamped over it.

"Hush, child. Madame Marie wants to find your mama and papa as much as you do. Let's go." She fought back tears, refusing to cry as the strange man carried her through the crowd and past all the Cotton Exposition's wonders and straight back to Marie Lalande's house. He left her sitting in the drawing room on a divan.

All the children were out at school and the house was silent except for the grandfather clock's ticking. Alethea wondered how much trouble she'd landed in for running away. A copy of the *Times-Democrat* sat on the table next to her. She picked up the big, floppy paper and turned to the second page. A box listed all the paper's editors including Mr. Hearn and it gave an address: 326 Camp Street.

Just then, Marie Lalande cleared her throat. Alethea looked up and tried to fold the paper back into a neat bundle but failed. She put the paper on the table beside her just as neatly as she could. Alethea expected to see anger on Mrs. Lalande's face, but instead, she just looked worried. Marie knelt down and brought Alethea into a hug.

"We were so worried about you, cher. Why did you run off like you did?"

Because I was scared. That would have been the honest answer. Marie Lalande and her Voodoo ways scared her. Madame Lalande's pirate husband who seemed to come back from the dead scared her too. She feared these folks wouldn't do everything it would take to get her mama and papa back.

"I need to let my daddy know momma's in trouble." Alethea wanted her words to come out big and brave, but they came out small and mousy instead.

Marie smiled and released the girl. Alethea didn't trust that smile. Sometimes it hid scary thoughts. "I'll be right back." Marie stood and strolled to the kitchen at the back of the house.

Alethea looked toward the door and tried to decide if she could make it outside before Marie returned. Alethea allowed her feet to swing back and forth while she thought. She needed to figure out where Camp Street was and whether she could get there on her own. A few minutes later, Marie returned with a glass of liquid that looked like lemonade, except that something white swirled around in it. It could be sugar or it could be one of Marie's Voodoo potions. She handed it to Alethea.

"Drink this, cher. Francoise will be here soon and she'll have the schoolwork you missed today and you can catch up."

Alethea lifted the glass to her lips and pretended to drink. It smelled like lemonade and herbs. She knew Marie wouldn't hurt her. Maybe the herbs would make her more cooperative, or make her go to sleep so she wouldn't run away.

"I'd like to go to my room now," said Alethea. "I promise I'll be good and drink this all down."

"All right, cher." Again, Marie flashed a smile that seemed to hide darker thoughts.

Alethea took the glass and walked slowly so she wouldn't spill any. She poured the drink into a potted plant beside the door, then continued on to the room she shared with Francoise. Maybe her friend could tell her the way to the newspaper office.

Fatemeh lay on the bunk in her cabin, heart pounding, staring up at the ceiling. She wore the raincoat and boots Ahmad brought and clutched an owl pendant around her neck. Ramon had given her the pendant during their first Christmas together, in San Francisco. They only remained in San Francisco for about a week, finding it too big and unwelcoming for their tastes, but he'd made the pendant himself, knowing she loved owls. She always wore it, no matter where she went.

She said a silent prayer, hoping Captain Turan had not changed his mind about helping her. Even if he did arrive, there would be great danger ahead. Although she had worked her way across the Atlantic pretending to be a boy on a merchant ship, she mostly followed orders and had learned little navigation. From the map Captain Turan had shown her, Fatemeh knew that, depending on where the captain set the boat down, there could be islands in most directions.

A short, sharp knock sounded at the door. Fatemeh hopped to her feet as keys rattled in the lock. For a moment, she worried Hamid had discovered her escape plans. She breathed a relieved sigh when the door cracked open revealing the captain. Without a word, he beckoned her onward.

The ship's corridors were eerily devoid of crew. All she heard was the engine's distant thrum, like a heartbeat. Bellows pushed air through the ventilation system like gentle breathing. As they walked, she reached out and brushed the wall with her fingertips, feeling a certain connection with the ship. She understood why sailors called ships "she." This one certainly seemed alive, albeit in a quiet slumber.

They ascended a ship's "ladder"—really a stairway to the upper deck. Even as far south as they sailed, the chill breeze reminded her that she'd been kidnapped in the middle of the night and she only wore a nightgown beneath the rain gear. She rubbed her arms, warding off the chill.

The captain stopped at an uncovered lifeboat, lowered to deck level. He turned and looked her up and down, then pointed to a mound of tarp-covered supplies. "You'll find a heavier coat, food and water for a week, a chart and a compass. All I can do now is wish you good luck."

Fatemeh wanted to gather the captain in her arms and hug

him even if it would make both of them uncomfortable. Instead, she held out her hand and they shook, then he helped her step across into the boat.

"What do you think you're doing?" Hamid Farzan emerged from the deck house's shadows into the moonlight. He aimed a revolver at the captain. "This is mutiny."

"Mutiny is an action against the master of the ship," growled Turan. "You are not this ship's master." He jabbed his thumb at his chest. "I am."

Hamid narrowed his gaze and flashed a dangerous smile. "Not anymore. He is."

A man Fatemeh didn't recognize stepped from the shadows.

"Dalir?"

The stranger nodded. "I'm sorry, Cap ... Mr. Turan," he rubbed his hands together. "Mr. Farzan made me a good offer and I couldn't turn it down."

"This ... *This* is mutiny!" shouted the captain. His voice echoed off the ship's structure.

Fatemeh came to her senses. While the men held each others' attention, she unhitched the ropes and began lowering herself toward the water. Captain Turan lunged toward the new man. She presumed Hamid must have promoted the ship's first officer.

A gunshot rent the night air and Fatemeh's grip on the rope slipped. The lifeboat canted over at a precarious angle, sending the supplies banging against one of the benches.

Captain Turan crumpled to the deck, shock etched into his features. Fatemeh vowed not to let his sacrifice be in vain. She adjusted the ropes and straightened the lifeboat. Just as she began to descend again, Hamid appeared at the ship's rail.

"Stop!" he ordered.

She did as commanded and glared up at him.

"Running away again?" He shook his head. "Don't you understand, I'm trying to give you a chance to make things right. Your father, your mother, they have no idea what happened to you. Your mother has been heartbroken for years. Your father has never been the same since you left. Don't you want to see them just one more time?"

"You're taking me back to face punishment." Fatemeh spoke the words through clenched teeth.

"Yes, I expect you to face the sharia court and I expect you to abide by their decision. In that way, you can make things right with God as well as your family."

Fatemeh pursed her lips. It had been a long time since she'd thought about her parents and she never wanted to hurt them with her actions. She swallowed and tears filled her eyes. As a healer, she'd vowed never to do anyone deliberate harm. She willed the tears not to flow, at least not in front of Hamid, this man who had just taken a life on this horrible quest. Two lives, she reminded herself. He'd killed Jacques Lalande. Poor Marie … Poor Francoise…

"I see you do have feelings for your parents after all this time."

Despite her efforts, a tear fell. She wiped it away, then continued lowering the boat. Hamid leveled the revolver at her. "I would hate to hurt your parents, and even more I would hate to see Alethea grow up without a mother."

Those words made the blood in Fatemeh's veins turn to ice. She looked up at Hamid again. "I have one demand."

"You are in no position to make demands." Hamid shook his head.

"You have searched for me a long time and if you shoot me you will lose me forever." She tied off the ropes and folded her arms. "I have one demand."

He lowered the gun and his expression softened. "All right, I'll listen."

"Come and speak to me. So far, all I know of Hamid Farzan is the man who was a rich man who wanted to impress a young girl with his wealth and make her a trophy. I know the man who is … a murderer who betrayed his captain's trust. Based on the man I've seen, I wonder which of us should face justice in the sharia courts."

The new captain, Dalir, eyed Hamid. From where she stood, below the ship's rail, she couldn't see Captain Turan's body.

"All right." Hamid holstered the gun. "I will come to your cabin and we will talk."

For just a moment, Fatemeh considered reaching for the ropes and continuing down anyway, but knew it would only take Hamid a moment to draw his weapon and kill her. "One more condition."

He frowned. She doubted he was in the mood to hear conditions from someone who had already been so much trouble, but pushed on anyway.

"Leave my cabin unlocked. Show me that I'm a guest and not a prisoner."

Hamid didn't answer for a long time.

"Where am I going to run?" she asked. "From the map Captain Turan showed me, this was my last chance to easily find safe harbor in a lifeboat."

At last he gave a small nod. He looked over at Captain Dalir. "Help her aboard and escort her back to her cabin, then get a detail of loyal men to help you with Turan's body."

"Aye aye, sir."

With that, Hamid disappeared into the shadows.

CHAPTER NINE
THE QUEST FOR TRUTH

"Do you know how to get to Camp Street?" Alethea lay in bed, across a darkened room from Francoise.

"That's easy." Francoise yawned. "Chartres Street here in the Quarter turns into Camp Street on the other side of Canal."

"And what about the offices of the *Times-Democrat* newspaper? Do you know where those are?"

"That would be Newspaper Row. It's just across the street from Canal. Mamá goes there all the time to place ads and sometimes they pay her to write stories for the society column. She gets invited to some fancy parties." The sheets shuffled as Francoise turned. Alethea noticed her bright eyes from across the room. "You're not thinking of sneaking out again are you? You gave mamá a big scare when you disappeared, and she gets scary when she's worried."

Alethea shivered. She didn't understand how Marie Lalande could both be warm and friendly, yet scary at the same time. What's more, she couldn't imagine Marie Lalande being scarier than normal. "My mom and dad are missing. I can't sit around and do nothing." Her voice seemed tiny, even as she thought the words sounded grown up.

Francoise pushed her blankets aside and padded across the floor. She climbed in next to Alethea and pulled her close. "I thought my papá would die. He was shot through the chest and I couldn't do anything about it. But he came out fine. There was a happily-ever-after. Your mamá and papá will be fine, too."

"Your daddy was always here in New Orleans and you had your momma by your side. I don't have anyone."

"You have us," said Francoise. "Now, relax and go to sleep.

We have school in the morning." Her voice grew heavy and soon her breathing deepened.

Alethea stared up at the ceiling, eyes wide. Her throat ached with a sob, but tears would do no good. She couldn't imagine going to school and concentrating on her books or math while she worried about her parents.

Newspaper Row didn't sound so far—not much further than the streetcar. She extracted herself from her friend's arms and climbed out of bed. She dressed, then removed a pillow from its case. She grabbed some clothes from the dresser drawer and put them in the case. Then, she opened the window and climbed into the courtyard.

The French Quarter was eerily quiet this late at night. A dog barked and some distant music jangled. The gas lamps cast bright rings on the ground, leaving deep shadows near the walls. Laughter and music grew louder as she approached Bourbon Street. She crossed at a run and a chill went up her spine as she heard catcalls behind her. She had no idea if they were aimed at her. She was only a little girl, but her mother told her drunk people didn't think straight. She ran and didn't stop for a block, where she fell against a brick wall and panted while her heart settled.

She looked up and realized her flat was close by. Tears threatened to gush forth as she thought about sleeping in her own bed and eating dinner with her mother and father. A gentle trill distracted her. She looked up into a nearby tree. A screech owl stood in the branches, its round eyes fixed on her. It reminded her of her father's gaze. Was it the same owl she'd seen with her momma just a few days ago?

It turned its head toward Bourbon Street. Alethea followed its gaze. Two strangers staggered into the lamplight. Alethea caught her breath. They were drunks and probably not after her, but she thought bad things might happen if they saw her.

Ruffling its feathers, the owl launched itself from the tree and flew toward the men. It circled around their heads. They shouted and swatted at it, then retreated up the street. Soon the owl resumed its perch on the tree. It said nothing but its glare held meaning. She curtsied, picked up her bag and continued on her way.

She cast a quick glance at her family's flat as she passed. A few minutes later, she turned at Chartres Street and continued on. Somehow, this street, closer to the river, seemed darker. Mostly, it held banks and some shops only open during the day. Not many people lived on this block. A cat screeched and knocked over an ashcan, causing her to jump backward. She took a moment to look around.

A fluttering of feathers told her the owl had followed, which made her smile despite her fear. She didn't know what the owl could do if someone wanted to do her harm, but at least it kept her company.

"Thank you for helping me."

It gave a whinnying cry, almost like a horse, which scared her almost worse than the cat's screech. She swallowed and continued until she reached Canal Street which marked the French Quarter's boundary. Bright lights revealed just a few people. A man slept in a doorway, holding a bottle like Alethea might hold a doll.

She ran across the street and looked up at the sign. Sure enough, she'd found Camp Street. The buildings here seemed blocky and plain, not multicolored and pretty with decorative railings like those in the Quarter. As she moved away from Canal, it grew dark again. The owl fluttered onto a tree branch ahead of her and looked around. It whinnied again. Although it scared her, she began to realize that was the owl's way of telling her it was safe.

As she walked, a great mechanical rumbling grew beneath her feet. Steam plumed from several buildings ahead. As she approached, she read the signs, which told her the buildings belonged to the newspaper offices. She found the *Times-Democrat's* building and noticed more light shining from the back than the front.

She crept around the building's side. The owl fluttered above her and perched on a fire escape. It gave its warning trill and Alethea slowed. She pressed herself against the wall until she could peer around the corner.

An enormous machine chugged and whirred. Newspapers moved along conveyor belts and dropped into neat stacks. Two glistening, shirtless black men heaved the stacks and loaded them onto wagons. One of them turned and gasped, as though he were more scared of her than she was of him. Then he laughed.

"What are you doing here, little girl?"

Her mouth went dry and she licked her lips, trying to get enough moisture to speak.

"I wanted to find Lafcadio Hearn."

The man erupted in a jovial laugh. "Mr. Hearn, he won't be here for a couple of hours yet. You come in here where it's safe and when we're done with work, I'll walk you home."

Alethea frowned. She didn't want the man to walk her back to Marie Lalande's house, but safe and warm sounded good. The man said it would only be a couple of hours before Hearn arrived. Maybe if she looked around a little, she could find a place to hide. She went inside the bright press room. The presses had great wheels that turned and pistons that went up and down. Every now and then, one of the black men would shovel coal into a boiler.

Alethea found a spot in the corner and settled in. The motion and rhythmic noise grew hypnotic despite the volume and she soon drifted off to sleep.

She didn't know how long she slept, but she awoke to voices. As her eyes fluttered open, she realized the sky outside had grown brighter than the light inside the press room. The black man talked to a tall, skinny white man with a drooping mustache and sleepy, almost sad eyes. She came suddenly awake, realizing the man was Lafcadio Hearn.

"She just wandered in last night, and I was going to take her home," said the black man. "She wants to talk to you."

Alethea leapt to her feet. "Mr. Hearn, I'm Alethea Morales. You wrote the book about my momma and daddy."

Hearn tugged at his trousers and crouched down next to her. "So you are, I remember meeting you the other day." He held out his hand and smiled.

She shook his hand, then plunged ahead. "My momma's been kidnapped and my daddy's out west trying to stop a war between Indians and settlers and I don't know what to do."

His brow creased. "Are you all alone?"

She turned her toe on the ground, then looked at him.

"Not exactly. My mother left me with Madame Lalande."

"Really?" He stood up. "We should return you at once. She'll be worried."

"Please, Mr. Hearn, would you hear my story? I came a long way to talk to you."

"All right," he said. "I'll listen. I won't promise not to take you home afterward."

"That's good enough for me." She smiled up at him.

He held out his hand. She took it and he led her to his office. "I think you have a lovely name, Alethea."

"My mom tells me it means truth."

He nodded. "My wife's name was Alethea, though I called her Mattie. May I call you Mattie?"

Alethea thought about it. She repeated the name then thought it sounded like a name they would use out west.

"Yes, that would suit me just fine, if you'll agree to help me."

Hearn chuckled. "You're very much your mother's daughter. I look forward to your tale."

Hearn pulled out a notepad. Alethea frowned, thinking he would doodle instead of listening carefully to her tale, but she plunged ahead. The reporter listened carefully, occasionally writing something on his pad. When she finished her story, she yawned. The long night caught up with her.

Hearn read his notes, then steepled his fingers. "Well, young Mattie, I have several choices. I could return you to Jacques and Marie Lalande…"

Alethea came wide awake and shook her head. "Please no. I like Madame Lalande and Francoise, but they don't think I can help my daddy."

The reporter chuckled and held up his hand. "Much as I admire your parents, I have reasons to question their choice of leaving you with the Lalandes. They have made, shall we say, interesting business choices."

"Oh, you mean how Madame Lalande has a Voodoo shop and how Monsieur Lalande works at something called the black market which my daddy won't take me to, even though they say you can get everything there."

The reporter's eyes widened. "Very perceptive of you, Mattie."

He sat back and read over his notes. "Your father is engaged in very important work." He reached over and patted a copy of *Owl Riders* on his desk. "I think it would be fascinating to see how he handles the situation in Arizona and it's probably best if I can return you to his care."

"That would be wonderful!"

Again, Hearn held up his hand. "Don't get your hopes up too high. This will not be easy to accomplish. Why don't you lie down and rest for a while and I'll go see what I can figure out."

Alethea didn't want to rest, but her eyes drooped in spite of her best efforts to keep them open. She lay down on the couch in Hearn's office and soon drifted off to sleep.

When she awoke, the light in the office had changed. Hearn sat at his desk, scratching notes on papers. When he noticed her, he smiled, then stood and went to the door. He called for a boy, handed him money, and told him to buy two po'boy sandwiches then returned to his desk to work some more.

By the time the man with the sandwiches arrived, she'd grown bored and worried. Hearn handed one to Alethea. She was so hungry she ate half the sandwich before she realized there were oysters on it. She made a face and forced herself to swallow, then set the sandwich aside. If Mr. Hearn minded, he didn't say. Instead, it looked as though he'd reached a decision.

"Alethea … Mattie, I need to take you back to your father," he explained. "It means taking an airship out west. Is that okay with you?"

Alethea couldn't contain her glee. "You're the best, Mr. Hearn."

Hearn held up his hand. "Don't thank me yet. I need to make sure my publisher agrees and I need to make sure I can afford tickets."

Alethea sighed and looked down at her sandwich. "I understand."

"Now, now," said Hearn. "Don't lose heart. I will do everything I can to reunite you with your parents. Just be aware, it might not be easy."

Hearn finished his sandwich and stood. "Stay here and don't call attention to yourself. I'll be back as soon as I can." At the door, he turned around. "Do you have something to occupy your time?"

She dug through her pillowcase and retrieved a copy of *The Authentic Life of Cowboy Charlie*. Hearn quirked an eyebrow but nodded. He put on a hat, grabbed his notepad, and stepped through the door.

Alethea thumbed through her book, mostly looking at the pictures. The men looked awfully mean and many of them had guns. She began to wonder if leaving Madame Lalande was such a good idea. Mr. Hearn sounded as though he really would help, but he asked so many questions. She wondered if he really believed her. She also wondered if he had what it took to stand up to such mean-looking men out west.

A fat man with slicked-back gray hair and a long, skinny beard opened the door. He wore glasses much like her daddy. "Hearn, are you in here?" His eyes fell on Alethea. "Who are you? Where has Lafcadio Hearn gone off to?"

Alethea swallowed hard. "I'm Alethea Morales, sir. Mr. Hearn left to run some errands. He said I should stay here."

The man frowned at her. "Come with me to my office. You shouldn't be here alone."

"Mr. Hearn said I should stay right here."

The strange man made a harrumph noise, then put on a forced smile. "Well, I am Mr. Hearn's boss. He listens to what I tell him. If you listen to him, then you should listen to what I tell you as well."

Alethea thought about that. It made some sense to her. She also liked the man's glasses. She packed up her book and followed the man. He spoke to a clerk on his way through the bustling newsroom. "Make sure Hearn comes to my office as soon as he gets in." He then led her into his office, which was much bigger than Mr. Hearn's. He let her sit on a couch under a big painting of a man with a lion's mane of white hair and a boring black suit. To her relief, the couch was in the corner of the office. The man returned to his desk and ignored her while he worked.

Alethea opened her book and began reading. As she neared the end of the first chapter, a knock sounded and Lafcadio Hearn appeared at the door. His eyes fell on Alethea. "Oh thank goodness you're safe."

"Hearn!" The reporter's boss stood up. "Where have you been and what are you doing with a child in your office?"

"I'm sorry, Mr. Hearsey. This is Alethea Morales, she's the daughter of the Assistant U.S. Attorney for the Eastern District of Louisiana. She's brought me a fantastic tale. He's gone out west to attempt to negotiate a peace between the Apaches and the white settlers." He then glanced back at Alethea and leaned forward and spoke quietly to his boss. She crept closer so she could hear. "...warrant out for his arrest. Something about the Persian ambassador catching him in some kind of impropriety."

Alethea fought to keep from gasping. Did he mean someone wanted to arrest her daddy? That made no sense. Her daddy was a lawman and an attorney who fought for justice. He didn't do bad things like the men in the Cowboy Charlie book.

"What's more, the girl's mother has been kidnapped. The Lalandes and their network are sweeping the Caribbean for her." He paused. "I think we have a fantastic story here with a local angle. I could take the young lady back to her father and send you a story right from the front lines of the Apache war."

The man called Hearsey tugged on his long beard. "I can get someone to cover your editorial responsibilities, but you're one of my best reporters. What happens if you get into trouble?"

"I don't intend to throw myself into the heart of any battles." Hearn held up his hands. "From what I know of Ramon Morales, his presence should have already calmed things down out west."

"I hope you're right." Mr. Hearsey tugged on his beard some more, then finally nodded. "All right. You can go." He held up a meaty finger. "I expect the best story you've ever written."

"Yes, sir." Hearn reached for Alethea's hand and led her from the office. Together, they went to the airship terminal and Hearn checked the schedule. The next airship west would depart the following day. He purchased two tickets. As he stepped away from the ticket counter, he found himself face to face with a man as big and intimidating as Mr. Hearsey, but even rounder as though he'd eaten too many beignets. He wore a long, black coat with a silver star on the left breast.

"Good day, Sheriff," said Hearn.

The sheriff lifted his chin toward the ticket counter. "Planning a trip, Mr. Hearn?"

Hearn placed the two tickets in his coat pocket. "I'm following a lead on a story."

The sheriff folded his arms. "Who is this little girl? I see you have two tickets. Is she going with you?"

"She's my niece. I'm watching her while my ... brother and his wife are away on business. I can't just leave her behind while I investigate a story."

The sheriff's brow furrowed. "I thought your family was back in Ireland and you didn't talk to them very much."

The corner of Hearn's mouth darted upward. "You seem to know a lot about me, Sheriff Jenkins. You should be a reporter."

"About your niece." The sheriff's gaze fell on Alethea and she scooted around behind the reporter's legs.

"I don't see how she factors into any official business we might need to discuss."

"I'm looking for Alethea Morales," said the sheriff. "You wrote a book about her parents, Ramon and Fatemeh Morales. This girl looks as though she fits the Morales girl's description."

Alethea swallowed hard.

"I know Alethea Morales and I haven't seen her." Hearn maintained a neutral expression. "But I'll be sure to let you know if I do." With that, Hearn pushed past the sheriff.

As they left the aerodrome, Hearn looked down at Alethea with a troubled expression.

"Young Mattie, I don't suppose you brought any clothes with you."

"I brought a change of clothes." She'd opened the pillow case to show him.

"Just one?"

"We can return to my house to get more."

He shook his head. "I'll send my secretary to the mercantile store to pick out a few suitable garments."

Since her escape attempt, a new young man brought Fatemeh's meals. She missed Ahmad and hoped he wasn't in trouble for helping her. At least Hamid finally sent down some proper clothes—three long-sleeved black dresses, about a size too big, but an improvement over her dirty nightgown. She had no idea where he got them, but suspected they were cargo he carried back to Persia. Did he expect them back at the end of the voyage?

The steward brought breakfast right at seven o'clock on the third morning after her escape attempt. He didn't speak and nothing about his demeanor invited conversation. She turned and looked out the porthole. She counted ten, then shot a glance over her shoulder and caught him looking with a wary curiosity. When he noticed her eyes upon him, he looked away. He poured a cup of coffee then left without a word.

Fatemeh sat down to a breakfast as good as the previous days. If she'd angered Hamid with her escape attempt, it didn't show in the meals he sent. Did the young man blame her for his captain's death? She didn't even know whether Turan had been a good captain to these men.

The captain's death still weighed on her. By not following through on the escape plan, had she shown cowardice and dishonored him? She sat back, wrapped her arms around herself, and wondered whether she'd always been a coward. She ran away from her parents without discussing her plans. She ran away from Hamid without giving him a verbal rejection. When she reached America and the townspeople of Socorro accused her of witchcraft, she ran away. When the mine owner Randolph Dalton pursued them, she kept running.

She sipped her coffee and attempted to reassure herself that she hadn't always run away. She'd assembled a team consisting of Larissa Seaton—then known as Larissa Crimson—along with Professor Maravilla, Billy McCarty, Onofre Cisneros and his crew to fly the Professor's mechanical owls in order to thwart the Russian invasion of Denver. She considered a prayer by the Bab, the prophet who foretold the arrival of Bahá'u'lláh.

"In moments of heedlessness, guide my steps aright through thy inspiration."

She closed her eyes. Soon after she'd told Ramon she was

estranged from her parents, she'd said she planned to return to Persia to attempt to heal the wounds between them. She hated the pain Hamid had caused Ramon and Alethea, but perhaps Hamid served a higher purpose, assuring she actually fulfilled her promise. She just wanted Ramon by her side. She felt stronger when he was nearby.

She finished her breakfast and coffee, then stepped to the door. True to his word, Hamid had not locked the cabin. She peered out into the corridor as she had several times over the last three days. A crewman slipped past, not paying her any attention. This time, she left her cabin and walked up the ladder to the deck above where crewmen worked in the light of day. She passed two men who scraped salt from the deck. A man hurried past and climbed the mast to relieve the lookout above. A group of sailors huddled together and spoke in whispers she couldn't hear in the wind. She suspected they discussed her because they shot occasional glances her direction.

She strode forward, passing the lifeboat she'd used for her escape attempt, noticing all signs of struggle had already been scrubbed from the deck. She continued to a spot where she could look out at the water and the sky beyond. Puffy white clouds floated over an undulating ocean. They were in the Atlantic, but she had no clue where.

As she looked out over the ocean, she became aware of a presence behind her. She glanced over her shoulder long enough to confirm Hamid stood there.

"You must think me a monster." His tone was gentle.

She reached out and grabbed the railing to steady herself and keep her hands from trembling. "I think you're obsessed with me. I'm angered that you pulled me away from my daughter. I'm outraged that you killed the ship's captain to keep me from escaping." She turned her head again to look him in the eye. "I do not see a monster. I see a human, albeit a human who has given in to terrible behavior."

To his credit, he neither laughed nor raged. He stepped forward and put his hands on the rail next to hers. He made no effort to reach out and touch her hands. "That's why I love you, Fatemeh. I'm a rich man and many men have offered me their daughters. Those men—and their daughters, too—saw my wealth and my power." He turned to look into her eyes. "You saw me as a human. When you left, I feared I'd lost you forever. When I discovered you'd married another, a rage burned within me and I had to take you from him. I am hurt that you don't feel the same for me as I do for you."

Fatemeh's knuckles on the railing grew white. She struggled to relax them. "And Captain Turan. Did he deserve to die for attempting to help me?"

Hamid snorted. "He committed mutiny. He deserved to be brought up on charges. There's a good chance he would have suffered the same fate."

"Your sympathy for him moves me." Fatemeh didn't bother to disguise the sarcasm.

He sighed. "Is there any way I can win you back?"

Fatemeh fought the urge to lash out. She looked out over the ocean and gave the question more serious consideration than it deserved, but she didn't want to put herself or any of the crew in more danger by angering him at this point. "Hamid, you must understand, you never won my heart at all. If you had, I wouldn't have left. I love Ramon Morales and won't leave him for you." She sensed his growing ire. Although bile rose in her throat, she reached over and placed her hand on top of his. "Despite all you've done so far, there are ways you could win me over as a friend."

He looked down at her hand holding his. He put his other hand on top of hers. His hands trembled, though from fear or suppressed rage, she couldn't tell. "That is a start, at least," he said. "Tell me what I must do."

"The best thing you could do is turn the ship around and take me back to New Orleans."

He shook his head. "I will not do that."

"I didn't think so." Fatemeh squeezed his hand, the hand that had pulled the trigger, murdering the ship's captain and withdrew it. "Barring that, take time to get to know me. Understand me as a person and my beliefs. You promised to come to my cabin, but you haven't kept your word."

"You would convert me to your heresy?"

She shook her head. "I have no interest in being an evangelist. I just want you to understand why we can't be together."

"I agree, as long as you agree to listen as well," said Hamid. "Perhaps I can convince you I'm a better man than you imagine."

Alethea's heart raced as she reached the airship terminal with Lafcadio Hearn. It hadn't helped when Hearn tried to help her brush out her snarled mass of black hair that morning. She screamed and cried until he stopped. Then she realized he looked so afraid that she laughed, which seemed to give him the courage to try again. Once he was reasonably satisfied he stood up. "Can you braid your own hair?"

"Momma always braids it for me."

Mr. Hearn looked as though he might faint.

"We can always put it up in pigtails," she suggested. "Do you have any ribbons?"

He shook his head, but then went to his desk drawer and retrieved two gutta-percha rings. "Will these do?"

She took the stretchy rubber rings and played with them. They were fun. Then she noticed the serious expression on his face. "Yes, I think I can make them work." She went to the mirror, put her hair up in pigtails, then faced Hearn.

He smiled and nodded. "Yes, that does nicely. It even changes your appearance."

At the aerodrome, several passengers sat on hard, wooden benches, awaiting the airship's arrival. Hearn reached the baggage counter and placed the bags on the scale while a clerk wrote out claim tickets. Alethea looked around and saw Jacques Lalande and two of his men walking toward them.

"Where are you going with that girl?" Lalande placed his fists on his hips and addressed Hearn. "She's supposed to be under our protection."

Hearn opened his mouth to speak, but no words came out for a moment. "I'm taking her to her father in Arizona," he said at last. As they spoke, the airship approached the mooring tower.

Lalande's eyebrows came together. "How do you know her father is still in Arizona?"

A throat cleared. "And what exactly has happened to the girl's mother?" Sheriff Jenkins tugged on a pair of over-strained suspenders as he eyed the three black men who confronted Lafcadio Hearn.

"That's none of your business, Sheriff," said Lalande.

"It's not, is it? You know this looks awfully suspicious."

"I don't care how it looks."

With the sheriff and Lalande engaged, Hearn reached back and took Alethea's hand. They slipped outside just as the airship lowered the stairway from the passenger cabin. Even before the purser walked down, Hearn bolted up, an iron grip on Alethea's wrist.

The purser stopped them at the top of the stairs and Hearn flashed his tickets. The purser took them, then let them pass. Hearn and Alethea continued up into the lounge. From there, Hearn took a seat. Alethea laughed.

"That was exciting."

Hearn held up a hand.

One of Lalande's men left the terminal and ran toward the stairway. The purser stopped him, then the sheriff emerged and called him back inside. Hearn didn't speak until the crew lifted the stairs and released the mooring line.

Alethea hopped from the chair and peered out the large windows. She gasped at the sight of the city tucked between the Mississippi and Lake Pontchartrain growing small beneath them. Hearn stepped up beside her.

"How can Monsieur and Madame Lalande be so nice and so mean at the same time?"

Hearn looked her in the eye. "I don't think they're trying to be mean. I just think they're trying to fulfill their promise to protect you."

"If they'll protect me, why are you taking me away?"

Hearn frowned and thought about her question. She decided she liked that about him. Most adults didn't take her that seriously. "I thought you wanted to go to your father?"

"I do. I just hope Madame Lalande will let me see Francoise again when this is all over."

"Your father is in Arizona because he's a good diplomat. I'm sure he can smooth things over with the Lalandes when we return home." He gave her a reassuring smile even though he looked as scared as she felt. "Let's go find our cabin, then order some lunch." She returned his smile and her thoughts brightened as she considered the adventure ahead.

CHAPTER TEN
DANGEROUS TERRITORY

Ramon pushed his glasses up on his nose. On one side of the table sat the Apaches—the Tsokanende—Lozen and Naiche. On the other side sat Wyatt Earp and Doctor Holliday. Masuda Hoshi sat on the far end of the table. On the table sat a map of Southern Arizona with pencil lines and a star on the site of the area where Earp wanted to establish a town.

"We should make a proposal to portion off this section of land as a separate county," said Earp. It struck Ramon that he could easily be Doc Holliday's brother. The two looked astonishingly similar and dressed much alike. "We could name it Cochise County in honor of your great chief."

Naiche and Lozen looked at each other and nodded their approval at the idea.

"We can set up the county seat here." Earp pointed to the town site. "We already know there's mineral wealth in the area. That means jobs for Apaches. There's also good farm land along the San Pedro."

Naiche held up his hand. "What about jobs in banks, mercantile shops, newspapers? Those are good jobs that towns have to offer. It almost sounds like you would have the Tsokanende serve as a labor class, supporting the town you wish to build."

A palpable tension filled the air and Ramon leaned forward. "I believe you also propose schools, open to all, isn't that right?"

Holliday toyed with a deck of cards, cutting it, drawing cards off the top of the deck, and putting them back. "Of course we would," he said. "It's always been our intention to make the Apaches productive members of society."

Naiche scowled. "It's not your place to make us anything. We choose our own destiny."

Hoshi cleared his throat. "You are right, of course. That

121

said, I believe it's reasonable that any schools built should have Tsokanende on the governing board."

Ramon quirked an eyebrow at Wyatt and Doc. "Is that agreeable to you?"

The two looked at each other. Doc winked at Wyatt who nodded. "I would be willing to discuss the idea further."

A knock at the door interrupted the discussions. Before anyone could rise to answer, General Miles let himself in.

Ramon rose and held out his hand to the general. "We haven't had the pleasure of your company in a while, sir. Please come in, I think we're making excellent progress toward an agreement."

The general's too-eager smile left a hollow feeling in Ramon's gut. "That's fine, good to hear," he said, "but I'm afraid your services will no longer be required." He held up a gloved hand and gestured behind him. Half a dozen soldiers filed through the door. "Sergeant, please escort Chief Naiche and Miss Lozen here to our fine guest accommodations."

"What is the meaning of this?" growled Ramon as the soldiers moved behind Naiche and Lozen.

Miles smiled. "Oh, you've been very helpful, Counselor. You've kept our friends here occupied while I've been moving troops into position. We have Naiche's band along the San Pedro surrounded and I expect good news from Fort Bowie within the week."

Naiche tried to lunge at the general, but the soldiers grabbed his arms. They escorted Naiche and Lozen out of the room. Lozen spat a Tsokanende curse as they left.

"I don't know what you're playing at, General." Ramon's fingers twitched. If he wore a six gun as he had back in his days as sheriff, he'd be tempted to draw it, no matter how foolish that might be. "I was brought in to negotiate in good faith. Now I find you've betrayed that faith by executing military maneuvers behind my back."

Miles shook his head. "You of all people should not lecture me on betraying faith." He withdrew a rolled-up paper from his belt and placed it on top of the map. "You're a wanted man, Mr. Morales. Sounds like some pretty high-ranking people want your head."

Ramon looked down at the wanted poster and pushed his glasses back up his nose. His picture appeared above the text: "Wanted for theft of Persian property."

"Persian property?" Ramon shook his head. "I haven't even been to Persia."

"That's not my concern." Miles waved the objection aside. "There's a U.S. Marshal on the way to question you regarding this matter. I'm afraid you'll be our guest as well for a time." The general gestured to the corporal with the bushy mutton-chops.

"This way sir."

Hoshi shot a glance at Wyatt Earp and Doc Holliday. "Aren't you gentlemen going to say anything?"

Wyatt held out his hands. "What can we do? Our hands are tied."

"You do not require the Apaches for your plans," sneered Hoshi. "So you will do nothing."

Ramon took a step toward the two businessmen who both sat up. "Did the two of you know about this?"

The corporal took Ramon's arm and led him out of the room before Holliday or Earp could answer. A sergeant met them in the next room.

They led Ramon out of the building and across the courtyard. Ramon tugged at his collar as sweat began to build up. They entered another building and continued into a back room—the stockade. Lozen and Naiche already occupied cells. The corporal opened the door of a third cell. "Let us know if we can make your stay more comfortable, Counselor. From what we hear, the marshal just got into town. You shouldn't be here too long."

Ramon entered the cell, then watched as the soldiers locked it and left. He turned to Lozen and Naiche and held out his hands. "I am so sorry."

Lozen folded her hands. "This is not your fault."

Naiche shook his head and stalked over to a cot and climbed up so he could look out a barred window. "We need to find a way out of here."

"How could I have been so blind?" Ramon sat on the cot in his cell and rubbed the bridge of his nose.

"You are a good man, Mr. Morales," said Lozen. "In my experience, good men can be naïve, expecting others to be as good as they are."

Ramon put his glasses on. "You're right. I've known generals who were good men. General Johnson in St. Louis, General Sheridan…"

Naiche hopped off the bed and whirled on Ramon. "Sheridan has blood on his hands, too. Be careful who you revere, Morales."

Ramon nodded. "I'm sorry and I should have known that." He shook his head. "The thing is, I know Sheridan well enough to know he wouldn't use me like this."

"Are you certain that's true?" Lozen's words silenced Ramon.

"The time for negotiation is at an end," declared Naiche. "War is now at hand."

"I'm sorry for your people." Ramon stood and walked over toward Naiche's cell.

"Miles is not the only one who has moved people and machinery while we've talked," said the chief. "Our position along the San Pedro has always been difficult to defend."

A catcall from the other room interrupted the conversation. A thud, a whump, and a clattering of furniture soon followed. Keys jangled and the door opened, revealing a tall woman about Ramon's age wearing a worn, undecorated army captain's hat and a once-white duster over a black jacket. Underneath the cap, brown hair stopped at the woman's neck. She strode forward and put her hands on her hips and peered into Ramon's cell.

"Well, if it isn't Marshal Larissa Seaton." Ramon couldn't suppress a smile. "When they said the marshal would come to question me, I never hoped it would be you." Ramon inclined his head toward the open doorway. "Trouble?"

"Some people still have problems with a woman marshal. Sometimes, I have to educate them." Her eyes locked with Ramon's and he noticed the lines around them. She was younger than him, so the job must be taking a toll. "How did you get labeled as some kind of pervert by the Persian ministry in Washington?"

"Pervert?" Ramon's eyes widened. "I thought this whole mess had to do with some kind of theft."

She shook her head. "The two go hand in hand." She glanced into the adjoining cells. "Do you care to introduce me to your friends?"

Ramon introduced Naiche and Lozen.

"I don't suppose you could get us out," said Naiche.

Again, she shook her head. "Sorry, I just came for Ramon." She turned her attention back to the attorney. "Is everyone okay back in New Orleans? There's been strange buzz on the wires for the last few days. Something about an abduction and pirates chasing a Persian freighter." She shrugged. "Sounded like something you and Fatemeh might be involved in."

"I haven't been able to send a message to Fatemeh since I got here." Ramon grabbed the cell's bars. "You said a Persian ship ... and the Persians are after me."

Larissa nodded. "Something fishy is happening and I don't like it. I'll take you into custody and we'll see if we can put the pieces together."

Ramon's shoulders slumped. "I can't leave now. If we could just stop the army, we could resume negotiations with Earp and Holliday. I think we were close to reaching an agreement."

Lozen stepped up and grabbed the bars of her cell. "Stop the army? I respect you, but that's beyond your power. I'm also convinced Earp and Holliday were just using you as a pawn in their plans. They are businessmen. All they care about is money. It doesn't matter whether it comes from white men or To-kanende."

"Wyatt Earp and Doc Holliday are involved in all this?" Larissa's eyebrows shot up.

"They are," said Ramon. "Holliday's not well, though."

"To be honest, I'm surprised he's still alive." Larissa shrugged. "Guess he's just too ornery to die." She opened the cell and let Ramon out, then looked at Lozen and Naiche. "I would release you if I could."

"We still have allies who are not jailed or cornered," said Lozen. "We have hope."

"Will your allies break you out of jail?" Larissa quirked an eyebrow.

"If they feel they must."

"Good. I'm not too fond of the army right now." She strode forward with Ramon close behind. As they passed through the front office, the guard was just coming to. Larissa tossed the keys toward him.

"Thanks for your cooperation." Without awaiting a response, she continued outside.

Several soldiers stood around, gawking at a machine on two wheels made of brass and black-painted iron with a lightning gun mounted between the handlebars. "That's quite a machine," said Ramon.

"It's my lightning wolf."

Ramon walked over and put his hand on the leather saddle. "Last I knew, the lightning wolf was a glorified, motorized safety bicycle."

"You're seeing eight years of improvements." Larissa flashed a smile. "You should get out from behind your books a little more often."

Hoshi emerged from the crowd of soldiers.

"I hate to leave you in a lurch," said Ramon.

Hoshi glanced at Larissa. "It seems you have no choice in the matter. Do not worry, I will do what I can to bring the dogs of war to heel."

Ramon patted Hoshi on the arm. "I know you will. I'll be in touch as soon as I can."

Larissa threw her leg over the lightning wolf's saddle and stomped the starter pedal. The machine roared to life and the soldiers retreated several steps. Larissa patted the seat behind her and Ramon climbed on.

"Hold on," she said.

Even before Ramon did as instructed, the lightning wolf shot forward, almost throwing him off the back. He reached out and grabbed Larissa around the middle as they shot through Fort Lowell's gates.

Lozen stared through the window of her cell. Activity at Fort Lowell appeared normal. Miles had done a masterful job of moving troops without Naiche or her seeing. She hoped she and Naiche had been as masterful in setting up their plans. If she was right, the army would have a surprise waiting when they reached Fort Bowie. Geronimo had been negotiating with factions within Mexico. Still, she hated to languish in a jail cell when she should be fighting alongside Dahteste.

The door to the cell block opened and the corporal allowed Hoshi and Doc Holliday to enter. Lozen's eyes widened at seeing the doctor. Naiche ran up to the bars of his cell and grabbed them, his knuckles turning white. "How dare you show your face in here?"

Holliday held up his hands. "This little adventure has not gone as I would have predicted. I brought Mr. Morales out here to help parlay with y'all, not knowin' he would be at the center of an international incident."

"Why are you here? To taunt us?" Lozen narrowed her gaze. "All you care about is getting access to the silver mines on our land. You don't care how that happens as long as it does happen."

"Ah but I do care." Holliday leaned against a wall, well out of Naiche's reach. "Yes, if Miles succeeds in his campaign we'll achieve our short-term goal, but there will be ramifications. Miles believes if he can stamp out the Apache threat here and now, it will end all the Indian uprisings."

Hoshi, who had been so quiet that Lozen nearly forgot about him, spoke up. "It rarely works like that. Every other tribe would be incensed. He might end the Apache threat, but the Navajo, the Papago, and more would rise up. I have heard the Indians are gaining sympathy in the Eastern states. You have started making alliances in other countries. Those other tribes could build on those relationships."

Holliday touched his nose. "Exactly, and therein lies the problem, we might get our land, but we'd have to fight to keep it." He turned to Naiche. "To answer your question, the reason I'm here is just to remind you that my associate and I had nothing to do with the general's plans. If he fails, we'd like to return to the negotiating table."

"In other words, you don't care who wins, you just want the land." Naiche scowled.

Holliday shook his head. "That's not true. I care very much who wins, but I can't argue with fate."

"If you care, then use your influence to get us out of here." Naiche rattled the cell door for emphasis.

Holliday opened his mouth to speak, but a racking cough interrupted him and he doubled over. After a moment, he stood straight. "I fear there is much that is beyond our control, but I will help if I can." With that Holliday tipped his hat and left the cell block.

"I believe there is an expression that applies to the good doctor," said Hoshi. "'He speaks with a forked tongue.'"

Lozen nodded. "He is a snake, but a sickly one. I don't think we can expect much help from him."

Hoshi folded his hands. "In that case, it's a good thing I can help. An old friend is on the way. She once captured a Russian airship in order to challenge the Japanese Emperor. Despite that, Ramon Morales and his wife helped her redeem herself in the eyes of the court and she now serves in the Meiji government."

Naiche relaxed his hold on the cell bars. "And exactly how will this friend of yours be able to help us?"

Hoshi looked toward the door. He seemed hesitant to speak too openly. "Do you know the tale of Kumamoto Castle in Japan?"

Lozen and Naiche shook their heads.

"Saigō Takamori was a samurai leader who thought he'd trapped imperial forces within their castle. He surrounded them and hoped to starve them out. However, he didn't know more imperial forces waited outside. General Kuroda Kiyutaka watched for weakness. When he saw it, he made a sortie from the castle through the samurai lines, allowing for reinforcements. Instead of being a position of weakness, it proved a position of strength."

"General Miles thinks he has our people trapped within Fort Bowie." Naiche smiled.

Hoshi stepped closer to the cell. "He thinks he has you trapped in here and if his campaign along the San Pedro succeeds there will be more of you at the fort."

"Interesting," said Lozen. "It seems we think along similar lines."

Larissa rode straight south for an hour and a half while Ramon took in the surroundings. Mountains rose to his right. To the left, scrawny trees clung to life near a stream with just a little water. Ahead, an old church came into view. Larissa accelerated. As they passed near the building, a loud whoosh followed by a second caused Ramon's stomach to clench. He'd hoped never to hear that sound again—bullets passing near his head.

Larissa hollered back at Ramon. "Reach back and hit the two switches on the control panel!"

Ramon looked around and threw the only two brass toggle switches he found. A hum rose to form an undercurrent to the wolf's ongoing roar. Two more bullets whizzed close to Ramon.

Without warning, Larissa turned to the right, whirling the lightning wolf's tail around. Ramon had to clinch Larissa's middle tight to avoid being thrown off. If she winced, he didn't hear. Once stopped, she lowered dark goggles from her cap to her eyes.

"Look away!" she called.

Ramon turned his head as Larissa aimed the weapon mounted to the wolf's handlebars. He couldn't tell how she aimed through such dark glass, but decided to save questions for later. A flash of light and a crack like thunder told him she'd fired. He looked around and noticed a scorched mark on the old mission's wall.

A moment later, another bullet whizzed by.

"Some people never learn." Larissa fired again without warning Ramon to look away. A bright electric arc flew from the gun toward the mission. Ramon blinked away spots swimming in his sight. He tried to see if Larissa had hit a fresh target. "I didn't think Apaches claimed land this far west."

"They don't," said Larissa. "These are Papago. They've increased their resistance since the Apaches began their fight. They don't have the Apache's hardware, but it's one reason the army wants to quash Naiche's uprising. If he gains concessions, then other tribes might think it's worth fighting back." She looked around. "We better get a move on before they regroup. Hold on."

Ramon faced forward again, and tightened his grip around Larissa's middle. "When we first met, did you ever think you'd come riding to my rescue?"

The first time they met was at gunpoint when Larissa worked as a bounty hunter for the mine owner Randolph Dalton, in Socorro. "Who says I'm rescuing you? I'm just taking you in for questioning. Depending on what I learn, I might be perfectly happy to dump your ass behind bars, especially if I find out you did something to hurt Fatemeh."

Fatemeh had recruited Larissa to her team of owl riders who fought against the Russian airships.

"If I hurt Fatemeh, I'll accept whatever punishment you see fit to dole out."

"That's why I like you and Fatemeh. Neither of you feel exempt from justice." She fell silent for a time and the wind blew through Ramon's hair and grit pelted his hands and cheeks. "You both taught me the meaning of justice and doing what's right no matter the cost." Her voice caught and she fell silent again.

Larissa's bounty hunting days ended after she met Ramon and Fatemeh. She teamed up with Professor Maravilla and learned enough science and engineering to build the prototype of the lightning wolf—originally just a bicycle with a motor and a lightning gun. The work she did brought her to Washington's attention and the president himself appointed her to the United States Marshal's service.

"You said you heard about some trouble in New Orleans." Ramon hoped Larissa heard him over the wind. "Did you hear anything about our daughter?"

"No." Larissa shook her head. "Means the world to me that you named her after my cousin who died."

"Your story touched us." Larissa originally became a bounty hunter because her cousin grew ill and died as a child. Although Larissa couldn't save her, she realized she could fight bad people to save other children from harm. "Besides, Alethea means truth. We liked that."

They reached a small town nestled in the hills. Ramon climbed trembling off the lightning wolf's seat, jostled more than he ever had been on horseback. He looked around, trying to get his bearings. Ears ringing from the wolf's constant, loud roar, it took him a moment to realize Larissa spoke to him again.

She shook her head and pushed past him to the saddlebags which hung on either side of the lightning gun's control panel. She reached in and pulled out a canteen. She took a swig of water, then handed the canteen to Ramon. He drank, then sighed.

Larissa returned the canteen to the saddlebag, then, almost as an afterthought, flipped the two toggle switches on the lightning gun's control panel. The hum in Ramon's ears subsided somewhat.

He glanced around at the buildings, some wood, some adobe, most with signs in Spanish. They reminded him a little of his hometown of Socorro, though the rolling countryside reminded him a bit more of his cousin's home in Palomas Hot Springs a little further to the south. Living most of his life in the New Mexico Territory, he'd grown accustomed to a few signs written in Spanish, but not this many.

"Where are we?"

"Nogales." Larissa planted her hands on her hips.

Ramon's gaze narrowed. "You took me over the border? Won't you get in trouble?"

"Town straddles the border. We haven't crossed." Larissa inclined her head toward a telegraph office. "I'll see if I can get those questions, and you can send a telegram to New Orleans to find out what's happening there." She brushed dust from her sleeves. "Then I think we should each find a room, get a bath, and get some food."

Ramon looked down at his fine clothes covered in dust, then sighed.

"How long are we going to be here?"

"Depends on what we learn."

Ramon couldn't argue with that. He followed Larissa to the telegraph office. After sending their telegrams, they went to the hotel.

Once in the room, Ramon took a little time to splash some water on his face. He vowed to avail himself of a bath after dinner. Without waiting for Larissa, he strode across the street to the telegraph office and found a reply

The telegram made his legs go rubbery like the gutta-per-cha tires on Larissa's lightning wolf. Marie Lalande said the owner of a Persian ship named Hamid Farzan had taken Fatemeh captive. What's more, Alethea had disappeared. According to the telegram, she got on an airship to Tucson with Lafcadio Hearn before Jacques could stop her.

Larissa entered the telegraph office looking much refreshed. Ramon held the telegram out to her.

"Fatemeh's in trouble. So's Alethea." Ramon's mind flew, grasping for a course of action. Fatemeh was in the Caribbean, or maybe the Atlantic. Alethea would be in Tucson soon, may already be there. "We should go back to Tucson."

She took the telegram from him and scowled. "The next airship isn't due into Tucson for two days. Let's take this one thing at a time. There may be a way for us to help them both."

"I'll go without you if I need to," growled Ramon.

"And do what?" She shook her head. "I have contacts here. Let's see if we can get you out of trouble first before you get into more trouble." She strode to the counter and asked about any responses to the telegrams she'd sent earlier. The clerk handed her one and she paid. Reading it, she snorted. "That's what all the fuss is about?"

"What?" Ramon narrowed his gaze.

"There's a cantina across the street. We can get something to drink and a bite to eat while we discuss this."

"What about Alethea?"

Larissa put her hand on Ramon's shoulder. "I'll head back to Tucson first thing in the morning and find her. I promise. What's more, you have friends here who can help you find Fatemeh."

"Friends?" Ramon's fingers twitched in indecision but his stomach rumbled a demand for food. He allowed her to lead the way across the street to the cantina where she held the door open for Ramon.

He glanced at her for a moment, unused to a woman holding the door open for him, then stepped inside the small, dim cantina. Ramon sat down at a small, wooden table with Larissa across from him.

"If you're going to spend time in this sun, you should get a hat." The marshal removed hers and ran fingers through her short hair.

A waiter in a dirty white shirt walked over and took their order. Ramon ordered carne asada and a beer while Larissa ordered tacos and an agua fresca made with whatever fruit they had in season.

"So, what's the Persian ambassador so desperate to know?"

Larissa set the telegram she'd received in front of her. "He claims you violated something they call sharia law when you married Fatemeh. Did you know she was betrothed?"

Ramon snorted and shook his head. He flashed back to the book *Owl Riders* and its mention of Fatemeh's fiancée back in Persia. "Sharia law is their religious law. It's like they want me arrested for lying during confession."

Larissa nodded. "I know, but if I can get some satisfactory answers to my bosses, maybe we can get the law off your tail long enough for you to go after Fatemeh."

Ramon removed his glasses and rubbed the bridge of his nose. "You're right. This Hamid has set things up well. If I went after Fatemeh now, our government would see it as an affirmation of their charges. If something happened, it would allow them to press for extradition." He replaced his glasses and nodded. "All right, I'll play along. I didn't know Fatemeh was betrothed until I read it in that new book about our exploits."

The waiter delivered their food. Ramon took a bite. He loved the food in New Orleans, but this reminded him of the food he grew up with. He sipped the beer and his nerves settled.

"Which book is that? Remember it takes a while for new books to make it out west." Larissa lifted a taco and took a bite. Meat dropped onto the plate. She scooped it up and dropped it into her mouth.

Ramon nodded. "It's a book called *Owl Riders* by Lafcadio Hearn. He interviewed us about our adventures during the Russian invasion."

"Did you say good things about me?"

"Can we talk about that part later?"

Larissa shrugged, then noted something on her paper and glanced at the next question. "Have you ever dealt with a man named Hamid Farzan?"

Ramon glanced at the pocket with the telegrams. "The man who kidnapped Fatemeh? No. The book mentioned him, and Fatemeh told me a little about him when I discussed it with her."

Larissa set down the taco and narrowed her gaze. "You mean Fatemeh never told you about this betrothal until after the book came out?"

"That's right." Ramon nodded. He sat back and folded his arms. "I didn't like learning about it from the book, but I also don't think Fatemeh gave him much thought after she left Persia."

"Fatemeh never loved anyone else … besides your daughter, of course." Larissa gave him a wistful grin. "I think this next question goes a little too far, but I'll ask it in hopes we can get things simmered down. Was Fatemeh a virgin when you consummated your relationship?"

Ramon's eyes widened and his cheeks grew hot. "As far as I know. How would I even know?"

"You've hung out with deputies and worked as a ranch hand. Surely men gab about such things…" Larissa lifted an eyebrow.

"They talked about saloon girls more than virgins." Ramon's eyes darted around the room, as he grew self-conscious about who might be listening.

"I'll just put down, 'yes, as far as you know.'" Larissa chuckled. "Old men sometimes think they know more about women's bodies than they do."

Ramon chugged a few gulps of beer, then tugged at his collar. "Any other uncomfortable questions?"

"Nope." Larissa shook her head. "As far as I can tell, Fatemeh seduced you and you had no knowledge you were breaking some religious law from a faraway land, but I suspect whoever came up with these questions already knew all that." She took a drink of her agua fresca.

"Okay, we've caught up with the questions, who are these mysterious friends you mentioned?"

"Onofre Cisneros has an airship hanger on the Mexican side of the border."

Ramon nodded in appreciation. "This Hamid Farzan is supposed to be a trader. Do you suppose Cisneros might know something about him? Maybe he knows a little about the extent of his business?"

"I wondered that myself." She pointed over her shoulder with her thumb. "I'll draw you a map and you can cross the border in the morning. I'll get back to Tucson and find Alethea. If you're with Cisneros, I should be able to get word to you."

"How did you know about Cisneros's hangar?"

"He makes the fuel for the lightning wolf. I come through here all the time."

Ramon didn't want to delay, but an involuntary yawn reminded him how tired he was and he had a long journey ahead. The bath and some sleep would be just the thing to help him prepare to take on Hamid Farzan.

CHAPTER ELEVEN
AIR SHARK

After breakfast, Larissa and Ramon walked to the stable she'd rented to store the lightning wolf. "I sent a wire to Washington with the answers to the questions. Hopefully that will satisfy the powers that be and keep the law off your tail." She handed Ramon a map to Onofre Cisneros's hangar. "I'll let you know as soon as I've found Alethea."

"How will you contact me? I left my clacker in New Orleans. Even if I had one, their range isn't far."

"Cisneros has a way. You'll see."

Ramon knew Onofre Cisneros well enough to know that was likely true.

His brow furrowed. "I want you to keep Alethea safe, but we also left a volatile situation in Tucson. I'll be back as soon as I can."

"Focus on getting your wife out of harm's way. I'll do what I can in Tucson." Larissa shook Ramon's hand, hopped on the lightning wolf, and the engine roared to life. Ramon stepped back and watched as she rode away in a spray of gravel and dust.

Ramon turned south on foot. As he walked through town, he grew self-conscious as people stared at him. He soon realized he still wore his fancy clothes from New Orleans. He would need something more suitable for the work to come.

If Larissa hadn't noted the international border on the map, he never would have known it. Some buildings even straddled the border. Once in Mexico, he entered a mercantile store and bought some new shirts and two pairs of denim pants plus a replacement carpet bag. Remembering Larissa's advice, he bought a hat as well. As he suspected, they gladly took his United States currency.

Donning the new hat, Ramon packed his clothes bundle into the bag and continued his southward walk. He looked up at the craggy mountains surrounding the town and tried to imagine an airship landing in the rugged terrain.

Soon the buildings thinned out and the mountains gave way to sand dotted with scrub brush. In the distance, a mooring tower stood like a sentinel beside a two-story brick warehouse. He stepped up his pace.

Outside of the warehouse, four men with long mallets stood around a set of hoops and sticks in the ground. A familiar cowboy swung at a ball with his mallet. The ball rolled into another which, bounced into a stick in the ground.

Ramon approached the men. He recognized the cowboy from New Mexico who once rescued him from Randolph Dalton's henchmen, then traveled with him to San Francisco during the Russian invasion. "Billy McCarty? Is that you?"

Billy flashed a lopsided grin and held out his hand. "Well, if it ain't Ramon Morales. Larissa said you might drop by." The two shook hands.

Ramon gestured around at the game. "What's all this?"

"Game's called croquet. I was just teaching it to the warehouse workers."

"Don't they have other work to do?" Ramon glanced at the men who shuffled uncomfortably under the gaze of a man in fancy dress. The lawyer realized he probably reminded them of their boss.

"It's not as though we have much to do until the airship gets here." Billy pointed up at a long orange sock sticking straight out in the wind. "Besides, the wind'll have to die down before it can land."

As if on cue, the wind tried to blow Ramon's hat off. He grabbed it, which caused Billy to laugh.

"Oye, debo ir ahora," he said in Spanish. "I've got to go now. We'll continue the game later."

The workers waved at him and spoke among themselves.

"Let's go inside and have some coffee," suggested Billy.

Ramon followed him into the warehouse. Offices lined one wall and Billy entered the first one. He added wood to a cook stove in the corner.

"So, when did you start working for Cisneros?" asked Ramon.

"Actually, I work for Larissa." Billy added coffee to a pot and set it on the stove top. "It's not regular. She just hires me now and again when she's got a job she needs doing."

"Are you still working for Hoshi as well?" Ramon realized he'd neglected to ask the farmer about their mutual friend.

"I like Hoshi, and he hires me when he needs some extra help, but he's been relying on Professor Maravilla's Jackalopes to do the hard work at his farm."

"Really?" Ramon raised his eyebrows. He couldn't imagine Hoshi trusting the mechanical rabbits to do so much work. Last he knew, Hoshi didn't trust much about the professor's inventions at all. Ramon's thoughts turned to Fatemeh. "Glad as I am to hear the news from Hoshi's farm, have you communicated with Onofre Cisneros at all?"

Billy sat down behind the desk as though he owned the place.

"I have. Turns out Cisneros also got word about Fatemeh's kidnapping." Billy plunked his boots on the desktop and leaned so far back, Ramon feared he would fall over. "He wanted to find you so he could put together a rescue party. It was lucky you came right here."

"Why's that?" Ramon sat down, placing his carpet bag next to the chair.

"He was on his way to New Orleans, but when he heard you were in Tucson, he changed course." Billy shrugged. "He should be here tomorrow." He looked out the window at the orange sock. "I sure hope the wind dies down by then."

"How in the world did Onofre Cisneros hear about my wife's kidnapping?" Ramon narrowed his gaze.

Billy opened the desk drawer and pulled out a pair of telegrams.

"These tell the story as best as I know it." He passed them over to Ramon, then grabbed two cups from a shelf near the cook stove. He poured coffee while Ramon read the story of Jacques Lalande and his men attempting to rescue Fatemeh and failing. When he read that Jacques had been shot, Ramon involuntarily grabbed his own shoulder, feeling guilty that he hadn't been there for his wife. Marie had not mentioned the incident in her telegram to Ramon.

Ramon paused. He had mixed feelings about the Lalandes. He knew from his work in the U.S. Attorney's office that Jacques had connections with several questionable businesses. Despite that, Fatemeh trusted and liked Marie. He wondered if that trust had been misplaced.

Ramon questioned his own plans again, thinking he should return to Tucson and retrieve Alethea before charging off to get Fatemeh, but taking his daughter on an airship into a dangerous situation didn't seem a wise course of action either.

Then there were the Apaches. The army still held Naiche and Lozen captive and Miles planned to recapture Fort Bowie. Hoshi would do his best to keep the situation from worsening, but what could he do to make it better?

Ramon sipped some of the coffee Billy placed before him. His eyes widened. He couldn't remember a worse cup of coffee. He gritted his teeth and took another sip, then read the second telegram. In it, Onofre Cisneros relayed that he didn't know much about Hamid Farzan, only that he was a trader who did business throughout Europe and the Middle East. He had a contract with a firm in New York and had ships which made the transatlantic journey nine months of the year. However European airship lines that traded overland with Persia would likely present Farzan serious competition in the near future.

"He's got money, and he's got guns," said Ramon. "He's also got an entire ocean to hide in. We'll be lucky if we can find him."

"We know where his home port is." Billy sipped his coffee as though it was the world's best brew. "In the worst case, we can get ahead of him. Meet him when he docks."

"I don't like it. That's his home turf." Ramon sipped more coffee and grimaced as much from the flavor as the situation.

Billy leaned forward. "We'll find a way to get Fatemeh back."

He finished his coffee, then showed Ramon around Captain Cisneros's warehouse. Bolts of cotton and wool, stacks of rebar, crates filled with cigar and cigarette boxes, all waited to be carried across the border into the United States. It was all so ordinary, it helped alleviate Ramon's anxiety about Fatemeh and the failed negotiations.

"It looks like the good captain has built up quite a business here." Ramon scanned the warehouse, hands on his hips.

"He has, and it gets even better."

Billy led Ramon up a staircase to another office. Inside, a man sat at a console with knobs and dials. "Hola," said the man, without looking up from a magazine.

Ramon responded in kind, then looked at Billy. "So, what's this contraption?"

As if in answer to Ramon's question, the machine began to chatter and clack, and a slot on the machine's surface extruded a paper ribbon. The man put down the magazine, tore off the paper, and read it to himself before handing it to Billy.

Billy read it, then handed it to Ramon. Written in Spanish, the message said the Airship *Tiburón* would arrive on schedule at eight in the morning. The paper instructed personnel to get fuel and ballast ready for the ship.

Ramon handed the paper ribbon back to the operator, then peered at the knobs, dials, and gauges. "I didn't see any wires outside. Is this some kind of wireless telegraph like the clackers?"

"Yes," answered the operator and Billy in unison.

"I thought clackers had a limited range—just a few miles." Ramon's eyebrows came together.

"That's right." Billy pointed to the panel. "Captain Cisneros built all this to translate Morse code into written language and improve the range. You can type a message into the machine and it'll encode and send it for you."

Ramon examined the machine, amazed. It had been too long since he'd taken time to ponder the marvels of developing technology. "So, this is what Larissa meant when she said she had a way to get a message to me." He turned to Billy. "So if you're working for Larissa, how do you have an office here?"

"Oh that." Billy shrugged. "It's just an office set aside for visitors. The captain said you and I could use it while we're here."

Later in the afternoon, Billy and Ramon took horses from a corral behind the warehouse and rode into town. They dropped

Ramon's bag at the hotel where Billy stayed and walked across the street to a saloon.

"Fatemeh would find the captain's operation fascinating." Just as he spoke the words, Ramon's neck muscles tightened. He'd almost let himself forget her danger. He drank a shot of watered-down tequila and slammed the glass to the table.

Billy patted him on the shoulder and Ramon forced his hand to relax.

He regretted the drink when his stomach began to churn. Ramon excused himself and returned to the hotel. Billy stayed behind to look for a card game and another drink or two. Ramon lay on the bed and stared up at the ceiling. He knew he needed to fall asleep or he'd be useless the next day, but his eyes refused to close. How could he have been so blind to the general's plans? If only he could get back to Tucson. But, Fatemeh needed him...

The next thing he knew, the room's door slammed and woke him up. Billy entered and undressed, then slipped into his own bed. Within minutes he started snoring.

Ramon next awoke as sunlight streamed in through the curtains. He stood up and walked over to the wash basin to clear the gunk from his eyes. His head swam in a muzzy, sleep-deprived haze, but he still managed to dress and pack his clothes. Once Billy arose, they ate breakfast then returned to the warehouse.

The wind had quieted and Ramon scanned the skies with a spyglass until the long, silver cigar-shaped craft came into view.

He remembered the large, bulky Russian airships with boxy gondolas from eight years before. This airship was lean and mean, with a streamlined gondola. A fin on the back reminded Ramon a little of a shark's fin.

"What does the dorsal fin do?"

"It's not a fin." Billy laughed. "It's an antenna. That's how the captain sends wireless signals from the ship."

"Why isn't anyone standing by at the mooring tower?"

"Keep watching." Billy pointed to the airship.

Ramon lifted the spyglass again. Hatches opened in the bottom and six craft emerged, tethered to the airship. The craft had flapping wings like the army's ornithopters. Much as the captain's *Tiburón* appeared predatory like a shark, the flapping craft resembled birds of prey.

They pivoted their wings in a way Ramon had never seen before and extended their talon-like feet, reminding him of owls coming in for a landing. As they descended, they pulled the airship along behind them. Soon they touched down. Winches took up slack in the tether lines until the airship floated just a short distance overhead.

A ladder descended from the gondola and Captain Onofre Cisneros emerged wearing a peaked white cap, a blue coat, and white trousers. Although comfortable, Ramon almost wished he'd bought something nicer than the gingham shirt and canvas pants he wore. He looked back toward the mooring mast, confused.

"He doesn't need to moor his ships?" Ramon lifted his eyebrows.

Billy patted him on the shoulder. "Not anymore." He ran forward and Ramon followed.

The captain extended his hand. "It is good to see you again, Ramon. It has been far too long."

"Indeed it has." Ramon's eyes widened at the strength of the captain's grip and the hardness of his hand. He guessed life on ships had strengthened the engineer-turned-merchant.

"So, I hear your beautiful wife is in trouble."

"Do you think you can help?"

Cisneros looked up at the airship and around at the ornithopters. He looked at his ground crew, running forward with fuel and ballast lines. He flashed a feral grin. "I'm ready to go hunting, my friend. The sooner the better."

A short time later, Ramon stood in the *Tiburón*'s gondola and watched as the owl ornithopters released their tether lines. This was the second ship called *Tiburón* that Onofre Cisneros commanded. The captain used the first in a misguided attempt to show how a submarine could be used in warfare. Alas, an individual committing acts of war at sea is called a pirate, and Ramon had been hired to help hunt him down. A successor to the submersible craft came in handy when Ramon and Fatemeh traveled to Japan. Without it, they may not have been able to stop the samurai air pirates who hijacked a Russian airship.

As the airship rose, Ramon realized Cisneros never operated a lone ship, he always brought auxiliary craft along. In the case of his ocean-going vessels, the auxiliary craft traveled under water. In the case of this airship, the auxiliary craft flew.

The wind continued to subside into the afternoon and the *Tiburón* drifted upward as she dropped ballast. Ramon tapped the windowsill impatient for the chase to begin. A slow ascent suited a vacation, or even a business trip where one needed to plan and think, but he worried about Fatemeh and wanted to get to her as soon as possible.

"Engage motors," called Cisneros behind him.

Ramon turned his head and watched as the crew pushed and pulled levers, turned knobs and flipped switches. He could just discern motors revving up far behind the gondola. The airship eased forward. Down below, the ornithopters launched themselves into the air on powerful, spring-loaded legs. With a few mighty flaps they ascended toward the airship.

Ramon wandered toward the gondola's stern where he found Billy looking at the ground in wide-eyed wonder. On other airships, the entire gondola sat below the rigid airship structure which framed the interior balloons. In the *Tiburón*, a door in the back of the gondola led to the crew and cargo compartments, all enclosed in the superstructure. Because of that, Ramon could not see directly aft, and as the ornithopters rose to match the airship's altitude, they disappeared from view, presumably entering the aft hatches.

Captain Cisneros called out a course heading then strode over to a chart laid out on a table near where Ramon and Billy stood.

The chart showed the Gulf of Mexico. Ramon recognized the Mississippi Delta and New Orleans. Cisneros traced an arc from New Orleans around Florida to an island chain labeled the Bahamas. "My contacts in New Orleans followed the *Fatemeh* this far. Their ships aren't equipped for a long voyage in the open ocean. That's where they lost her."

"*The* Fatemeh?" Ramon's brow furrowed, as he wondered whether Cisneros misspoke.

"It's the name of Hamid Farzan's ship," explained the captain.

Ramon caught his breath. "Hamid was Fatemeh's betrothed, according to the book *Owl Riders*." He pounded his fist on the chart table. "I should never have gone."

"It wouldn't have made a difference." Cisneros's arm rose in a strange jerky motion and landed on Ramon's shoulder. "He must have been the one behind the trumped up charges against you. He'd already taken steps to get you out of the way."

"All right." Ramon removed his glasses and rubbed the bridge of his nose. "We know he planned this well, but how do we find them?"

Cisneros smiled and pointed to a series of arrows on the chart which ran along North America's east coast to Newfoundland, then crossed the Atlantic. "It's almost certain he'll follow the Gulf Stream across the ocean, then ride the currents around Spain and into the Mediterranean."

"He's got a steam ship, though, doesn't he?" Billy's brow furrowed. "Why can't he just tear directly across the Atlantic?"

Cisneros shrugged. "He could, but I bet he thinks he's home free. Even a steamship owner won't waste more fuel than he needs powering through the middle of the ocean when the current will do much of the work for him."

Ramon replaced his glasses and did his best to focus despite his emotions. "I can see how knowing his path will help, but we don't know how fast he's going..."

"Ah, but we have a good idea," Cisneros held a finger aloft, "because the pirates got a good look at the ship. That allowed me to look up her specifications."

"Unless it's slow, I don't know how much that helps us," said Ramon. "He's got quite the head start."

"Being an airship, we aren't constrained to follow his exact path." He traced a line from Nogales across the continental United States to a point over the eastern seaboard. "We'll go straight across and meet him here." A red "X" had been penciled onto the map at that point. "I've already done the calculations."

"Still sounds like a long shot to me." Billy rubbed his chin.

"We'll be lucky if we hit the mark exactly," admitted Cisneros, "but we have one advantage. The ornithopters." He looked to Billy. "Do you remember how to fly?"

"I was afraid you wouldn't ask." Billy's face broke into a wicked grin.

Ramon frowned. "I'd like to help, but I never learned how to fly."

"Don't worry." Billy patted him on the back. "I'll teach you!"

Ramon caught his breath. "What if I can't figure it out?"

Billy shook his head. "You got one of them fancy law degrees, from Harvard no less, right?"

Ramon gave a slight nod.

"If I can learn how to fly those things, you can." Billy jerked his thumb toward his chest. "Let's get you suited up."

Alethea Morales thought she knew heat until she emerged from the airship in Tucson. The sun beat down from an unbroken, blue sky onto her bare skin and evaporated the sweat almost before it could form. Dust settled in her lungs and tickled. Even Mr. Hearn started coughing. She looked up at him and saw worry in his eyes. She tried to give him a reassuring smile, then looked around at the horses, wagons and people.

They entered the terminal and retrieved their baggage then went outside. Several horses and buggies stood ready to carry passengers into downtown Tucson, about five miles away.

"About five miles farther than I want to walk," grumbled Hearn. He hired a wagon and it carried them to a hotel across the street from the rail depot.

Hearn paid the wagon driver and gave him a generous tip, then entered the relative cool and dark of the hotel lobby. Alethea blinked a few times, before she could see well. Hearn led the way to the front desk. After the airship engines' continuous roar and the wagon's rattling, Alethea found the lobby's quiet strange.

"I'd like a room for my niece and I." Hearn's voice sounded too loud.

The clerk turned the guest register book around and indicated Hearn should sign, then retrieved a key.

Alethea tugged on Hearn's coat. "Can I have my own key?"

"You're a small child." Hearn shook his head. "You shouldn't go out unaccompanied."

The clerk rang a bell and a bored porter ambled over and grabbed their bags. He led them up the stairs to a room.

"It doesn't look as though you have much business," commented Hearn.

"No." The bellhop set the bags down and unlocked the door. "It's been quiet ever since the Indians blasted the rail line."

"What about the airships?" piped in Alethea.

"Not many people can afford the airships and they only come through once a week." The bellhop carried the bags into the room.

"Do you know where I could find..." Hearn's brow furrowed and he glanced down at Alethea. "...the man who hired your father."

It took Alethea a moment to realize Hearn wanted information. "You mean Doctor Holliday?"

"Yes." Hearn nodded. "Doctor John Holliday." He handed the bellhop a generous tip.

The man stuffed the money in his pocket without a glance. "You'll most likely find Ol' Doc Holliday running a faro game down at the Congress Hall Saloon."

Hearn took out his pocket watch and glanced at it. "At this time of morning?"

The bellhop shrugged. "He was there last night. He may not have gone to bed yet."

Hearn asked for directions and the bellhop provided them.

"I'm hungry," said Alethea after the bellhop left.

Hearn looked at his watch again. "We ate breakfast on the airship. We'll get lunch when I get back."

"I want to see a real old west saloon! Do you think there'll be a shootout?" Alethea held out her fingers like guns and let her thumbs—the pretend hammers—fall.

Hearn cleared his throat. "I think it would be best if you remained at the room while I go look for Doctor Holliday.

Saloons are not suitable places for young ladies."

"Ahhh...." She looked down at her feet for a moment, then looked back up at Hearn. "I know what Doctor Holliday looks like."

Hearn considered that, then nodded. "All right, but please don't call attention to yourself."

It turned out, the Congress Hall Saloon was just one block away from their hotel. Hearn and Alethea strolled down the street and entered the establishment. Even though the clock hadn't yet struck noon, several people already occupied the saloon, though most of them ate a late breakfast rather than nursing alcohol. Only one man had a shot glass at his elbow and he appeared to be sound asleep. A piano sat in the corner, but no one played.

A man with a black suit sat at a faro table amusing himself shuffling cards. A woman in a pink corset and small dress sat next to him, her hand on his leg and her head on his shoulder.

Hearn's cheeks turned a funny shade of pink as he looked down at Alethea. "Is that Doctor Holliday?"

Alethea tried to remember the doctor from her brief encounter at the Cotton Exposition. The black suit looked the same, as did the mustache. "I think so." She didn't feel at all certain.

Nevertheless, Hearn approached the two. "Doctor Holliday, I presume?"

"Who's asking?" The man spoke in an even tone, even though he sneered.

"My name is Lafcadio Hearn, I'm a reporter with the New Orleans *Times-Democrat*."

"Irish?"

Hearn nodded.

The man snorted. "Democrat? Is that your political persuasion as well?"

"More the political persuasion of the South." Hearn shrugged.

The answer seemed to suit the man and he invited Hearn and Alethea to sit. "From New Orleans, you wouldn't happen to be following Ramon Morales would you?"

Alethea sat forward at the mention of her daddy's name.

"I would. Do you know where to find him, Doctor?"

"Sorry." The man held out his hand. "Forgot to introduce myself. Name's Earp, Wyatt Earp."

Alethea's cheeks grew warm and she shrank back, embarrassed by her mistake.

Hearn seemed unperturbed. "I'm so sorry for the confusion." He reached out and shook Earp's proffered hand.

"Don't mention it." Earp put down the cards, then kissed the woman on the cheek. "Why don't you get us some coffee? Maybe a root beer for the girl."

She smiled at him, then stood and went to the bar. Hearn retrieved a pencil and notepad from his pocket.

"Marshal came in and took Morales away." Earp tilted his head back in Fort Lowell's general direction. "Most of the Indians are holed up at Fort Bowie. They have Chief Natchez locked up in the stockade. Doc'n I offered him a deal, but General Miles has other plans. It's possible you've just waltzed into a war zone."

Hearn scratched some notes, then glanced over at Alethea before returning his attention to Earp. "Do you have any idea where Morales went?"

"None whatsoever." Earp pursed his lips, disgusted. "I had such high hopes he could get the Indians to talk to us. God only knows where he is now."

Hearn narrowed his gaze. "What marshal took him away for questioning?"

"Her name's Larissa Seaton." Earp shook his head. "God knows why they'd ever hire a woman to be a marshal."

Alethea brightened at the mention of Larissa. She hadn't dreamed of seeing Auntie Lyssa on this trip. Hearn scratched more notes on his pad.

The woman who'd been sitting next to Earp returned with a tray containing two cups of coffee and mug of root beer. She handed the cold root beer to Alethea, then passed a coffee cup to Earp. She kept the other for herself. She didn't offer anything to Hearn.

Alethea sipped the root beer and savored its spicy sweetness.

Hearn sighed. "Thank you for your help." He put his

notepad away, donned his hat and stood. "Come along, Mattie."

"Where are we going? I haven't finished my root beer."

"Never mind that." She took a big gulp of the root beer, then followed him out of the saloon.

"So, why didn't she bring you a coffee?"

"Probably because I'm Irish."

"Is that like being black or Mexican?"

Hearn shot her a bitter smile. "For some people, it's even worse." He walked across the street to the train station and hired a buggy to take them back to the airfield.

"Where are we going? We just got here."

"I think it would be prudent to have return tickets in case we can't find your father."

As they approached the aerodrome, Alethea noticed the airship still loomed over the field. They entered the terminal, went up to the window, and Hearn asked about tickets.

"No idea when the ship will be leaving, much less returning to New Orleans." The clerk shrugged. "General Miles has commandeered the ship for a top secret mission. All passengers have been ordered to disembark."

Hearn gritted his teeth, but thanked the man. The buggy waited outside and Hearn had the driver return them to the hotel.

Outside the hotel, a strange motorized bicycle stood next to the hitching post. Hearn knelt down beside it, taking a closer look. He took out his notepad and made a quick sketch. Alethea's heart began to beat faster. Wyatt Earp said Auntie Lyssa was nearby. She'd never seen the lightning wolf before, but this sure looked like a machine Lyssa would ride.

Sketch complete, Hearn led the way into the hotel. Larissa Seaton sat on the circular banquette in the lobby. Alethea ran to her. Larissa stood and scooped her into her arms. "Thank God I found you."

Hearn stepped up. "Who might you be?"

Larissa narrowed her gaze at the reporter. "Larissa Seaton, U.S. Marshal. You must be Lafcadio Hearn. You're in a lot of trouble, Mister."

"You don't know the half of it," said Hearn.

"Try me," said Larissa. "We should find someplace to talk."

CHAPTER TWELVE
OWL RIDERS

Ramon lay awake on his bunk aboard the *Tiburón*. Now that Captain Cisneros took him to Fatemeh and Larissa had sent word that she'd found Alethea safe and sound, his mind returned to the Arizona crisis. There had to be a way to turn things around. He couldn't believe General Johnson, his old friend who served as the commander of western forces, had given Miles permission to deploy troops in the middle of negotiations. This meant Miles either moved troops without permission or had phrased his request in such a way that Johnson did not have a complete picture.

Unable to sleep, Ramon climbed out of bed and folded down a small desk from the wall. He lit the room's battery-powered lantern and pulled out a piece of paper. He composed a brief message to General Johnson telling him his side of the story. He urged Johnson to order Miles to stand down. He read it over, crossed out some words, and added a few more.

Satisfied at last, he grabbed his trousers and put them on over his nightshirt, then walked forward to the gondola. Only a few dim electric lights provided an aura around the instrument panels. Captain Cisneros stared out the forward windows at the moonlit landscape through a pair of binoculars.

Ramon cleared his throat.

The captain turned. "Ah, can't sleep, I see." He pointed out the window. "We're approaching the coast. We'll be over the ocean soon."

Ramon held up the paper. "I'd like your permission to send this message to General Johnson in St. Louis using the shipboard wireless telegraph."

The captain shook his head. "The range might be a problem. I'm not sure it'll get through."

"We've got to try. I've got to give Naiche and Lozen a fighting chance to make negotiations work." Ramon stepped up next to the captain. "If those negotiations fall through, I may not get paid. Hell, I may not have a career when this is all over. My reputation may be in tatters."

Cisneros held out his hand. "Give me the message. I'm willing to try."

Ramon passed him the paper.

"Thank you, my friend."

With that, he went back to the cabin, dropped into the bed, and fell into a dreamless sleep, only to be awaken by the sun streaming in through the porthole a few hours later. After dressing, he went to the galley, where he found the captain nursing a cup of coffee.

"We sent your message. No reply yet."

"You'll let me know if you hear anything?"

The captain gave a curt nod.

After breakfast, Ramon walked aft to the ornithopter bay. He pulled goggles over his eyes, adjusted his leather helmet, and swallowed hard. Billy had been giving him flying lessons for four days. The time for his first solo flight had arrived.

"You have nothing to worry about, we're over the ocean," Billy said with a smile.

Ramon narrowed his gaze. "That doesn't exactly reassure me. I've never been a good swimmer."

"If you go down into the water, just grab your seat cushion," explained Billy. "Captain Cisneros designed them to float. It'll keep you on the surface long enough for someone to come get you."

"How would that do any good if I fell over land?"

Billy didn't answer. Instead, he pointed to the ornithopter. Ramon sighed, climbed inside, and performed the preflight checks as he'd been taught. He wound the ornithopter's clockworks, then gave Billy a thumb's up. The young cowhand cranked a winch, which opened the landing bay door. The wind rushed in from outside and took Ramon's breath away. He pushed the lever which brought the fuel rods together, then pushed another lever which set the owl-shaped ornithopter's springs in motion.

Ramon gritted his teeth and tensed up. A clacking sounded in his ears—the code for "relax." He looked up. Billy stood to the side, tapping on the clacker. Ramon loosened his muscles just as the springs in the owl's feet released. He screamed as the owl shot from the bay and plunged toward the ocean below. Furious clacking erupted from his headset. He forced himself to focus. "Pull up!"

He reached for the main control lever and pulled it back. The air caught the wings and the bird shot forward. He almost screamed again, but the wind sucked the breath from his lungs. He struggled to remember his lessons. A lever near his right arm controlled the flapping. He pushed it forward, the ornithopter's flight smoothed out, and he gained some altitude.

Ramon took several deep breaths and began to relax. He looked around. The Atlantic Ocean spread out before him like a textured green-blue blanket. The *Tiburón* floated above and behind him. He used the foot pedals to move the rudder. The little craft turned and he just discerned America's East Coast on the horizon. They had flown over Maryland in the predawn hours.

What news he had from Arizona, indicated a stalemate. The forces surrounding Fort Bowie found Geronimo commanding two more battle wagons than they expected. Ramon had some hope he could get back before things blew up even further.

More clacking sounded in Ramon's headset bringing him back to the task at hand. He worked out the words. Billy reassured him he did fine. Ramon then remembered he had his own signaling device. "I'm getting the hang of it," he responded.

As Ramon flew over the ocean, exchanging signals with Billy, he thought about Legion, the visitor from the stars. Legion was a swarm of clockwork automata, so tiny no one could see it. It had wanted to help humans achieve peace by breaking down the barriers between nations, and encouraged the Russians to invade the United States as a first step toward that goal.

Legion had shown Ramon visions of flying through the air and beyond to a point where the atmosphere thinned out so much, stars surrounded him even though the sun still illuminated Earth's globe below. Legion lived a life where up and down were as commonplace as left, right, forward, and back. Ramon loved the freedom this new dimension offered.

Back during the Russian war, Ramon had not bothered to learn how to fly the ornithopters. He wondered now if he would have ever gone on to study law if he had. He could have become as devoted to these machines as Billy.

Clacking in his ear brought his mind back to the task at hand. "I'm coming out to join you," Billy signaled.

Ramon turned as an ornithopter dropped from the airship's hatch. Unlike his fearful plummet toward the ocean, Billy's craft made a careful spiral until he flew a course level with Ramon. "Try speeding up," came the next set of clacks. Billy shot ahead.

Ramon pushed the control rod forward. They shot out over the ocean. He yelled again, but more from excitement than terror. His mouth dropped open as he looked over his shoulder. The airship fell far behind. Looking forward, he noticed an ocean-going ship on the horizon. Billy already steered toward it.

Ramon accelerated. He flew lower than Billy and studied the ship as he approached. It was a freighter, flying the Persian flag. Ramon swallowed. He pulled back on the control lever to gain altitude, then clacked a message to Billy. He dropped down and swooped as near the bow as he could.

"I took a photograph," the cowhand clacked back. He rose up level with Ramon's craft and pointed back toward the airship. "Check your fuel gauge."

Ramon did as instructed, then swallowed hard. He'd used more than expected, but still had plenty to reach the airship if they didn't dawdle. He pulled back on the control rod and the two returned to the *Tiburón*.

As they approached, Billy slowed his craft and brought it to a gentle skid in the landing bay. Ramon didn't slow his quite enough and it bounced off the floor and threatened to topple over. He gave the wings a quick flap, then pulled the lever disengaging the fuel rods. The ornithopter came to a stop and Ramon stumbled out, trembling.

Billy opened a compartment in the ornithopter's bird-like head and pulled out a black cartridge.

An airman eyed the skid marks behind Ramon's craft as he ran back to close the hatch.

"That was a pretty rough landing." Ramon removed his flight cap and his cheeks warmed.

"They say, any landing you can walk away from is a good one." Billy pushed the goggles to the top of his head. "Let's get this plate to the photo lab and then join the captain on the bridge."

Ramon and Billy walked forward and dropped the photo cartridge off with a technician at the lab, then proceeded forward.

As they passed the wireless telegraph room, the technician stopped Ramon and handed him a sheet of paper—a response from General Johnson. Ramon's heart pounded as he read the brief message. Johnson would travel to Arizona and had ordered Miles to hold his troops in position. "Will try to keep things calm until you can return."

Ramon took a deep breath as he folded the telegram and put it in his pocket. It may not be much, but it allowed him to focus on the task at hand. He felt sure the ship he'd seen must be the one holding his wife captive. He continued forward with Billy. The captain frowned as he listened to their report. When they finished, he bent over the chart and pointed to a spot near the red X.

"Almost too good to be true," he muttered. "But, it's where I thought she would be."

"We nearly ran out of fuel getting to her." Ramon pushed his glasses up his nose.

Cisneros frowned, but nodded. "If it is the *Fatemeh*, we'll get closer in the airship, then launch our attack."

"What do we know about their weapons?" asked Billy.

Cisneros rubbed his chin. "They have four deck guns, effective against the pirate cutters that pursued her through the Caribbean. They might give the owls trouble, but they're a merchant ship. I'm guessing they don't drill much. We'll want to launch as many owls as we can to give them multiple targets. The *Tiburón* can hover out of range."

As the captain finished, the lab tech arrived with a developed image. The captain opened a side drawer on the chart table and pulled out a note his contacts in New Orleans sent him with the ship's name as it had been written in Persian. Ramon leaned in close. The characters in the photo matched those written on the paper. They'd found the *Fatemeh*!

Captain Dalir entered Hamid's office and handed him a sheaf of papers. Hamid scanned the documents and nodded. "We are making good progress." He looked up at the new captain. "How is the crew's morale?"

Dalir frowned and shook his head. "It could be better. Few believe Turan would commit mutiny … not without a good reason."

"And you? What do you believe?" Hamid sat forward and folded his hands.

"Captain Turan challenged your authority." Dalir shrugged. "You're the owner. You gave us a job. Captain Turan worked to sabotage that job."

Hamid narrowed his gaze.

"And now, your job is to make sure the crew knows that."

"I'm trying." The captain swallowed. "May I ask you a personal question?" Dalir's eyes darted to the chair across from his desk. Hamid relented and invited the captain to sit. "Was this job to capture the woman in New Orleans only for personal gain?"

"Some causes transcend personal gain." Hamid had been deciding how to address this question for some time and he delivered his practiced answer to the new captain. "Early in my career, a man named Kazem Karimi provided fine navigational tools at a price I could afford. The woman we captured is his daughter and she left him. I vowed a long time ago to bring her home so she could face her father."

Dalir pursed his lips as he considered. "She's betrothed to you, is she not?"

"She is, but she committed zina."

"Would you forgive her?"

"I haven't decided." Though honest, he didn't admit he still wanted her. Even tainted by another man's touch, he still desired her … to the point a small, dark corner of his brain even toyed with the idea of forcing himself on her. He thrust those dangerous thoughts aside. He already walked a fine line with the ship's crew. Dalir took a deep breath, then blew it out in a huff.

"I'll do my best to speak to the crew again." The captain stood, donned his cap and left.

Hamid stared at the papers before him, but found he couldn't focus. His thoughts kept returning to Fatemeh. He stood and strode through the ship to her cabin and knocked. When she acknowledged, he entered.

"I hoped you would have time to see me."

"I have nothing but time." Her words came out like a sigh.

Hamid held out his hands as he sat at the table across from her.

"Of all the women I courted, only you looked me in the eye. I saw a spark there, a spark of desire."

"I didn't desire *you*." Fatemeh closed the book she read and set it aside.

That remark stung. "I know. You desired to see the world and I desired to show it to you."

"Why? So you could have someone to fuck on your journeys? You don't need me. You always have your hand."

Her blunt, filthy words took Hamid's breath away. He blinked at her for a moment before remembering she had committed zina. She deserved to be punished. The dark thoughts surfaced again. If he had her now, no one would blame him. Then he remembered the crew, already uneasy, and tempered his thoughts. "No." Hamid choked out the word. "I honestly wanted to show you the world."

"To control how I saw it?" Her piercing green eyes cut right into his soul and refused to waver.

"The world is a dangerous place for women. I knew you would go anyway, I wanted to keep you safe."

"I don't need someone to keep me safe." Fatemeh spoke firm and even, unlike Captain Dalir, whose words carried uncertainty.

A warmth rose within Hamid. "What about this Ramon who you married? Right there, in the book's first chapter, he saved you from people who you dared anger with your open words." To his shame, the dark thoughts pushed closer to the surface, feeding arousal as his words gave Fatemeh pause.

She blinked and for the first time looked away. "It's true, I need the friendship and help of good people who desire justice and peace. That's what Ramon is and I'm lucky I found him." She looked at him again. "I think you could be that, if you would let yourself."

The dark desire quelled just a bit, but before Hamid could answer, an explosion rocked the ship. The deck guns fired. Without further word to Fatemeh, he leapt up and ran through the corridor, then up the ladder to the deck above.

Mechanical birds circled the ship. A lightning bolt flew from one. It scorched the deck near his feet and he smelled burnt wood. He leapt backward into Fatemeh, who had followed him.

A crewman loaded a shell into a swivel gun, took aim and fired at a mechanical bird. The shot flew true, smashing the craft and sending the pieces into the ocean. However, another bird fired. The gunner sizzled as the lightning struck him and his hair smoked before he toppled over, dead.

Hamid gritted his teeth. He pushed Fatemeh ahead of him, leading her down the ladder. She resisted and he shoved harder. She stumbled down the steps and sprawled at the bottom. For a moment, he feared she'd broken her neck. Then she looked up at him with intense fury. Another blast rumbled through the deck.

He grabbed the rail and ran down the steps. He yanked her to her feet, and led her to the cabin. He locked her in. At the rate the battle progressed, Hamid knew men from the flying machines would storm the decks soon. He ran toward the bridge.

Ramon circled high over the *Fatemeh*. More experienced pilots flew closer, attacking with the lightning guns. He groaned when the swivel gun blew an ornithopter from the sky, but punched the air when another ornithopter's lightning bolt destroyed the deck cannon.

People ran around on the deck, pointing. A man threw open a locker and handed rifles to the crew. The lightning guns swept the decks, clearing them of armed defenders. Despite his anger at the crew, Ramon's heart sank as he considered the lives lost.

Soon, all four of the *Fatemeh's* swivel guns fell silent and most people on deck ran for cover. One ornithopter flapped its wings harder, ascending to Ramon's elevation. Billy gave him a thumb's up, then pointed down. It was time to board the ship.

Ramon tried to figure out how to land the ornithopter on the deck. There just didn't seem to be enough room without hitting a mast, railing, or other structure. Still, he followed Billy down. As they descended, the first ornithopter landed, followed by a second. They each set down on a large afterdeck hatch.

Just as Billy made his approach, the ship lurched, dropping below him, forcing him to dive further. He missed the rearmost mast and set down just behind the ship's superstructure. As Ramon came down, waves lifted the ship higher. Ramon caught his breath and rolled the ornithopter away from the heaving vessel. He tried to flap, but that sent the craft into a spiral, plunging into the ocean. The impact rippled through his body, intensified by the cold, Atlantic water.

Ramon took a breath, aborted when he swallowed sea water and realized the ornithopter's weight dragged him under. He struggled with the restraints, then despaired as he didn't know how to free himself. Then he remembered Billy's words about the floating seat cushion. He wrenched it up and pulled it free.

It seemed to take forever, but the cushion did float and lifted him toward the surface. He gulped fresh air as he broke free. Looking around, he discovered he'd crashed into the water just ahead of the ship, which bore down on him. He turned and kicked as hard as he could to get out of the way.

As the ship passed, a man called out to him. He looked up. Billy unrolled a rope ladder from the deck's side. Someone pulled Billy away from the railing, but he reappeared a moment later. Ramon had to kick hard to keep up with the ship.

Holding onto the seat cushion with one hand, he reached out with the other. He missed the ladder the first time, but grabbed it the second.

Grasping the ladder, the ship pulled him through the water. He forced himself to let go of the cushion and latched onto the ladder with the other hand, then pulled himself from the water.

The climb up the ship's hull in sodden clothes took every ounce of strength he had left. When he reached the deck, Billy helped pull him aboard. He dropped to his hands and knees, panting. A few inches away, one of the crewmen lay on the deck, knocked cold.

Billy helped him to stand. "No time for that. We've got to move."

Ramon nodded, rose to his feet, and looked around, noting more than a dozen charred and smoking corpses where the lightning guns had exterminated people from a distance. For a moment he thought he would be sick. Still, he almost expected more crewmen on deck protecting the ship.

"Where is everyone?"

"Many who were on deck are dead. Those who survived went for the superstructure over there." Billy pointed. "Some went below decks. I think they're regrouping to protect the bridge and the cargo."

"Probably the engine room as well." Ramon reached up and lifted the goggles onto his helmet and adjusted his glasses.

"Captain Cisneros has taken some of his men to see if they can take the bridge," said Billy. "That leaves the staterooms for us."

"I hope you're right about the freighter's crew going to guard the cargo."

Ramon followed Billy to the superstructure where they found a ladder that led below decks. A gunshot and shouts sounded from above. Ramon ducked involuntarily as he descended the ladder into a corridor. In their conference before battle, Captain Cisneros noted that this class of ship had just a few staterooms near the stern.

Their strategy was for Ramon and Billy to try the staterooms, reasoning it likely that's where Fatemeh would be held.

Cisneros would lead a team to attempt to take the bridge, figuring someone there would know Fatemeh's location if they
guessed wrong. If Ramon and Billy found more guards than
they could deal with, they would attempt to regroup with Cisneros.

Billy opened a door. Inside were tools, gears, and pipes—a
workshop.

The next door proved to be a hastily abandoned stateroom
with rumpled bed and a trunk hanging open with clothes
strewn over the edge. Ramon spared just a moment to wonder
whether the owner of those clothes still defended the ship or
had become a blackened corpse on the deck above.

Ramon opened the next door and stopped cold, his insides
turning icy to match his sodden clothes. Fatemeh gasped her
surprise. In front of her, a big man held a revolver aimed right
at him.

Ramon struggled to keep his voice from trembling. "Hamid Farzan, I presume."

He nodded. "Stop right there."

Billy crept close to Ramon and whispered. "I think I can
take him out."

"Stop this. Ramon, Billy, get out of here." Fatemeh spoke
the words through clenched teeth. "I'm willing to go with Hamid."

"Put your weapons on the deck." Hamid's aim didn't waver.

Ramon looked into Fatemeh's green eyes, rimmed with
dark circles. She appeared unharmed, just tired and a little
unkempt. She wore a strange, baggy dress that ill-suited her,
but he'd feared he might find her chained and naked. Ramon
placed his gun on the deck.

"Keep your hands where I can see them!"

Billy crouched low, his gun already on the deck, one hand
in his pocket. "I've got another weapon in here. Sure you don't
want me to put it on the deck?"

"Slowly," said Hamid.

Billy withdrew his hand. In it was a croquet ball. He placed
it on the deck and gave it a gentle nudge.

Hamid's eyes followed the ball as it rolled toward his feet.

He took an involuntary step backward to avoid the ball.

Fatemeh grabbed Hamid's arm and yanked it to the side. Trembling from the dunking and adrenaline, Ramon leapt forward and jumped on Farzan. The revolver dropped from his hand and all three tumbled to the deck.

By the time Hamid pushed Ramon off, Billy held both his own six-gun and Hamid's revolver. He handed the revolver to Ramon, then grabbed Hamid and brought him to his feet. "Over there." He pointed to the far wall.

Footsteps sounded from the corridor outside and Ramon prayed that reinforcements weren't coming to Hamid's rescue. He breathed a sigh of relief when Onofre Cisneros entered. His eye was swollen and blood trickled from a cut lip. "The bridge is ours. One of the men spoke enough English to confirm our suspicions Fatemeh would be here."

Ramon handed him Hamid's revolver, then turned and grabbed Fatemeh in his arms. They kissed even as Farzan released a low moan.

"I've been so worried about you, Corazón."

"And you, too." If she minded his wet clothes, she didn't say.

"This is piracy!" shouted Farzan.

Cisneros shook his head. "No, we're just here to collect what belongs to us. Trust me, I'm something of an expert on piracy."

Fatemeh cleared her throat. "No one here belongs to anyone else."

"You got that right." Billy turned to Farzan. "I should plug you right now for what you done."

"No, Billy," growled Fatemeh. "That would be unnecessary revenge. Besides, Hamid is correct in one thing. I need to make peace with my parents. I need to go to Persia."

CHAPTER THIRTEEN
BUSHIDO

Alethea followed Larissa Seaton to Tucson's schoolhouse. Larissa explained that Alethea's education didn't stop because they were in Arizona. A roar from above resounded from the surrounding buildings. A great pink and festive airship resembling a caged paper lantern passed overhead on its way to the landing field.

"It's beautiful," remarked Alethea. "Do you know what those squiggly lines are?"

"I think that may be Japanese writing," said Larissa.

"Can we go see it up close?"

"I'm taking you to school." Larissa put her hands on her hips, but seemed drawn by the airship as well.

"I've already missed lots of days, what's one more day going to matter?"

Larissa gave a sharp nod. "All right, we'll go take a look." She knelt down and pointed a finger at Alethea. "But if there's even a hint of danger, we're leaving. Got it?"

"Got it!" Alethea smiled and thought Auntie Lyssa was the best.

They strode back toward the rail station. Although the rail line was out, a few buggies and wagons stood by for any stranded travelers looking for transport. They found Lafcadio Hearn talking to a driver perched above and behind the passenger compartment of a hansom cab. Hansoms had become more common in America as aerodromes began to spring up on the outskirts of cities.

Larissa tapped Hearn on the shoulder to get his attention. "Are you going out to get a closer look at the oriental airship that just passed over?"

"I am indeed. Would you care to join me?"

Larissa looked down at Alethea as though she were having second thoughts, but finally nodded.

Hearn handed the cab driver money, then lifted Alethea into the cab's seat and climbed in beside her. Larissa climbed in on the other side.

"Take us to the aerodrome. I suspect that's where the ship will come down," said the reporter.

"We'll get there quick as we can." The driver snapped the reins and they took off through the streets. "Where do you suppose it's from?"

Hearn glanced over his shoulder through the small hole which allowed him to communicate with the driver. "I'm guessing Japan, by the look of her."

They soon cleared the city's buildings and, as expected, the airship vented gas and descended to the ground near the *City of New Orleans*. As they approached, Alethea could make out more details on the new airship. American and Russian airships were sleek, silvery gray machines with few external features to distinguish them from each other. Kind of boring, actually.

This oriental design was much different. Deck railings with gun mounts surrounded the rigid exoskeleton that held the colorful gas bags. "It's very pretty," remarked Alethea. "I like it better than the *City of New Orleans*."

Hearn pulled out his notepad and scribbled some notes. "The pink makes it rather audacious, don't you think?"

Larissa studied the airship for a moment. "I'm not so sure. The pink and white color scheme would make it difficult to see as it flew low on the horizon at sunset or sunrise." She pointed up to a few puffy clouds. "Might be just as hard to see against clouds." She shrugged. "Pink might be the color of a warship in this case."

Alethea liked that. She didn't always like to wear pink, but she might ask for some new pink dresses when she saw her momma and daddy again.

The hansom cab reached the aerodrome as a ramp descended from the structure hanging below the balloon. Hearn climbed from the cab, then held his finger up to the driver. "Please stay nearby. We may want to move on quickly, depending on how this develops."

"I wouldn't miss this for the world," said the cab driver.

Larissa helped Alethea out of the cab and instructed her to hold hands at all times. They moved closer, but Alethea had a hard time seeing with all the adults around. She tugged on Larissa's duster. "Can you lift me up to your shoulders?"

"Sure thing, sweetie." Larissa hefted her up.

It didn't take long before something happened. A woman wearing what looked like a pretty robe strode down the ramp. Alethea couldn't tell how old she was, only that she walked upright and proud like Madame Lalande. Two men in military uniforms followed her. An aerodrome official met her at the bottom of the ramp.

"Welcome to Tucson, ma'am. I'm afraid your ship's arrival wasn't on our timetable."

"Never mind that," she said in heavily accented English. "I wish to meet with General Nelson Miles, Ramon Morales, and ... Masuda Hoshi."

Larissa gasped.

Hearn scribbled something on his notepad, then glanced back at Larissa. "Did you notice that? She paused before she mentioned that last name."

"I know Masuda Hoshi. He's a farmer in Las Cruces." Larissa shook her head. "What's he doing around these parts?"

The aerodrome official shook his head. "I don't know those last two folks, but you'll find General Miles at Fort Lowell. I don't think he's in a mood for visitors, though."

"How do I reach Fort Lowell?"

Hearn put his notepad back in his pocket and returned to the hansom cab. Larissa lowered Alethea back to the ground and followed.

"Where are we going?" Alethea asked. "I want to stay and see what happens."

"I think things will be far more interesting at the fort," remarked Hearn.

Larissa grasped him by the arm. "Is that really the best place for Alethea?"

"Before you joined me on this excursion, you were taking the young lady to school. I daresay she'll get a better education if she's with us than she would stuck in a schoolhouse."

Larissa looked torn as they reached the cab. Hearn gave instructions to the driver. Like Alethea, he hated to leave, but a little extra cash convinced him the trip would be worthwhile. Despite her misgivings, Larissa helped Alethea into the cab. As the driver turned to leave the aerodrome, a vehicle on treads appeared at the top of the ramp.

"You do realize the fort is locked down because of the approaching battle." The cab driver spoke through the hole. "We can't go inside."

"I suspected as much," said Hearn. "Just find us a good place to watch, somewhere near the main gate, and let's hope the sentries aren't too trigger happy when it comes to bystanders."

The cabby swallowed a gulp and Larissa glared at Hearn who wiped sweat from his brow. They soon reached the fort and the cab pulled off the main road and stopped so they could see what transpired.

A horseman approached the gate and spoke to the guards. Alethea could just make out some shouts from within. She tapped Hearn's shoulder and pointed. A dust cloud appeared down the road.

The dust's source soon proved to be a strange vehicle. The closest thing Alethea could think of was a Roman chariot on tractor treads. Instead of a horse, a mechanical man pulled it. Her momma and daddy had told her stories about the Japanese mechanical men. They had a lot in common with Jackalope Harvesters, except they could do a lot more. Her daddy said the Russians bought them to do work in factories as well as on farms. Alethea thought they must be very smart machines indeed.

Three soldiers appeared at the gate bearing rifles. The woman in the fancy robes stepped from the vehicle and approached the soldiers. "I wish to speak with General Miles."

"And who might you be?"

"Imagawa Masako, official representative of the Japanese Emperor, here on a peacekeeping expedition." As she spoke, more of the strange chariot-like machines pulled up and Japanese soldiers leapt out, taking up positions behind her.

Alethea shook her head. "This doesn't look all that peaceful."

Larissa placed her arm around Alethea's shoulders. "Some people say peace requires a strong hand."

A man from within the fort ran up and spoke with the soldiers. Their leader nodded. "The general will see you." He held up his hand and glanced at the other soldiers. "The general agrees to see *only* you."

The woman called Imagawa bowed and followed the soldiers inside the fort.

Larissa shot a pointed glance at Hearn. "I think we should leave, before things turn ugly."

"I think she's amazing." Alethea beamed, her eyes locked on the gate.

Hearn sighed, but he agreed things could turn dangerous. He made a few more notes, then instructed the cab driver to take them back to Tucson.

Lozen watched through the bars of her cell as soldiers led the dignified woman in flowery robes through the courtyard to the general's office. The woman carried herself much like Hoshi, and Lozen felt a kinship with this new arrival.

A few minutes later, a soldier left the general's office and walked toward the stockade. Lozen climbed down from the cot and walked to the front of the cell.

Naiche sat on his cot. "What do you make of this new arrival?"

"I suspect this must be the Imagawa that Hoshi spoke of. It will be interesting to see what transpires."

A moment later, the guard came in from the other room followed by the soldier who recently left General Miles's office. "The general has a guest who has requested the pleasure of your company at a meeting," said the guard. "I don't want you to try any funny business."

Lozen narrowed her gaze. "Trust me, after several days in your stockade, I have no interest in 'funny business'."

The guard released a bitter laugh as he unlocked first Lozen's cell, then Naiche's. The two warriors followed the guard and soldier out into the sunlight and back into the general's office. The general and his visitor both stood. The woman bowed.

"Madame Counselor, may I present Chief Natchez and Lozen, an Apache warrior." The general maintained a dignified, polite tone. He must respect this woman from Japan.

The Japanese woman maintained a neutral expression as she bowed. "I am honored to meet you," she said. "I am here on behalf of the Meiji Emperor and the Ritsuryō—the Ruling Council." She retrieved a paper from the wide belt around her mid-section and handed it to the general. "As we understand, the United States has negotiated treaties with the sovereign Indian nations."

The general glanced at the paper. "I think there may be a misunderstanding about our government's position on the ... sovereignty of the Indian nations."

"Then let there be no misunderstanding about the Japanese government's position. We recognize the Chiricahua Apache Nation as a sovereign power whose interests align with the emperor's. I am here to negotiate a trading deal with said government. However, we also understand there are tensions between your government and that of the Chiricahua Apache Nation. We wish to take steps to prevent those hostilities from interfering with our good faith negotiations."

General Miles snorted a laugh and dropped into his chair shaking his head. Lozen failed to see what the general found so funny.

"Miss Imagawa, I do not know who put you up to this, but you really must go. I have no time for jokes, even elaborate ones involving Japanese princesses and airships."

Imagawa stiffened. "This is no joke, General Miles, and I have no intention of presenting myself as a 'princess.' I am of the ruling council, but not of a noble house. In my position as a member of the ruling council, I would suggest that the United States of America would face many difficulties should you continue your battle against the Chiricahua Apaches. I have asked Chief Naiche and Lozen to be here so we may resume our negotiations without needless delay."

Lozen appreciated how Imagawa used Naiche's proper name and not his name interpreted as Spanish.

Miles sat forward and put his hands in front of him, but he did not invite anyone in the room to sit.

"Miss Imagawa, I will explain this once, and then I expect you to leave my office. Even if your government accepts the Chiricahua Apache Tribe as a sovereign nation, these people—" he held out his hand to Lozen and Naiche "—have committed several acts of aggression against the United States. They have captured an American fort and they have damaged an American rail line. We are justified in taking action against them."

Naiche took a step forward and lifted his chin. "My people took those actions after you violated your treaty and took our land. If we are to speak of justification, I think we have some as well."

Lozen took a step toward Imagawa. "We welcome the Japanese government to the negotiating table."

A knock at the door interrupted them. The general nodded to the guard beside the door, who opened it a crack. "General, are we interrupting?" said a man at the door.

"No, I think you should come in." General Miles folded his arms.

The guard opened the door and Wyatt Earp and Doc Holliday entered. Lozen noted how Imagawa's eyes took them in without being obvious. The general introduced the newcomers to Imagawa.

"Counselor Imagawa Masako at your service." She bowed.

"Charmed I'm sure." Holliday seemed as amused as Miles.

"As I understand, you recruited Ramon Morales as an emissary for the Apaches," said Imagawa. "I hope to persuade the general that negotiation is still an option. Chief Naiche and Lozen appear willing to resume talks."

"Well, Missy," began Earp, "we invited Mr. Morales when we thought we could persuade our friends here to take a nice little patch of farm land we had picked out for them. Maybe we could work out a deal where they farmed the land and the miners paid them in the gold for their food, kind of like one of them Daimyo arrangements in your country."

"Interesting." Imagawa considered Earp's words.

During his visits to their cells, Hoshi had told Lozen and Naiche a little about his past and the old Daimyo system under the Tokugawa Shogunate. In the system as described, the Apaches would be the peasants. No doubt there would either be rent or a tax on the land. "You would be like the samurai," Imagawa concluded.

Earp pursed his lips and nodded, apparently taking her assessment as a compliment.

Lozen hated how these people minced words. "We were making good progress until General Miles used our negotiations as a distraction so he could attack our people. Fortunately, Geronimo brought in more battle wagons and kept him from devastating us."

Earp narrowed his gaze and steel slid against leather. Imagawa drew her katana and pressed it to Earp's throat before he'd withdrawn his six-gun from the holster.

Designed to transport cargo, the Airship *Tiburón* possessed just four private cabins—one for the captain, one for the first mate and two guest cabins. Cisneros gave one guest cabin to Ramon and Fatemeh. Despite its name, the guest cabin on the *Tiburón* proved smaller than the cabin Ramon shared with Doc Holliday aboard the *City of New Orleans*. Now reunited with Fatemeh, he didn't mind.

Ramon sat on the bunk next to Fatemeh and held her, delighted to feel her reassuring presence next to him. For a few heart-wrenching minutes during Fatemeh's rescue, Ramon feared she wouldn't return to the airship with him. He had heard stories of prisoners who grew too close to their captors and began to align themselves with their desires.

Despite that, she had watched quietly while Billy led Hamid away. Captain Cisneros sent up signal flares. The airship approached and lowered a ladder to the deck. Fatemeh climbed, nimble as ever, and relaxed when she reached the airship's deck. Ramon hated to break the comfortable silence, but he knew they needed to decide their next course of action.

"We should get back to Tucson and Alethea. Larissa pulled me away from a volatile situation. I need to get back and put things right before it gets worse."

Fatemeh considered that. "I want to get back to Alethea as well, but Hamid is right that I need to face my parents. Also, the Persians told the U.S. government you committed a crime. Even if you're cleared, someone could still use that as an excuse to question your credentials." Ramon opened his mouth to speak, but Fatemeh placed her hand on his chest. "Going to Persia will allow us to put an end to this nonsense once and for all. We should do that sooner than later."

"All right, I accept we should go to Persia, but I still think we should return to Tucson first."

"You may be right, but there are two other matters to consider." Fatemeh swallowed. "First, what exactly do you propose to do with Hamid now that you've captured him?"

"Take him back to America. Prosecute him for kidnapping." Ramon smacked his fist in his palm.

"But you have to go negotiate with the Apaches. What are you going to do with him while you take care of that?"

"Drop him in jail somewhere." Ramon shrugged. "Washington, New Orleans, both are more or less on our way back. We can work out the details with Captain Cisneros."

"You might do as well just letting him go." Fatemeh continued before Ramon could object. "When I was aboard his ship, the crew were on the verge of mutiny because they saw his actions kidnapping me as getting in the way of their profits. He would be lucky to make it home in their care." She stood and walked to the window. "Besides, how many of his crew did you kill?"

Ramon closed his eyes on the memory of the blackened corpses on the deck of Hamid's freighter.

"He took the law into his own hands and you did the same." She sighed. "It might do the most good just to let him contemplate what he's done on the long voyage home."

"It's also possible he'd stew in his defeat. His hatred could grow more intense and he could rally his crew against us." Ramon shrugged. "We could be tried as pirates when we got to Persia."

A knock at the door interrupted them.

"Compliments of the captain." First Mate Gonzalez stood at the door and held out a garment bag. "We had some dresses from Ensenada in the cargo hold. The captain thought Mrs. Morales might like to try these on."

Ramon took the garment bag and handed it to Fatemeh who smiled.

"Please give my thanks to the captain," she said.

The first mate tipped his hat and Ramon closed the door. "You said there's something else to consider."

Fatemeh reached out and took Ramon's hand. They sat down together on the bunk.

"Hamid is right about one thing. The time has come for you to meet my parents and for us to explain what we've done." She squeezed Ramon's hand and seemed to gain strength. "I feel we need to do that soon and not once we return to our busy lives."

Ramon blinked. "I thought you didn't like your parents."

"My father and I don't agree on matters of faith." Fatemeh gazed into Ramon's eyes. "I imagine this journey will be difficult, but it needs to happen."

Ramon frowned, but nodded. "I can talk to the captain. I think he's willing to take us to Arizona. I don't know if he'd want to go there and then all the way to Persia again."

She considered that for a moment. "I might have an incentive for him."

"And what do we do with Alethea when we go back to Persia? Take her with us, or leave her with the Lalandes?"

Fatemeh turned away and stared out of the porthole for a long moment. When she turned back to Ramon, a tear ran down her cheek. "Jacques Lalande died trying to save me from Hamid. Several of his men were seriously injured."

Ramon blinked at her and swallowed. "Oh," was all he managed. Then he remembered the telegram he'd read in Nogales. "Jacques is all right. Marie sent the captain a telegram. He's expected to make a full recovery."

Fatemeh caught her breath. "Oh, I'm so glad to hear that." She grabbed Ramon into an embrace. "But do you see why I have no doubt—no doubt at all— Marie and Jacques would do everything in their power to keep our daughter safe?"

Ramon nodded as he tightened his hold on his wife. He silently vowed to do what he could for the Lalandes upon their return. "We still have to ask Captain Cisneros if he's willing to make this trip."

"I'm sure he's waiting to hear what we want to do, why don't you go talk to him?" She glanced back at the garment bag. "Besides, it will give me a chance to try on these new dresses."

"I'd enjoy watching."

She slapped Ramon playfully on the shoulder. "As though there's room in here."

Ramon embraced Fatemeh, then stood and walked forward to the gondola where he found Captain Cisneros staring at a chart. His eye had turned a bright shade of purple and his lip began to swell.

"I have a course that will take us to New Orleans with a short layover so you can hand Hamid over to the authorities, then I can have you back to Arizona so you can resume negotiations."

"Fatemeh made a case to me about letting Hamid go home on his ship." Ramon shoved his hands in his pockets.

The captain rubbed his chin. "That's actually not a bad idea. We don't exactly have a brig here on the *Tiburón* to securely lock him up. He could break out and make trouble before we get to a port."

"Do you think he would?" Ramon's eyes widened.

"I don't think it's beyond him. We should be careful while he's aboard." The captain made a strange one-shouldered shrug. "Still, I agree with you. He should answer for his crimes."

Ramon nodded, glad for the captain's agreement. "Fatemeh would also like to go to Persia once we finish our business in Tucson." He looked up hopefully.

Cisneros held up his hand and shook his head. "I like you and Fatemeh, but I'm not your personal coachman."

"I suggest you contact Behzad Mazdaki in Shiraz." Fatemeh stood in the gondola's stern wearing one of the new dresses. It suited her well. Ramon held out his hand and she stepped forward and took it. "He's a trader who works with my father. He might be a good partner in your business, Captain."

Ramon lifted his eyebrows. "But wasn't Hamid a trader who worked with your father?"

"Mr. Mazdaki is the trader who helped me leave Shiraz.

He bought me a ticket to Paris. From there I was able to travel to the United States."

Ramon nodded, understanding. "Then we owe Mr. Mazdaki a debt of gratitude."

The captain retrieved a clipboard hanging from the chart table. He consulted several sets of figures, then dropped a ruler onto the chart, marking out the distance to a set of islands in the Eastern Atlantic off the coast of Africa. Then from there to Shiraz in Persia.

"It'll be an expensive trip." Cisneros laughed and then grabbed Ramon's shoulder. ""But I'm willing to contact Mr. Mazdaki during our flight back to Tucson and see what he'd arrange. I've been looking for an excuse to open up trade with some Mediterranean ports. This is as good an opportunity as any."

"Thank you, my friend." Ramon put his hand on the captain's, finding it cold despite the warm gesture.

"Come to my cabin and share a drink?"

"I'd be honored," said Ramon.

Fatemeh shook her head. "I'm exhausted and would like to get some sleep." Ramon also knew that Fatemeh's Bahá'í faith prohibited drinking. He really wanted nothing more than to take her back to the cabin and help her remove that nice dress, but he also knew she needed her sleep. Better to go with the captain.

The captain stepped beside the helmsman and issued orders while Ramon kissed Fatemeh good night. They walked hand-in-hand to the window and watched as the *Tibúron* turned away from the *Fatemeh*, on a return course for the United States. Once satisfied with the ship's condition, Onofre Cisneros led the way back to his cabin.

Fatemeh kissed Ramon on the cheek and left the men to their discussion.

Cisneros opened a cabinet, retrieved a bottle and poured two glasses of tequila. "I've never enjoyed the piracy game," he admitted. "I prefer building things and figuring out how to make them work." He flexed the fingers of his right hand.

Ramon sipped the tequila and tried to work out why his hand seemed so strange.

A knock sounded at the door. "Yes," called the captain.

The first mate, Ernesto Gonzalez, stood at the doorway. "Sir, the prisoner is making a ruckus. The crew's getting edgy."

Cisneros sighed. "Right. I'll see what I can do." He shot a glance at Ramon.

"Thank you, sir." Mr. Gonzalez turned and walked forward, toward the gondola.

The captain downed a gulp of tequila.

"Are you sure we shouldn't leave him back on the ship?" Ramon took another sip of his tequila. It burned its way down his throat.

"We could just toss him overboard. Say he escaped." The captain gave a bitter chuckle at his own dark humor. He donned his hat and left the cabin. They'd locked Farzan in a small cargo hold near the airship's stern, away from the crew bunks, but Ramon could still hear his shouts.

"The guy's a loudmouth, that's for sure." Ramon shrugged. "Our friend Hoshi would invoke the Samurai's Bushido code, which speaks of benevolence and compassion. Unless Hamid poses a threat, killing him just seems like the wrong thing to do. Much as I would like to for what he did to my wife."

"I promise I won't be the villain here."

Another shout sounded from down the corridor.

Ramon and the captain reached the cargo hold. Cisneros banged on the door. "This is the captain. Shut up or I'll put you in irons."

"Come in here and face me, you coward!"

The captain rolled his eyes, then looked toward the ship's tail. Two ruddermen stood nearby. He summoned them over. "If he gets past us, stop him. Got it?"

When they nodded, he unlocked the door and entered. Farzan looked ready to pounce, but held his place. "I demand to know where you're taking me."

"We're taking you back to New Orleans," said Ramon, "where we'll hand you over to the authorities."

Farzan chuckled to himself. "What good do you think that will do? I'm not a citizen of your country."

"Doesn't matter." Ramon narrowed his gaze. "You committed the crime on U.S. soil and there are witnesses to put you at the scene. We've got you."

"I have friends in high places," said Hamid. "Your charges won't stick."

"Then you have no reason to keep shouting," said the captain. "Behave yourself and you'll be out of our custody in a few days."

"And what if I don't 'behave myself'?"

"There are many hungry sharks in the waters below us, my friend." The captain's weariness and battered expression lent a certain credence to his words.

Farzan stared into the captain's eyes for a moment, then looked away. "And what of my ship?"

"We've let them go. They'll continue on their way and arrive in Persia in due course." Cisneros shrugged.

"All right, I'll be good." Farzan sneered. "But I'll do everything in my power to have you hanged as a pirate at the first opportunity."

"Better men than you have tried." Cisneros tipped his hat, then left the cargo hold followed by Ramon.

CHAPTER FOURTEEN
SHOWDOWN

Lozen didn't want Imagawa to gut the man called Wyatt Earp. She sensed a kindred spirit, albeit one possessed by greed. Things turned ugly fast. Doctor Holliday, the general, and the soldiers drew their side arms. Most were leveled at Imagawa but she and Naiche would be caught in the crossfire. "Drop the pigsticker right now, lady," said Holliday.

"Why should I?" Imagawa narrowed her gaze. "If you shoot me in these close quarters, you'll kill your friend." Miles attempted to cut around the desk. "Stay put, General."

"It seems what we have here is a Mexican standoff." Holliday narrowed his gaze, evaluating options.

"No standoff at all, Mexican or otherwise." Imagawa grinned. "All you have done is delayed my return to the *Issa*, which means a signal has not been sent."

Lozen knew what to expect and remained calm. Naiche tensed and she feared he telegraphed what would happen.

"And what signal would that be?" Miles lowered his service revolver slightly.

As if in answer to the general's question, an explosion rent the air causing the men to stagger backwards. Imagawa took advantage of the distraction and whirled around, pushing past Doc Holliday and out into the front office. Lozen followed with Naiche at her heels. Gunfire sounded from the courtyard, followed by a crack and a tremendous pop. The clerk and guards in the front office had bolted to the windows and didn't pursue Imagawa, Lozen, and Naiche as they darted outside.

An automaton's chest cannon had blown the fort's front gates inward. Soldiers fired, but their bullets plinked off the machine's armor.

The Airship *Issa* rose high overhead. Its lightning gun

fired, turning first one ornithopter, then another into fireballs. "The light from one candle is transferred to another." Imagawa flashed a wry smile.

Lozen raised an eyebrow. She knew Japanese airships were named for poets. "Is that from a poem?"

"A haiku by Buson."

Automata rolled through the compound, herding soldiers into groups. Though numerous, the soldiers hadn't had time to organize. The Japanese automata strove to keep them from harm's way, but also away from the armory.

An explosion behind her caused Lozen to take a step to keep her balance. A battle wagon rolled through a hole at the compound's eastern side. Mexican soldiers followed behind.

Miles, Holliday, and Earp ran up behind her and took in the situation. "What is the meaning of this?" Miles pointed at Imagawa. "This is an act of war."

Imagawa nodded. "The war started when those from Europe rolled across this continent and took land from those who already lived here."

"Savages!" shouted Miles. "You're siding with savages!"

"And yet, I believe Wyatt Earp here attempted to pull a firearm on me, a woman armed only with a blade." Imagawa shook her head. "I believe any truly civilized people would regard that as an unmitigated act of savagery."

Lozen wanted to shout a war whoop in support. Instead, she turned her attention to an American lieutenant who shouted orders. A company of soldiers formed up near the mess hall. They raised rifles and fired at the battle wagon. The wagon's turret turned and fired a shell, which exploded in front of the soldiers' position, knocking the first row off their feet and sending the back row into three automata who politely requested their rifles.

The battle wagon rolled up to the general's office. The door opened and Hoshi emerged. Imagawa cast him the briefest of smiles. Naiche turned to Miles. "General, my people now control Fort Lowell and demand your surrender."

The general stood straight, reminding Lozen of a Bantam Rooster. "I will not surrender to the likes of you!"

"Then you give me no choice." Naiche reared back and

landed a punch on the general's jaw, sending him sprawling into the wall. "Fort Lowell is ours now, as is Fort Bowie. With these two fortifications, we now control our territory."

Wyatt Earp's nostrils flared and his eyes widened. Holliday put his hand on his friend's shoulder, then stepped forward and addressed Naiche. "The general's right. This is an act of war. Your tribe is now spread awfully thin having taken two American forts. Are you prepared to stand up to the entire U.S. Army?"

Lozen stepped forward. "I believe I see Japanese and Mexican soldiers here as well. Is America ready to fight three opponents when so little is really at stake, just meager farm land and some minerals in the Arizona desert?"

"We'll see about that." Miles leaned against the wall and rubbed his jaw.

The *City of New Orleans* rose behind the *Issa*. Lozen evaluated the situation. Sharpshooters on the civilian airship fired at the exposed decks surrounding the *Issa's* gasbag. Several men went down. Lozen wished she had her binoculars so she could see whether the men had been hit or just dove for cover.

"Your 'gas of the rising sun' is no match for the hydrogen gas we use to lift our airships." General Miles stepped beside Imagawa and folded his arms. "Helium doesn't give you the lifting power. We'll always have the altitude advantage."

The *City of New Orleans* rose higher than the *Issa* while still approaching. From that vantage, they could drop a bomb or continue to strafe the Japanese airship at will. Lozen hoped the *Issa's* captain recognized the danger as well.

Apparently he did, since two rockets launched from the *Issa's* flanks. One missed, bursting off the *City of New Orleans'* port side. The other penetrated the gasbag, setting it aflame. Despite the flames, the American airship continued forward. Once over the *Issa*, someone lobbed five small, round objects from the gondola.

Three bounced off the exoskeleton, but two hit *Issa's* balloon and the craft erupted in flames. The small objects must have been incendiary devices. Both airships began to sink to the ground. Lozen's instincts told her to settle into a crouch. Naiche, Imagawa, and Hoshi followed suit.

As the airships descended, the hydrogen in the *City of New Orleans'* gas cylinders caught and the entire ship exploded, knocking Miles off his feet.

Wyatt Earp held onto a pillar as the explosion blew his hat off. "Oh my God!"

"Well I'll be damned." Holliday leaned on the door frame with a wistful look in his eye, but the dust cloud from the blast sent him inside, coughing.

General Miles rolled onto his back and laughed. "You may have won the day, but you've just lost the advantage in any war, unless you happen to have more airships."

Naiche summoned a warrior and barked instructions. The warrior grabbed Miles and led him away.

Lozen turned to Earp. "You and your friend are civilians. You're free to go. You may return if you're willing to work with us to discuss a settlement."

Wyatt Earp narrowed his gaze. "We'll consider our options." With that, he stepped inside to see how his friend was doing. The sound of coughing could be heard and it didn't subside for several minutes.

The cannon fire that breached Fort Lowell's gates caused the hansom cab driver to pull back on the reins and look around. "My God, what was that?"

Hearn and Larissa hopped out. Alethea followed. Mechanical men rolled into the fort, oblivious to soldiers firing at them. She looked up at Larissa, who lifted Alethea back into the cab and climbed in after them. "Get in here, Mr. Hearn," called Larissa.

"For God's sake, keep driving, man," said Hearn as he hopped in next to Larissa. "We need to keep this child safe." Alethea bristled at being called a child, but she had no problem with going somewhere safe.

"Best place is back at your hotel," said the driver.

"Then move!"

The cab driver snapped the reins and continued down the road to Tucson. Another explosion rumbled through the earth.

Alethea glanced out to the side. The Japanese airship had lifted from the airfield. It started its motors and drifted to the fort. She leaned out of the cab and looked behind them just as a lightning bolt flew from the upper deck into the compound. Larissa pulled her back into the cab. "That's not safe, Alethea."

"But the airships..." She didn't even know how to put it into words.

Hearn looked over to the airfield and gasped as the *City of New Orleans* showered the ground with water ballast and shot into the air. Its motors fired up even before it reached its full altitude. This time, Hearn leaned out of the cab and looked behind. Larissa tried to get him to turn around but had no luck, so Alethea turned around and looked back as well. By this time, trees and buildings obscured the view, so Alethea turned and faced forward. She noticed Hearn had as well.

When they reached the San Xavier Hotel, all three hopped out, anxious to reach Hearn's second-floor room for a better view. The cab driver coughed and Hearn stopped.

"So sorry, my good man." He pulled out a coin and handed it to the driver, then the three ran upstairs to the room. They reached the window just in time to see the Japanese airship, in flames, settling to the ground. Flames also engulfed the other airship. Alethea couldn't stop tears from flowing. How could people harm such magnificent aircraft?

Just as the question formed, a flash blossomed causing Alethea to jump backward. A heartbeat later an explosion rattled the window. Alethea's breathing came fast. She wanted nothing more than for someone to explain what had just happened and why. She sat on the floor and hugged herself, wishing her momma and daddy were there. Hearn and Larissa just stared spellbound out the window.

A moment later, Larissa turned around. She beckoned her to come to the chair and sit in her lap. Hearn kept looking out the window, occasionally shaking his head. Finally he walked over to a small writing desk and removed his notepad. He sat, thinking.

Alethea sat in Larissa's lap and held on tight until the tears subsided and she could speak. "What happened?"

Larissa shrugged. "It would seem the Japanese attacked

Fort Lowell, but I can't imagine why."

"That woman's name sounded familiar. I'm pretty sure my momma told me about her."

Hearn looked up from his notepad, then gave a slow nod. "Yes, Imagawa Masako, the lady samurai your mother and father met in Japan. She was also friends with Masuda Hoshi, the Japanese farmer from Las Cruces."

The reporter turned back to his notepad and began writing. Alethea could imagine gears turning just like the machines she'd seen at the Cotton Exposition.

"Could the Japanese have allied themselves with the Apaches through Hoshi?" asked Larissa.

Hearn looked up and nodded. "It would make sense."

"I don't know what most of that means." Alethea's brow furrowed.

Larissa chuckled. "It means this fight has just gotten bigger."

Alethea frowned. "I wish we could make them stop fighting."

"To get people to stop fighting, you have to get them talking." Larissa shrugged. "One side has to see the other side's point of view."

"I know." Alethea hopped off Larissa's lap and walked over to her bag. "That's why I took these herbs from Marie Lalande."

Hearn blinked at her. "You took herbs from Marie Lalande? Voodoo magic?"

Alethea nodded and her stomach clenched. She realized she may have made a mistake telling Hearn and Larissa about the herbs. She feared she was in trouble and wished she could take back her confession.

Larissa held out her hand. "What do the herbs do?"

Alethea tucked the bag behind herself. "Am I in trouble?"

Larissa chuckled again and Alethea wished she wouldn't do that. "No, not at all. Tell me, what do those herbs do?"

"My friend Francoise said they make people see your point of view."

Hearn turned around in his chair and steepled his fingers as he sometimes did when interested in something. "And who is Francoise?"

"Madame Lalande's daughter." Alethea's voice became whisper-quiet.

Hearn seemed satisfied with the answer and gazed out the window. "It would be helpful to know just what happened at the fort."

"We saw what happened. The Japanese and Americans fought and both airships caught fire." Alethea shook her head. Adults could be so dense sometimes.

"Yes, but who controls the fort? Were the Indians involved? It could all be decided at this point and depending on how, it could be a very long time before we get back home."

Alethea shrugged. "You could always go back to the fort and find out what happened. That's what reporters do, right?"

Hearn quirked a smile. "I think the fort could be quite dangerous right now, no matter who has the upper hand, but I know one place where I might get answers and if your herbs are effective—and given their source, I have every reason to believe they are—I might also have some ideas about how to put them to use."

"You're not going to use them to interview people for a story are you?" Alethea put her hands on her hips, suspicious of the reporter's motives.

He shifted under her gaze, confirming her suspicions, but smiled after a moment. "I do want to write a good story, but I also want to reunite you with your parents. I'll do what's necessary to make that happen." He rubbed his chin, thoughtful. "May I see the herbs?"

"Promise you won't take them."

"I promise." Hearn held up his hand as though prepared to take an oath.

Alethea handed them to Hearn. He sniffed them, then took a negligible amount of the crushed leaves and put it on his tongue.

"Kind of minty."

"You better be careful with that." She held out her hand for the bag and Hearn gave it back.

"I'm just considering the best way to use these." He took out his pocket watch and glanced at the time. "I'd better go."

"I think we oughta come along," said Larissa.

Hearn shifted uncomfortably under Larissa's gaze. "I was thinking of going to the Congress Hall Saloon. People will be talking there."

Larissa nodded. "I'll watch out for Alethea. I think we owe it to her to see what happens."

They left the room and went back downstairs. Alethea didn't like the saloon. It smelled of smoke and puke and there wasn't much for kids to do there. She could hear the voices from the Congress Hall Saloon long before Hearn and Larissa pushed through the batwing doors. Groups of men clustered around speculating about what happened at Fort Lowell less than an hour before, wondering what it would mean for the work on the railroad and whether the *City of New Orleans'* destruction meant the end of air service as well as rail.

Alethea watched as Hearn drifted among the clusters of men. She recognized shopkeepers, mill workers, rail workers, and even some ranchers, but no one wore a soldier's uniform. No one sat at the game tables and few people drank. They all sounded worried about the future. Hearn returned to the table where Alethea sat quietly next to Larissa. "Learn anything?" Larissa asked.

Hearn shook his head. "Nothing I don't already know."

Just then, the batwing doors flew open and in walked Wyatt Earp followed by Doc Holliday. The room fell silent.

Wyatt held up his hands. "The Apaches have just taken Fort Lowell with the help of the Japanese and the Mexicans."

The words set off a commotion. Alethea didn't know the Mexicans were involved. Her head began to spin and she thought it was from more than the smoky air.

Several people nearby voiced disbelief.

A clamor in one corner overtook the rest of the room's buzz. A cowboy stood up, "Let's form a posse and take the fort back!"

Cheers and applause echoed around the room. Despite the cheerfulness of the sound, Alethea shivered.

Wyatt held up his hands again. When no one settled down, he unholstered his six-gun and fired it into the ceiling. Larissa grabbed Alethea and held her close. Plaster rained down on those nearby. The bartender cringed, then looked up at the damage and sighed.

"The Indians had help from the Japanese," explained Wyatt.

"But their airship fell from the sky, burning," called a shopkeeper.

Wyatt shook his head. "They only had a few people aboard. Most are at the fort—and they've got automata. They rounded up the soldiers. They say all the land east of Fort Lowell and west of Fort Bowie, south of the railroad and north of the Mexican border belongs to the Apache."

Again a roar erupted from the crowd. As Wyatt waited for the crowd to simmer down, Alethea noticed something was wrong with Doc Holliday. The doctor seemed awfully quiet under the circumstances. Sweat streamed down his face and he struggled to unbutton his collar. Alethea had never seen a man so pale.

The woman who'd accompanied Wyatt Earp at the faro table the other day sat down next to Larissa and Alethea. Hearn leaned over to her. "What does Mr. Earp like to drink?"

The woman shook her head. "He doesn't drink."

Hearn's eyes widened. "He plays faro in here all the time."

"And that encourages other people to drink, so they're glad to have him."

Undeterred, Hearn pressed the woman for more information. "Surely he must drink something. He can't spend hours without some refreshment."

"Coffee mostly." The woman narrowed his gaze. "Why are you so curious?"

Hearn shrugged and smiled. "I thought he deserved something for getting away from the fort to share the news."

The woman shook her head. "If you want to get something special for Wyatt Earp, go across the street."

Hearn seemed puzzled, but Alethea knew what she referred to. "The ice cream parlor!"

"The man loves his ice cream." She looked as though there was more she wanted to say, but she glanced at Alethea and Larissa and remained quiet.

A man at the far end of the bar rapped for attention. Wyatt Earp spoke again. "The Indians say they'll let us continue work on the railroad and they'll let the trains through."

"Do you believe them?" shouted a man in a cravat, a fine suit, and a bowler hat.

Wyatt considered that a moment, then nodded. "I believe them, but it's not much consolation. The Indians now control all the mineral wealth down in that part of the territory."

"The army won't let this stand, will they?" asked a man in clothes so dusty Alethea couldn't tell what color they originally were.

Wyatt shook his head. "Probably not, but who knows what a war would mean."

Hearn smiled for some reason. He motioned for Larissa and Alethea to follow him. Even before they left their seats, Doc Holliday doubled over, coughing and hacking, splattering his hand with more than a little blood. Wyatt ran to his side and helped him into a chair. He looked up, frantic. "Is there a doctor in the house?"

A man in a pinstripe suit held up his hand and rushed over. He examined Doc Holliday and shook his head. They spoke too softly for Alethea to hear. At last Wyatt stood up. "Clear the way. We have to get my friend to the doctor's office."

The doctor and Wyatt carried Doc from the saloon. After they departed, the buzz of conversation resumed. Some men went to the bar to buy drinks to console their fears.

"I don't think we'll learn anything else," said Hearn. "Let's go across the street and I'll buy you both some ice cream. You can help me decide what would go well with minty herbs."

"You're not thinking of using that Voodoo potion on Mr. Earp, are you?" Larissa narrowed her gaze at Hearn.

"I think someone needs to listen and be cooperative, or we'll be stuck here a very long time."

Larissa stood and held out her hand for Alethea. "I didn't think reporters were supposed to get involved with their stories."

He considered that a moment. "We're supposed to write, and that's just what I will do ... after we get some ice cream."

"What about you, Auntie Lyssa. Marshals are supposed to get involved."

"You got me there, Partner." As they stepped out to the

street Larissa gazed in the direction of Fort Lowell. "If we have a way to set things right, I'm all for it."

As the *Tiburón* approached New Orleans, Ramon and Fatemeh went to the ship's wireless communication's room to pick up messages. He learned that the Japanese and Mexicans had helped the Apaches take Fort Lowell. The standoff continued at Fort Bowie. The Apaches requested Ramon's return to negotiate a proper treaty between nations—not the worthless scrap paper that had been negotiated between the United States and Indian Nations before.

"This is likely to set a whole new precedent," said Ramon. "If Apaches have risen up, I wouldn't be surprised if others follow suit."

"Yes, but the Apaches had the battle wagons." Fatemeh shrugged. "Other tribes don't have that advantage."

"I suspect it's just a matter of time before they seek it out."

Ramon leafed through the other papers. Sheriff Jenkins would meet the airship when it docked to take Hamid into custody on kidnapping charges. He gave no indication whether or not he would attempt to take Ramon into custody as well.

Captain Cisneros docked the ship at the New Orleans aerodrome. Soon after, Ramon, the captain, Billy, and First Mate Gonzalez led Hamid down the ramp to where Sheriff Jenkins waited with his deputies. At the bottom of the ramp, Jenkins placed handcuffs on Hamid.

"You should handcuff Morales as well," growled Hamid. "My government wants him for questioning."

"Not anymore." Jenkins shook his head. "Washington received satisfactory answers to the inquiry and the Persian envoy's going home soon."

"I want to contact the Persian envoy." Hamid maintained an even tone, but Ramon could see the muscles in his neck working.

"Behave yourself and I'll consider it." The sheriff tipped his hat and he and the deputies led Hamid away.

Captain Cisneros released a relieved sigh. "Glad to be rid

of him." He turned to Ramon. "I just need a little time to get some fuel and restock supplies. I know you're anxious to get back to Tucson but with the *City of New Orleans* destroyed and the rail line out, they could probably use us to take some cargo westward. It'll also help me offset the expenses of our extended voyage."

Fatemeh walked down the ramp and joined the men. She took Ramon's hand and he looked from her to the captain. "There's some business we should tend to while we're here. How long do you need?"

"Give us about three or four hours, then we'll get going."

Fatemeh and Ramon walked into the French Quarter to Marie Lalande's small shop. Marie stood behind the counter and her mouth fell open as she caught sight of Fatemeh. She rushed around the corner and embraced her friend.

"I feared I would never see you again after those evil men took you away."

"I'm back, thanks to Ramon and many other good people." Ramon breathed in the comforting, familiar aromas of the shop.

Marie sighed and stepped away from Fatemeh. "I'm so sorry about Alethea. We tried to keep her safe, but she was bound and determined to go out west and help."

Ramon glanced up at the painting of Marie's grandmother who seemed to watch them with stern disapproval.

"We've heard and we're heading that way. Alethea's in good hands. We'll get her back." Fatemeh approached Marie and took her hand. "How is Jacques? Is he…."

"He recovered and he is well, but we feel we have failed you."

Fatemeh squeezed her friend's hand. "You haven't failed us and Alethea has the amulet of protection you made for her."

"I fear the amulet only works when she's in range of those who can keep her safe." Marie glanced up at the painting of her grandmother. Ramon wondered what emotion Marie read from the painting.

"She has plenty of people to look after her where she is." Fatemeh spoke the words with conviction. Ramon agreed. Alethea was in good hands with Larissa.

Ramon put his arm around Fatemeh's shoulder. "She's like

her mother. You can't keep her down when she's decided to do something. You did your best."

Ramon and Fatemeh said their good-byes and left. They stopped at the Blessed Life Apothecary. Fatemeh smiled at the veritable rainbow of liquids in the shop's window indicating no major infections sweeping through the city. Lazare Picou stood behind the counter cleaning glassware and reported business had been fair.

"It's good to see you, Madame Morales."

She looked to Ramon and then back to the man behind the counter. "I wish we could stay. It looks like we need to leave for a few more days."

Picou shuffled from one foot to the other. "Biggest problem is the rent is due."

Fatemeh chuckled. Ramon found it ironic he asked permission to pay, even though he was the building's formal renter. "Do you have enough money in the till to cover it?"

"I do," he said.

"Then go ahead and pay the bank," said Fatemeh. "Let them know we'll be back soon."

"I will."

With that, Ramon and Fatemeh walked down to their flat and checked in. They found the door to their rooms had been repaired and several letters on the floor, dropped through the mail slot. Among the mail messages was one from Lafcadio Hearn and one from Alethea sent while they were en route to Tucson.

Ramon tore the first open while Fatemeh read another. Again, they exchanged glances. "At least it sounds like she was safe in Mr. Hearn's care," said Ramon. "I'm glad Larissa was able to meet them."

"Agreed." Fatemeh rapped her fingers on the kitchen table. "Mr. Hearn is a good man, but he doesn't seem like he's spent much time caring for children."

Ramon nodded. He looked around at the flat and sighed. It was good to be home and he longed to put his feet up and rest, but he worried about Alethea and he hoped he could still do some good in Arizona.

He stood and held out his hand. Together, Fatemeh and

Ramon left the flat, locking it behind them. They returned to the airship. On the way, Fatemeh pointed out a screech owl. It whistled at her and she whistled back.

"So, what exactly did the owl say?" asked Ramon.

"Just another friend who missed us and our little girl." She looked from Ramon to the owl. She had a wistful smile.

"What are you thinking?"

"Marie once told me that the loa of an owl watches out for me and Alethea. I hope those spirits' influence extends out to the wild west."

"You know they do, Corazón." He kissed her and they continued back to the aerodrome.

Alethea sat at a table eating ice cream with Larissa when Lafcadio Hearn and Wyatt Earp entered the parlor. Alethea's heart pounded. She knew this was all part of the plan. Hearn introduced Alethea and Larissa to Earp. "Mr. Earp here has agreed to join us for some ice cream."

"I can't stay long, I have to get across the street. They're expecting me to run a faro game." He took off his hat and sat down.

Alethea watched Hearn as he went to the counter and ordered two ice creams. The clerk placed a scoop in one bowl and handed it to Hearn. While Larissa made small talk with Earp to keep him distracted, Hearn reached in his pocket and sprinkled some of the Voodoo herbs on the ice cream. He took the spoon and swirled it around. The clerk handed him the second bowl and collected the money.

Hearn brought the two bowls to a small table. "How is your friend, Doc Holliday?" he asked.

Earp took the bowl and shook his head. "Not well. The doctors don't hold out much hope. There's some medicine that could ease his suffering, but they haven't finished repairing the eastbound rail and the trains from California are reluctant to come this far with the Apache war in progress." Despite Earp's calm demeanor, the circles under his eyes betrayed his concern.

Larissa nodded. "I hear the army is mustering forces up in

Prescott, hoping to recapture Fort Lowell." She took a bite of her ice cream.

If Earp noticed his ice cream was a bit of a mush, he didn't say, but Alethea knew ice cream got kind of melty in Tucson's heat. Earp tasted the ice cream and made a face. He blinked and took another bite.

"Something wrong?" Hearn shifted in his seat.

Earp shook his head. "No, not really. Tastes kind of minty." He pondered for a moment. "Chocolate mint ice cream might just catch on. That's interesting. I'll have to ask for it again next time I come."

Hearn cleared his throat. "I get the impression you could make a deal with the Apaches that might get them to give up the fort without shots fired."

Earp considered that as he ate his ice cream. "We tried to talk to the Indians. They don't trust us and we don't trust them."

Larissa leaned forward. "You're not offering them a square deal."

"No, ma'am," said Earp. "No one ever has."

"I have it on good authority, Ramon Morales is on his way back." Hearn took a bite of ice cream and swallowed it down. "I interviewed him and his wife extensively for a book I wrote. They're good and honorable people. Morales might help you find a path that would work for both you and the Apaches ... if you just go and talk to him."

Earp finished his ice cream and nodded, his gaze thoughtful. "I might just do that." He reached over to the adjoining chair and grabbed his hat. "Thank you for the ice cream."

CHAPTER FIFTEEN
DEALING A NEW HAND

Lozen asked Imagawa to show her how to use a katana. Imagawa showed her several basic strikes in the predawn cool of Fort Lowell's parade ground. Imagawa emphasized that the Katana should serve as a natural extension of the arm. After half an hour, sweat glistened from her skin and Imagawa called a halt. Lozen walked over to a nearby well and ladled out water, letting the cool breeze dry the sweat. She handed the ladle to Imagawa. She missed Dahteste, but the Japanese warrior was good company.

"Do you think we will win?"

"If our objective is to assure that the Americans negotiate with your people as a government, then we have already won." Imagawa drank. "They will either negotiate or fight."

"I think fighting is more likely." Lozen took the ladle back. "More to the point, I'm worried about our survival if the Americans do fight."

"The challenge is not one of winning and losing battles. It is assuring that the win or loss happens in such a way that the Tsokanende keep the land they want."

Lozen considered that. "Hoshi told me you once stole a Russian airship in order to overthrow the Japanese emperor."

"There are many samurai on the Japanese council. They have taught me how to prioritize my objectives and make sure the most important ones are achieved." Imagawa walked over to a bench and sat down. "As a council member, I have found ways to improve the lot of women in modern Japan. Before, I did not see a way to do that without a Shogun's strong hand. Now I see that many hands working together can be strong."

"We have no airship." Lozen quirked an eyebrow as she returned the ladle to the bucket.

"Another is on the way."

"Yet I fear the Americans will strike before it arrives."

Imagawa nodded. "That is possible, but it is not the most important weapon in our arsenal."

"What do you see as the most important weapon?" Lozen narrowed her gaze.

"Persistence and patience."

A young Tsokanende warrior ran up. "Sorry to interrupt," he said in English so Imagawa could understand, "but a man named Wyatt Earp has just arrived. He allowed us to disarm him. He said he wants to talk."

Imagawa grinned at Lozen. "As I say, I believe we have already won."

A short time later, Lozen sat next to Naiche at a long table in Fort Lowell's mess hall. Imagawa and Hoshi sat next to them. Wyatt Earp sat across the way. The map from the earlier negotiations with Ramon Morales sat on the table between them.

Earp pointed to the map and indicated the silver deposits discovered in the Mule Mountains near the San Pedro River.

"We would like access to these mountains to the east of the San Pedro," said Earp. "I propose a boundary line for Apache lands bordered by the railroad on the north, along the river to Latitude 31.8 degrees. The border will run east to longitude 109.7 west."

Lozen noted that Earp asked for just enough to serve his self-interest, but not more. This boded well compared to the Earp's original plan to sell land to the Apaches.

"The San Pedro River flows to the North," said Naiche. "I understand that you need water for your town, but mining contaminates river water. We will not have good water to drink or good water for our crops."

Earp nodded. "I understand. We'll use the mining machines in the mountains. They do use water to process the ore, but we don't have to put the waste water back. We can treat it as sewage."

Lozen folded her arms and glared at Earp. "You would have a fleet of your mining machines which are easily converted to battle wagons? What will keep you from overrunning the Apaches when you find you want more land?"

Imagawa cleared her throat. "You saw how our automata overran the American soldiers in this camp. The Japanese government would be pleased to sell you farming automata which you could convert to defensive machines. You would have your battle wagons and you would have the automata, putting you on equal terms."

"Sell, sell, sell," growled Naiche. "It's always about selling us things—taking advantage of us. We have little money to feed into your coffers."

Hoshi cleared his throat. "When I first encountered the Jackalope Harvesters on my land, I thought they were an abomination, but they proved essential to my farm's success. They were created by Professor Maravilla, who also invented the mining machine. He is often looking for new ways to test his machines. If you allow him to build new machines for you, I feel certain he would provide them for the cost of materials."

Naiche narrowed his gaze.

"Would this professor be so selfless?"

"He wandered without a home for years." Hoshi folded his hands on the table. "He only wants to conduct his researches in peace." He shrugged. "I perhaps take too many liberties speaking for him, but I would be happy to send him a telegram to see if he would be amenable."

Naiche and Lozen huddled together and considered the idea. Naiche was skeptical, but Lozen saw promise in the idea of working with this Maravilla. Across the way, Earp's mustache enhanced his frown, showing the depth of his worry. He wanted to resolve this soon so help could be brought in for his friend. Lozen wasn't sure if much could be done for Doc Holliday, and she suspected if Holliday died, Earp's willingness to negotiate would fade fast. She made that point to Naiche and the warrior gave a sharp nod, reaching a decision.

"This sounds promising. Send a telegram to your friend and see what he is willing to do."

Imagawa blew out a breath and nodded.

"Presuming that is agreeable, the next step will be to present this to the government and negotiate a formal agreement. Ramon Morales is on his way back."

"We'd be willing to work with Morales," said Naiche.

"In that case, I will send a telegram to Professor Maravilla and confirm his willingness to provide farm machines to the Tsokanende." With that, Hoshi stood to send a telegram.

As they adjourned, army soldiers approached the fort under a white flag. Lozen recognized the contingent's leader as General Wilberforce Johnson, formerly of Fort Bliss in El Paso. Naiche granted him permission to enter. Lozen joined Imagawa, Naiche, and Hoshi by the gate where Johnson and his men dismounted. A civilian with a large mustache and sad eyes accompanied them. From the way he watched everything with keen interest, Lozen suspected he must be a reporter.

Johnson gave a slow nod when his eyes wandered over Hoshi. "Why am I not surprised to see you here?"

"Perhaps it's because I'm asked to get involved every time the army has made a mess of things."

"Usually it's Washington's orders that make the mess." Johnson's lip curled upward in a hint of a bitter smile as he dismounted. "All right, I need to know who's in charge here."

Naiche stepped forward and Lozen accompanied him.

"I speak for the Tsokanende," said Naiche.

Johnson removed his riding gloves and tucked them into his belt. "We come prepared to fight, but we hear that may not be necessary."

"We are prepared to make a gesture of good faith." Naiche motioned for Johnson to follow him. The war chief led Johnson and his entourage to the stockade and the cell where they held General Nelson Miles. Lozen didn't know what to expect when the cell door was opened, so she gripped the handle of her knife.

The general emerged, blinking in the sunlight, hands open at his sides. He looked over to General Johnson, his superior officer, snapped to attention and saluted. Johnson returned the salute.

"We are prepared to surrender Fort Lowell and Fort Bowie back to the United States Army," said Naiche, "under condition that the informal agreement we've made with Wyatt Earp is drafted into a formal treaty by Assistant U.S. Attorney Ramon Morales."

The civilian accompanying Johnson had a pad of paper out

and scribbled notes, adding to Lozen's suspicions about him being a reporter.

Johnson looked from Miles to Naiche and narrowed his gaze. "I'm not authorized to accept terms. You must surrender unconditionally."

"I suggest your choices are limited." Naiche took a step closer to Johnson and Miles. The soldiers who accompanied Johnson put their hands on their side arms, but Johnson held up his hand to still them. "We'll allow you to use the fort's telegraph to wire Washington for further instructions. If you would rather fight, we can return General Miles to the cell and we'll see what bloodshed happens."

Imagawa approached. "Not only that, but more fighting will further damage relations between America and Japan."

The reporter took a keen interest in Imagawa's words.

Johnson looked from Naiche to Imagawa. "You seem awfully sure of yourselves. What makes you think Washington will agree to these terms? I feel confident we have the manpower to win an engagement if we need to."

"The actual cost of fighting has been high so far." Lozen released her grip on the knife. "We have shown good will by allowing the rail lines to be repaired through the Dragoon Mountains. Negotiating will further cement the alliance between Japan and the United States. Continuing to fight will drive a wedge in the alliance, something I don't think the United States wishes to risk given the strength of Asian air power."

Johnson considered those words and nodded. Lozen had heard Johnson was a reasonable man and suspected he'd already considered these points, but wanted to test his opponents' resolve. The generals didn't want to admit the Tsokanende could form alliances outside the United States and then use them in an effective campaign, but they had, leaving Johnson and Miles few options but to comply with Naiche's demands.

"Very well," said Johnson, "we'll send a telegram for further instructions."

Miles led the way to the telegraph office with Lozen, Naiche, Hoshi and Imagawa close behind. They sent their message, then two warriors escorted Miles and Johnson to the base commander's office where his clerk and aide-de-camp waited. Naiche left them behind closed doors to talk among themselves, free but watched. The reporter didn't enter the office with the soldiers. Instead, he remained outside.

Lozen and Imagawa walked away from the office. They climbed the stairs leading to the ramparts and gazed out at the surrounding desert and the palo verde trees lining the tiny Rillito River. "Do you see a day when your people and the white settlers trust each other, or will you always watch each other warily, waiting for the other to strike?" asked Imagawa.

As Lozen considered her answer, the reporter who'd accompanied Johnson appeared on the ramparts nearby. He stood silent as Lozen answered.

"I suppose that all depends on the people involved." Lozen shrugged.

The civilian stepped forward and spoke in an Irish accent. "This country is one of many cultures coming together, clashing and working to live together." He held out his hand. "My name is Lafcadio Hearn and I'm a reporter who has been watching these affairs with great interest."

Satisfaction swelled within Lozen at hearing the man's profession confirmed. Knowing the white man's custom, she reached out and shook his hand. Imagawa bowed.

"I hoped..." Hearn faltered, words failing him. "I hoped perhaps when the time came, I could accompany you to Japan and learn more of your story. I think it would be fascinating and provide great insight to American audiences."

Imagawa narrowed her gaze, then nodded. "You would be welcome."

Hearn's mustache lifted, revealing a broad smile. "Thank you very much. I will, of course, need to send my latest report back to my paper and let them know where I'm going."

Lozen looked around and noticed a warrior emerging from the telegraph room. The warrior approached Naiche and Hoshi, then turned and went toward the general's office with the senior warriors close at hand.

Lozen nodded to Imagawa and the two climbed down from the ramparts followed by Hearn and entered the general's office where Johnson already scanned the telegram. The general handed the telegram to Miles, then put his hands behind his back. When Miles read the telegram his face puckered as though he'd eaten something sour. He returned the telegram to Johnson who folded it and put it in his pocket.

"We accept your surrender." General Johnson clasped his hands behind his back. "We expect all Japanese combatants to leave the area immediately. The Apaches may leave a contingent of delegates, but otherwise must clear the fort and retreat to a position to the east of the San Pedro River."

Lafcadio Hearn's shoulders drooped, much as his mustache seemed to. Lozen suspected he worried that events had transpired so quickly, he wouldn't be able to accompany Imagawa after all.

"Ramon Morales will be here within twenty-four hours. He's already drafting a formal agreement," announced Johnson.

Hearn's eyes brightened. He leaned toward Imagawa. "How long will it take you to depart?"

"We will wait until Morales's arrival and the departure of the Tsokanende forces to assure a peaceful transition." Imagawa looked toward the general. "Is that acceptable?"

Johnson nodded. "That's acceptable. Washington is eager to settle this affair."

Ramon Morales didn't know what kind of reception to expect when the *Tiburón* arrived in Tucson. Given the aerodrome, Cisneros didn't utilize the ornithopters for landing. The ground crew moored the ship and Cisneros ordered the cargo gangway deployed. Ramon grasped Fatemeh's hand and the two descended to find a small crowd gathered around.

Alethea ran from the crowd and jumped into her father's arms. He whirled around as much from the momentum as from delight to see her, then handed her over to her mother, who shed a tear of delight.

Larissa Seaton stepped up followed by Lafcadio Hearn. Ramon wasn't quite certain whether he wanted to hit the man or shake his hand.

"I am so sorry for the worry I caused." Hearn held his

hands out to his sides, ready to accept whatever fate befell him. "I only brought her here because I thought it would be better to reunite her with one of her parents than leave her in—" he struggled for the right word "—uncertain hands back in New Orleans."

Ramon understood the sentiment. He reached out, clasped his hand, and shook it. "Thank you. I just wish there had been better communication between us."

Fatemeh turned to Larissa. "Thank you for stepping in and helping out."

"Returning runaways to their parents is all part and parcel of my job." Larissa tipped her hat and winked. "Besides it was my pleasure. Duties were light and the U.S. Marshal Service appreciated my reports from the scene of the Apache crisis."

Just then a familiar man with platinum blond hair and a long blond mustache approached. He wore epaulets with stars on his blue uniform jacket. "Ramon Morales, it's good to see you again."

"Colonel … no General Johnson." Ramon reached out and shook the general's hand. "I thought you were stationed in Missouri these days."

"I was, but the president put me in charge of the Tucson situation." The general clasped his hands behind his back. "I gather the Indians want you to draw up a formal treaty."

Ramon reached up and tugged on his collar. He'd grown used to wearing a gingham shirt and denim pants. Once again, he found himself in trousers, waistcoat, jacket, and cravat. "I sent out some messages on the way over here. It won't be quite as neat and tidy as anyone wants, I'm afraid. The powers that be in Washington aren't willing to cede United States territory to the Apaches."

Johnson nodded, looking neither happy nor distraught. "I'm not surprised. The question is, how do you plan to break the news?"

Ramon shrugged. "The only way possible, truthfully and directly."

The general began to escort them toward a wagon, when Wyatt Earp approached the group. He removed his hat and addressed Fatemeh. "Mrs. Morales, I presume?"

"Yes." She narrowed her gaze and evaluated the man.

"I am told you are a healer of some skill. I have a friend who is in dire straits and I would appreciate it if you could come and help out, if possible."

Earp displayed much more humility than the last time Ramon had seen him. He suspected the friend was Doc Holliday, but doubted Fatemeh could do much for him. Like dealing with the Apaches, the only answer would be to deliver the truth as kindly as possible and hope for the best. Fatemeh looked toward Ramon.

He nodded. "You go, see what you can do."

"What about Alethea?"

"We'll go get some ice cream," said Larissa. She looked toward Fatemeh. "I'll meet you after you attend to your errand."

Fatemeh gave a curt nod. "Do you hear that, Alethea joon? Stay close to Larissa." She set the girl down on the ground.

"You bet I will." She reached up and took Larissa's hand.

Fatemeh, Larissa, and Alethea followed Wyatt Earp to a carriage and Ramon watched as they rode toward Tucson.

Ramon and Hearn climbed in the wagon with General Johnson and rode to Fort Lowell. A Japanese airship patrolled overhead. A soldier hustled Ramon and Hearn into General Miles' office. Naiche and Lozen sat waiting.

Imagawa stood at the head of the table. She acknowledged Ramon and Lafcadio Hearn with a nod.

Ramon sat across from the Apache warriors and opened a packet he carried with him. "I'm sorry to say, the United States government has refused to recognize the Apache secession."

The Apaches banged on the table. Lozen growled something in Apache while Naiche said, "We should have known."

Imagawa held up her hand for silence. "Hear him out, see what he has to say."

"The U.S. Government will allow a new territory to be portioned from New Mexico and Arizona territories, in keeping with the precedent set by the creation of the Indian or Oklahoma Territory north of Texas."

Naiche and Lozen looked at each other, then turned their attention back to Ramon.

"Before you agree, you should consider this, many back

East were all too willing to let the Arizona and New Mexico territories be split up. It makes them smaller and will take longer for them to be admitted to the union as states. A better option might be to form yourself into a self-administered Federal reservation in the boundaries selected. In which case, any other Indian tribes who choose to live there will bolster the territories' population, meaning Arizona and New Mexico might achieve statehood sooner, which might actually give you a greater voice in Washington than you'd have as a small territory."

"And how would that help us?" Naiche leaned forward, brow furrowed. "New Mexico and Arizona would still have majority white populations."

"You would get representatives in Congress if the territories became states. I can't guarantee a small Indian territory in this part of the country will be granted statehood. At least not in our generation."

Naiche and Lozen looked at each other. "We want to take this proposal back to our people and see which is the most acceptable to them."

General Johnson cleared his throat, getting Ramon's attention. "This is going to stick in Wyatt Earp's craw."

"He'll have to negotiate with the Apaches no matter what's decided." Ramon pursed his lips and turned to Naiche. "Are you willing to work with him?"

"We will give him as fair a deal as he would have given us," said Lozen.

The reporter, Hearn, leaned close to Ramon. "Talk to Mattie," he whispered. "I mean Alethea. She ... helped me find a way to get Wyatt Earp to see reason."

Ramon narrowed his gaze, but the reporter's expression convinced him not to pursue the matter right away.

"I'll have papers drawn up either way you decide. Shall we reconvene here in say, three days?"

"That will be acceptable to us," said Naiche.

All parties stood from the table and shook hands. Imagawa bowed to Naiche and Lozen. "The time has come for me to depart. I bid you well in your continued discussions."

"Thank you," said Naiche. Lozen returned Imagawa's bow.

Ramon followed Imagawa, Hearn, and General Johnson out through Fort Lowell's gates. The Japanese airship hovered just over the ground and had lowered a ladder. Hoshi stood next to the ladder and bowed to Imagawa. "It was good to see you again. I hope one day you will return to America for a more social visit."

Imagawa looked around, then returned the bow. "There is too much open space for my taste. Be well." She climbed up the ladder.

Hearn looked around at the others. "It's also time for me to bid you farewell. Imagawa has graciously invited me to go to Japan aboard the *Buson*." He indicated the airship.

Ramon reached out and shook Hearn's hand. "Thank you for taking care of Alethea for us."

"She is a wonderful girl, but I would have been hard-pressed to do it alone. I'm grateful Miss Seaton was able to meet us and help." Hearn's eyes glistened with unshed tears.

Imagawa barked a command in Japanese from above. Hearn turned around and clambered up the ladder. As soon as he boarded the airship, the crew withdrew the ladder and the engine roared to life. Ramon stood with Hoshi and Johnson, and waved until the airship had flown out of sight.

Fatemeh emerged from Doc Holliday's room and faced Wyatt Earp, who stood wringing his hands. "There's not much I can do for him," she said. "His tuberculosis is quite advanced. I've done what I can to make him comfortable."

"Is there anything we could have done for him if we'd not been cut off from the rest of the country?"

Fatemeh shook her head. "I don't think so. Actually, given his hard drinking, I'm surprised he has done as well as he has for so long." She reached out and took Wyatt Earp's hands. "Working to make peace with the Apaches and not exploiting them, that leaves a lasting legacy and tribute to him. You're going to build a town. Why not name it for him?"

Earp quirked an eyebrow. "Holliday, Arizona? It has a certain ring to it."

"It seems friendlier than the name the Apaches gave it ... the land of the Tombstone."

"It may prove to be his tombstone." Wyatt looked down and shook his head.

"Let it be his monument." With that, Fatemeh gave Wyatt's hands a squeeze. She slipped past him and left the saloon where Doc Holliday lived. It was still early enough that just a few people sat in the saloon, most eating a quiet lunch.

Fatemeh found Alethea and Larissa across the street at the ice cream parlor. They'd just finished. "Now, young lady, you should show me where you've been staying so we can pack."

Alethea looked crestfallen. "But I was having a good time staying with Auntie Lyssa."

"I imagine your Auntie Lyssa would like a little time to herself."

"I think your daddy has his work cut out for him for a few days yet. I'm not going anywhere till this is all settled. We'll still get to spend time together." Larissa reached out and tickled the girl. She looked up at Fatemeh. "How is Ol' Doc Holliday?"

Fatemeh shook her head. "Things don't look good. I don't think he has long to live."

A rumbling engine interrupted their conversation. They looked up as the *Buson* flew overhead. Alethea and Larissa waved at the airship. Fatemeh did as well and wondered whether anyone could see.

Once the airship had vanished from sight, Larissa tipped her hat at Fatemeh. "I really do need to check in and see if there are any telegrams. I'll see you soon."

"Thank you." Fatemeh turned to Alethea. "Now, show me to your hotel room."

Alethea led the way down the street. "So, what happens when you die?"

"If you've led a good life, I believe you get to enter the presence of God."

"Forever and ever and ever?"

"There you will find infinite beauty and infinite knowledge." Fatemeh smiled. "Enough to keep just about anyone occupied forever and ever and ever."

"Even someone like Dr. Holliday?"

Fatemeh considered that, then nodded. "Dr. Holliday is complex. I'm sure he'll be kept ... busy in the afterlife."

Alethea led Fatemeh to the hotel where she'd stayed with Larissa. As she packed her bags, she found a note from Hearn addressed to Fatemeh.

Fatemeh tore the note open and read it. "I am dreadfully sorry for any pain and confusion I caused bringing your daughter out west, but she is a delightful child and I would not trade the adventure we shared for anything. I will remember you and your family fondly as I embark on my new adventures to the Far East."

Fatemeh folded the note and placed it in her bag. "What I don't understand is why Mr. Earp and Dr. Holliday decided to let the Apaches have land free of charge. Usually men consumed of such greed are not so willing to let their plans go."

Alethea bore a somewhat guilty expression, but didn't say anything as she packed a pouch that looked suspiciously like those Marie Lalande used to send herbs home with her customers. Fatemeh realized the time had come to teach her daughter about herbs and medicines and how to use them without causing harm. She had a sense her daughter already had the instincts of a healer.

Once Alethea had packed, they left the hotel and returned to the *Tiburón* to find out how Ramon's negotiations had gone.

Two weeks after their arrival in Tucson, a formal agreement had been reached between the United States and the Chiricahua Apache. To celebrate the formal signing of the treaty, Billy McCarty set up a croquet pitch on Fort Lowell's parade ground. A gentle breeze mitigated the late morning heat. Ramon, Fatemeh, and Alethea joined Billy and Larissa. Naiche and Lozen looked on, curious. Billy explained the rules and Lozen decided to try her hand at the game. Ramon and Larissa also decided to play.

Hoshi stood next to a pale and drawn Wyatt Earp. Doc Holliday had passed in the night and his body had gone to the undertaker. Wyatt's gaze held a faraway look.

The train had come through from California. Among the shipment were lemons, which the cooks at the fort turned into lemonade. Fatemeh took a glass to Wyatt and he savored the sweet-tart flavor.

Ramon glanced over to the Apaches, standing tall and proud. Rather than form a reservation, they had decided to break off into a new territory, which they named Cochise to honor Naiche's father. Ramon wondered whether they had chosen the best option. He also wondered how the Federal government would attempt to exert control in the coming years, but for now, it was land they could call their own and develop as they chose.

Billy took the first turn at the game, knocking a wooden ball through the wicket. Larissa followed and gave her ball a good solid whack, which knocked Billy's off course.

Lozen wagged her finger at Larissa. She knocked her ball just behind Larissa's. "Competitive play is not necessarily the best strategy in this game."

Ramon took a turn and knocked his ball into Lozen's, pushing it a little closer to the next wicket. His ball blocked both Larissa and Billy's. Billy attempted to send his croquet ball beside Ramon's, which then knocked Larissa's backwards, but also pushed Lozen's further forward.

"I don't think the point of this game is to win or lose." Wyatt finished his lemonade and smacked his lips. "It's to be outside with friends on a nice day." This was not a man who would cry openly, but no one doubted he wished for another friend's presence.

Naiche and Lozen both glanced toward Earp. "Does this mean you consider us friends?"

Wyatt struggled to smile, but couldn't. "We're learning to work together, which is the first step to being friends. I appreciate that you're willing to sell me land in the Mule Mountains for a reasonable price. I've wired my brothers in Dodge City so they can start raising the funds."

Alethea walked over and tugged on Ramon's shirt. He lifted her into his arms. "This is why you came here isn't it? To help people work together?"

Ramon smiled at her. "It is indeed."

"So, what about Hamid Farzan?" Larissa placed her hands on her hips.

Ramon heaved a deep sigh. That was the one aspect of the last two weeks that galled him. Hamid Farzan contacted Haji Hossein-Gholi Khan in Washington. The envoy pulled strings and got him released from jail. All Sheriff Jenkins could tell them was that some Persian officials came and retrieved him.

Fatemeh folded her hands and closed her eyes. "It would take much work on his part to earn my trust. He has worked to isolate himself and in the process has weakened himself."

"You are far more forgiving than me, Corazón. There is no way he could earn my trust." Ramon walked over to Fatemeh. "Are you certain you still want to travel to Persia to see your father and mother?"

"Now more than ever," said Fatemeh. "They need to know what has happened before Hamid gets a chance to spin the tale his way. It will be difficult enough to make peace with my parents as it is. After Hamid speaks to them, it may be impossible."

Lozen took her turn and knocked her ball through the second wicket. She let out a war whoop which caused Alethea to cover her ears and the others to laugh. Ramon then took a turn, aiming wide and missing the wicket.

"There is a reason you are a diplomat and not a warrior," teased Naiche.

"I spend too much time in an office." Ramon patted his belly, thin again after their recent adventures.

"Perhaps we should get a croquet set and play in New Orleans," mused Fatemeh.

Alethea bobbed her head in an enthusiastic nod. "That would be fun."

"And then we'd get to play with the alligators," said Ramon.

Larissa made the next shot. "That would be a bit more exciting than this."

"I think we've all had enough excitement in the last few weeks." They all looked up as Captain Cisneros approached. He'd taken advantage of Ramon's negotiations to return home and take care of business and stock up on supplies before making the extended voyage across the Atlantic. He grabbed a glass of lemonade, and took a sip. He tipped his hat back and rubbed the cool glass against his forehead. "I'm looking forward to new adventures."

Billy leaned on the croquet mallet. "The owl riders fly again!"

The group all looked at Billy.

He shrugged. "After all, we've fought in the Battle of Denver with the owl ornithopters. Then we took Hamid's ship. We're becoming an outright force for justice. Whenever you need help, just call for the owl riders!"

Larissa looked off toward Mt. Lemmon and smirked. "You know, it's not a half-bad idea. An international force for peace and justice."

Captain Cisneros held up his hand. "Let's not get carried away. After all, I got involved to help a friend. I only agreed to our new journey because of Mr. Mazdaki's interest in forming a trade partnership."

Wyatt folded his arms. "Well, I, for one, am grateful to you owl riders. I nearly lost everything in the war here in Southern Arizona. If you ever need a new recruit, I'd be happy to apply."

"You'd be welcome, Mr. Earp," said Billy.

Earp smiled at that. "Maybe next time. One of the first things I'll do in the town of Holliday is set up a sheriff's office to keep order—that and open a shop that serves mint chocolate ice cream."

Ramon and Alethea shared a guilty look under Fatemeh's withering gaze.

Cisneros held up his left hand. "I think the winds are shifting. It's about time for us to go." He looked to Ramon and Fatemeh. "Are you ready?"

"Let's get this show on the road," said Ramon.

Billy looked from Ramon to Fatemeh to Captain Cisneros. "Hey, who's going to help me pack up the croquet set?"

They looked at him and blinked.

"Well I'm coming along, too! I wouldn't miss this for the world."

CHAPTER SIXTEEN
REUNIONS

It took a week and a half for the *Tiburón* to reach Shiraz in Persia. Ramon worried about taking time to go to Shiraz. He might get back to New Orleans and find he no longer had a job. He might have to apply for a job in the city attorney's office, or maybe Sheriff Jenkins would hire him as a deputy.

As the airship descended toward Shiraz, Ramon found Fatemeh in their cabin, tying a scarf around her head. Alethea sat in front of the cabin's mirror admiring a similar scarf around her own head. Ramon's stomach fell as he remembered a conversation he'd had with Fatemeh soon after meeting. He stepped up behind her and put his hands on her shoulders. "Corazón, does returning to your home mean you and Alethea need to wear a veil?"

Fatemeh shook her head. "The veil is more a fetish among rich men like Hamid and men who aspire to wealth such as my father. Still, Alethea and I should cover our heads to avoid attracting … undue attention."

Alethea smiled up at Ramon. "Besides, it's pretty!"

Fatemeh turned around and took Ramon in her arms and put her head on his chest. He could feel the tension in her muscles, but she looked up and smiled. "I need to do this."

She took his hand and led him to the gondola where they watched the airship descend over the narrow Khoshk River. The river reminded Ramon of the Rio Grande, silt and mud with little water, but still a lifeline for Shiraz's people. The captain selected a landing site in the desert just north of the city, next to the river, near a mountain. The ornithopters launched, tethered to the ship. Once they landed, they reeled in their lines, bringing the ship down.

Once the airship reached a position close enough to the

ground, gangplanks deployed. A small but curious crowd emerged from the city and surrounded the ship. Cisneros eyed them from the gondola. "I suspect it won't be long before some official arrives wondering what we're doing here."

"You want to establish a port for your ships and a trading deal with Mr. Mazdaki." Fatemeh shrugged. "I think the best approach is to tell them the truth. A small bribe tactfully given wouldn't hurt."

The captain took out a clacker set and handed it to Ramon. "You can use this to communicate with the ship if you get in trouble."

Ramon looked at it and sighed, thinking of the clacker he wore at the office in New Orleans. "You're not coming with us?"

"Not this time. I think it's better if I wait with the ship, at least until the first curiosity seekers go about their business." He looked from Ramon to Fatemeh. "I'd feel better though if Billy went with you."

Ramon considered the recommendation. He had sharp eyes and could keep an eye out for danger, but he could also offend people of a different culture unawares. Then again, the same could be said for most of Cisneros's crew. Billy stood near the gondola's window, as curious about this new land as those on the ground were about the airship. He came this far and risked his life rescuing Fatemeh. He had every right to go along.

Ramon shook the captain's hand, startled once again by the strength of his grip, then followed Fatemeh to the ladder and climbed down. Billy and Alethea followed. The crowd pressed close as they approached. Fatemeh spoke to them in her native language. She smiled at certain comments and answered questions. Other times she shook her head as she declined trinkets passed to her.

As the crowd thinned, Alethea looked up. "What are they asking, momma?"

"Most of them are just curious. They wonder what it's like to travel in an airship. They wonder where we're from and why we're here. Some want to sell us souvenirs. I told them no thank you."

Once they left the crowd and entered the city, Ramon

thought he'd found an oasis in the desert. Both pine and palm trees lined the streets. Flowers bloomed everywhere. Brown buildings surrounded them. At first, the buildings reminded Ramon of the adobe structures back in New Mexico, but the elaborate tile work and unfamiliar alphabet adorning the signs told him home was far away.

For the first time in eight years, Ramon longed for Legion's company so he could understand the language. So far, no one had built a machine that could provide instant translations the way Legion could. Billy and Alethea looked around in wide-eyed wonder.

As they strolled through the streets, the sun reached its zenith and a voice cried out from the top of a nearby building, haunting and lyrical. Ramon's breath caught. "What is that?"

"The building's called a mosque and he calls the faithful to prayer," explained Fatemeh.

Billy's brow furrowed. "Is this a Bahá'í thing?"

She smiled and shook her head. "No, it's a Mohammedan thing."

A shopkeeper nearby closed his door, set out a small rug, then faced the southwest. He held his hands up beside his head. Fatemeh led them to a quiet alley to watch. They noticed several other people on the street doing the same thing.

"Will we be in trouble if we don't join them?" asked Alethea.

Fatemeh shook her head. "No, but we should respect them. Allow them time to say their prayers."

The prayer time did not last long and soon Fatemeh led the group past the mosque to an enormous enclosed market place. "It's called the Bazaar Vakil. My father's shop is near here."

Ramon swallowed, realizing he'd never asked what Fatemeh's father did. All he had known was he did business with traders. She entered the bazaar with its tall, vaulted cathedral-like ceiling. Billy asked a question that had just occurred to Ramon. "Are you sure your father's still in the same place. You left a long time ago. He could have set up shop somewhere else."

"We'll cross that bridge when we come to it."

They passed stalls selling everything from rugs to pottery

to hookahs, which Ramon had read about but never imagined he would see. Some men sat together and smoked. Others drank coffee. He enjoyed the camaraderie but worried about the stares that followed them as they walked through the marketplace.

They came to another doorway. Fatemeh turned right and entered a building nearby. Pocket watches lined a narrow table just inside the door. An assortment of clocks hung from the back wall. Between them, a pair of telescopes with their clockwork drives stood like sentinels. Against a side wall, Ramon recognized sextants and compasses. In the back corner, a man with a gray beard haggled with a customer. After they went back and forth half a dozen times, the customer paid some coins and left with a pocket watch.

Fatemeh cleared her throat. "Papa, I've come home."

The man looked up and his eyes widened. Then he stiffened and turned, closing his eyes tight. Despite that, a tear leaked through and trailed down his cheek.

"Is that grandpa?" asked Alethea. "Why's he sad?"

Billy took her hand. "Let's step over here. I think we should let your ma and pa sort this out." He led her over to a display of watches.

Fatemeh stared at her father's back and wondered what went through his mind. Would he turn around, raging and yelling? Would he ever turn around? She wanted to go up to him, but her limbs trembled and she couldn't move. She jumped as someone touched her. Ramon took her hand and her breathing eased.

Off to one side, Billy picked up a pocket watch. He evaluated it, then instead of returning it, he eased it toward his pocket. Alethea smacked his hand and shook her finger at him. He returned the watch.

At last, Fatemeh's father turned. "Who is this man who touches you so brazenly?"

"He's my husband, Ramon Morales. He's an attorney in New Orleans ... in America." She added the last as an afterthought, though she suspected her father, the maker of navigational instruments, knew just where New Orleans was.

Her father snorted. "You married well after all." Then he shook his head as though he had more important matters to discuss. "Have you ... have you returned to the teachings of Mohammed?"

"I never stopped believing in Mohammed's teachings." Fatemeh clasped her hands together. "I'm still Bahá'í."

Her father's face drooped, more sad than angry. "And this man, this Ramon?"

"He's Christian." The words emerged quietly but with confidence. "And we have a daughter." She held her hand out and Alethea stepped forward.

Her father looked dumbstruck, then Alethea curtsied. A hint of a smile passed across his lips, then his Adam's apple bobbed and he closed his eyes. When he opened them, no trace of emotion remained. "Why do you return at this time?"

"Hamid Farzan..." Fatemeh struggled to find words even though she'd rehearsed what she would tell her father several times on the voyage over from Tucson. "He found me in America. Kidnapped me. Wanted to bring me home to face justice." She pointed to Ramon and Billy. "My friends ... they rescued me. But I realized Hamid was right and I needed to come home and see you and mother again. I needed to tell you what had happened."

Her father sighed. "It broke Hamid's heart when he learned you'd run away. I told him you'd renounced Mohammed and we didn't hold him to the betrothal. I offered to return his dowry and I told him he should find another, but he wouldn't hear it."

Fatemeh stood, torn. Part of her wanted to rush forward and embrace her father. Another part wanted to run away, never see him again. "I never renounced Mohammed. I still love the Prophet's words." She closed her eyes and found strength to continue. "I also love the words of Bahá'u'lláh."

Her father looked as though he'd just bitten into one of Shiraz's famous sour oranges. He looked up and met her gaze for the first time. "You should see your mother."

Fatemeh's stomach fell, as though she were aboard an air-ship that just hit turbulent air. No "I love you" or "I missed you" or "I was worried about you." Just cold dismissal. Nevertheless, she'd seen the tear. She knew he cared. She'd hurt him, but whether by leaving or returning, she couldn't tell.

"We live in the same house. Your brother and sisters will want to see you as well."

Fatemeh gave a sharp nod. Without further word, she led the others away from her father's shop. They wound their way through Shiraz's crowded streets to a nearby neighborhood. She approached a wooden door and knocked. A moment later, a woman with a headscarf pulled around her mouth and nose answered. Fatemeh found herself staring into green eyes so much like her own. "Fatemeh joon, is it really you?"

"Yes, mama. It is."

Anahita Karimi gathered her daughter into an embrace and held her for a long time. "I thought you were dead." Her mother stepped back at last, tears glistening in the corners of her eyes.

A banal apology caught in Fatemeh's throat. She looked up and glimpsed a boy, in his late teens, behind her mother. "Is this Arshad?" asked Fatemeh. "He's grown so!"

The boy whirled around and stormed away. Again, Fatemeh's stomach lurched. She wanted to run after him. "He has been listening to your father's anger for many years. I know he misses you even if he doesn't show it." Her mother reached out and took Fatemeh's hand.

A screech sounded from the main room. Fatemeh looked over her mother's shoulder. "Sah-bum! You're still alive." She ran into the house, calmed her breathing and screeched at the Persian eagle owl perched on a stand.

Alethea ran up beside her mother and screeched as well.

The bird screeched back and looked them up and down. The bird had welcomed them. Fatemeh beckoned Ramon and Billy to enter and she introduced them to Sah-bum and her mother.

Ramon looked around at the colorful wall hangings, potted plants and elegant vases decorating the Karimi home. Alethea and Fatemeh joined Anahita in the kitchen. They spoke, but Ramon couldn't make out the words. Alethea knew some Persian words, but he wondered if his daughter followed the conversation. His neck muscles tensed. The occasional forays he made into Mexico never seemed so strange. At least there, he spoke the language and things seemed little different from New Mexico where he grew up.

Billy walked over to Fatemeh's gray owl with black spots. He reached out to touch it, but it squawked and lunged at him. He backed away and straight into Fatemeh's brother, Arshad. The boy dropped a fig and shouted at Billy in Persian.

"Yeah, what's it to ya'?" Billy's hands went down to his belt where his gun would normally ride, but, of course, Fatemeh made him leave it aboard the ship. She wouldn't appreciate him plugging her brother.

Ramon put his hand on Billy's shoulder and eased him away from Arshad. The teen picked up the fruit and stormed off to another room.

"You seem on edge, Billy." Ramon led him over to a chair and sat down across from him.

"I don't know what's going on. Fatemeh's dad don't seem all that interested in her one way or the other. Her mom is talking to her and we're not in on the conversation. I guess I don't know why we need to hang around doing nothing."

"We're here to support Fatemeh. What's more, we don't know where Farzan is, for all we know, he could be lurking around somewhere."

"If that were true, I wish Fatemeh woulda let me keep my gun."

"If she'd let you keep your guns, you might have killed her brother just now."

Billy laughed. "I woulda stopped myself."

"Why don't we take a walk around the house," suggested Ramon. "I could use some fresh air after all the time cooped up in the airship."

"Sounds like a plan." Billy nodded. They walked outside.

"I just realized I don't know much about your folks, Billy.

Fatemeh met you in Silver City, is that right?"

"My pa died back east when I was a little baby." Billy sniffed, then rubbed his nose. "My mom married a man named William Antrim. I even used his last name for a time, but people kept calling me 'junior'. Might not'a been so bad except Mr. Antrim always seemed to prefer my brother's company to mine."

"What about your mom?"

"Ma? She died a while back. I even went to Mr. Antrim to pay my respects. All I got was a lecture about how I needed to find a real job and quit drifting around the countryside. He didn't even care that I'd been a hero in the Battle of Denver or helped to stop the Russian invasion. All he cared about was that I didn't have steady work."

Ramon patted him on the shoulder. "Sounds like he cared in his way."

"Maybe, but I still don't know why anyone'd go outta their way to go home." Billy shrugged. "Didn't do me much good."

Billy shoved his hands in his trousers' pockets. He and Ramon continued their walk. Five people approached the house. Ramon soon realized Fatemeh's dad accompanied two women, a little younger than Fatemeh, and two men.

"'Spose those two purty fillies are Fatemeh's sisters?"

Ramon cast Billy a sidelong glance. "Seems likely."

"What about the fellers with 'em? Fatemeh's sisters couldn't be married, could they? Too bad if they are. They're kinda cute."

"If Fatemeh's dad is home, it must be about supper time." Ramon tugged on Billy's shirt sleeve, leading him back inside the house.

Alethea met them and led them to a dining room where a bowl of stewed chicken in a reddish brown sauce studded with pomegranate pips, trays of fruit, some rice and flat bread had been set out. Ramon's stomach began to rumble.

Fatemeh called Ramon and Billy over.

"I'd like to formally introduce you to my father." Then she spoke in Persian to him.

Kazem Karimi looked at Ramon and Billy unimpressed. Ramon held out his hand and Fatemeh's father gave him a surprisingly gentle and warm handshake. He then grabbed

Ramon in an embrace and kissed both of his cheeks. Ramon's eyes went wide, even though he knew that was the custom in much of the world. He then nudged Billy and pointed his chin at Fatemeh's father. Billy took the hint. When he backed away, he lifted his hand as though tempted to wipe away the kisses, but seemed to think better of it.

"So, does this mean he likes us?" asked Billy.

Ramon shrugged.

"I don't think he hates us."

Fatemeh then led Ramon and Billy over to the two women who accompanied her dad. She introduced her sisters, Kiana and Leila. Unlike Fatemeh's mom, their head scarves didn't obscure their faces. Billy smiled at the two young women, who appeared to be about his age. He held out his hand and the two women held up their hands and laughed. Kiana glanced back at the men who'd accompanied them. The big man took a step closer. Ramon led Billy back toward the table.

At that point, Kazem Karimi, indicated they should all sit. Billy pulled out the chair next to Leila, but Mrs. Karimi tapped him on the elbow and shook her head. She pointed sternly at the chair next to Ramon.

Mr. Karimi held out his hands and Fatemeh said, "Guests should start before family."

Ramon reached out and took the bowl and served himself, then passed it to Billy. Ramon leaned over to him.

"She says this is fesenjoon—chicken in a walnut pomegranate sauce. Be sure to try a little of everything. Fatemeh says, to be polite."

"I'm so hungry, that won't be a problem at all," said Billy.

"Don't clean your plate." Ramon held up his finger. "It's considered rude, but be willing to take seconds."

Billy scowled. "Careful, pard, I think you're starting to take this diplomat thing a little too seriously."

"I'm taking this married to a Persian thing seriously." Ramon smirked and dove in to his food. Sweet spices danced on his tongue. Between time in Tucson and aboard the airship, it had been too long since he'd had Fatemeh's cooking. Her mother's, if anything, was even better. He watched the conversation between Fatemeh, her parents and siblings. Her mother had moved the scarf from her face so she could eat. Her brother said little, not surprising for a teenager. Her sisters plied her with questions. The two men, who indeed proved to be Fatemeh's brothers-in-law, sat silent, almost befuddled by these new people in their lives. Alethea also sat in silence, watching everything in wide-eyed wonder.

Fatemeh's father interjected a few times. He pointed to Ramon and asked a question. Fatemeh swallowed hard, then answered. Her father eyed Ramon for a while, but nodded at last and resumed eating.

As they finished their meal, Kiana and Leila served strong coffee. Ramon sipped it and his eyes widened. Only then did he realize Fatemeh deliberately weakened her coffee for his tastes. He let the coffee slide down his gullet. At which point, he admitted he wanted to run several circles around the family house.

At last Fatemeh's father delivered a grave message. Fatemeh nodded and looked to Ramon and Billy.

"My father says there's only room for me and Alethea to stay the night as guests. You will have to return to the airship."

"Do we have to be separated, Corazón?" Ramon's fingers inched toward Fatemeh.

She looked down at his hand, then up at her father and didn't reach out.

"It's probably for the best."

Ramon sighed, but nodded. Billy gazed at Leila. Ramon guessed Billy would like to get to know her better. When her eyes drifted away and Ramon saw a hint of a blush, he realized leaving for the ship was probably best after all.

Mr. Karimi and Fatemeh accompanied them to the door. Billy leaned on the frame as Fatemeh and Ramon took hands under her father's hard gaze.

"Believe it or not, you impress him," whispered Fatemeh. She squeezed his hands and they parted. Before they left, Kazem gave them a password to use should they encounter any policemen. Knowing police patrolled the streets gave Ramon some comfort. Alethea leaped up into Ramon's arms and hugged him tight, then gave him a big sloppy kiss on the cheek. Ramon laughed and gave her a big sloppy kiss in return.

With that, Ramon and Billy entered the darkening streets. Billy led the way through Shiraz's narrow streets, claiming he remembered the way.

"So, what's going on?" asked Billy. "Will Fatemeh be all right?"

"I think her father is disappointed she left the Mohammad-an Faith, but he's relieved that she's all right. He's angry with her, but he loves her. He loves his wife and feels good that his wife now has closure on what happened with his daughter."

"And Fatemeh had time to tell you all this?"

Ramon shook his head. "No, but I'm a dad and a husband. I think it's a lot like how I'd feel." Ramon looked around. "Are you sure we're going the right way?"

"Positive." Billy pointed ahead. The courtyard with the bazaar lay before them. Just before they turned off the narrow street, Hamid Farzan stepped into their path from a side alley. "How very good to see you again," he said.

Billy reached for the nonexistent gun at his hip.

Ramon held up his hands. "You're home, Farzan. We have no further qualm with you."

"Perhaps..." Farzan spoke the word slowly, letting the final syllable fade away in a sibilant hiss. "But I still have a 'qualm' with you. I meant to see you punished for your crimes. It will happen."

"And how will you make that happen?" Billy took a step forward.

Just then, Ramon realized at least four large men had emerged from the alleyway behind him. Billy started to lunge toward Hamid when one of the men grabbed his collar and threw him to the ground and kicked him. Before Ramon could run to help him, something impacted his skull and everything went dark.

Fatemeh lay on a nearly forgotten bed in a nearly forgotten room and stared up at the ceiling listening to the quiet whispering of palm trees outside and the gentle chirp of crickets. Alethea shared her room and she lay curled up, snoring softly.

She almost wished for her sisters' chattering, but their husbands had walked them home right after Billy and Ramon left.
She laughed to herself thinking about Billy's flirtations and
how they irritated her brother-in-law. She shook her head. She
couldn't even remember his name.

A loud banging and a shout brought Fatemeh from her
half-doze. Sah-bum screeched in response and the owl's excla-
mation told her Billy had returned alone. She sprang to her feet
and ran from the bedroom into the house's main room. Her
father reached through the doorway and helped Billy inside.
Blood streamed down the side of his face and already turned
the front of his shirt brown.

She rushed up and helped her father lead Billy to a couch
where they lay him down. Alethea emerged from the bedroom,
rubbing her eyes. Fatemeh examined Billy's head wound then
looked at her father. "Bring me bandages and some water right
away."

"It's not proper for you to touch a man who is not your
husband so intimately." His eyes did not hold the fire of his
words, though.

"I'm a healer and I'll do what I can for him. Move it, papa."

He left the room to get the items required. Alethea woke
up enough to become cognizant of the situation and sprang to
Fatemeh's side.

"What happened? Will Billy be okay?"

"I'll do everything I can for him." Fatemeh hugged her
daughter, then led her back a couple of steps and looked at
Billy. "Who did this to you?"

"It was Hamid," he croaked. "He got a bunch of his friends
and jumped me and Ramon."

Fatemeh's father arrived and she fought to focus on wet-
ting a cloth and cleaning Billy's wound even as her hands
trembled.

"What about Ramon?"

"I don't know." Billy struggled to get the words out. "They
jumped us near the market. I think I was out for a while."

"It's lucky he didn't bleed out," said Fatemeh's father.

Fatemeh frowned as she dressed the wound.

"Head wounds bleed a lot. It must have clotted soon after

he was knocked out, then reopened while he walked here." The clinical analysis helped her focus. She looked into Billy's dilated eyes. "Are you hurt anywhere else?"

"Sore all over," said Billy. "Would feel better if your sister sat beside me."

"Doesn't sound like he's too badly hurt." Alethea giggled.

Agreeing with her assessment, Fatemeh leapt to her feet and poked her finger into her father's chest.

"What do you know about this? Are you working with Hamid to seek your own brand of justice?"

Her father looked hurt at the accusation. He shook his head.

"I admit, I am disappointed you followed such an unorthodox path in your life. I am angry that you left and hurt … your mother … your sisters." Either he hadn't been hurt, or he couldn't admit it.

"What about Hamid? Where has he taken Ramon?"

"I don't know, but you and your friends should find him soon. Hamid was hurt most of all when you left. I can forgive you, but I'm not sure Hamid can." Her father frowned. "He is also rich enough that he can buy help—as much as he needs."

Fatemeh simmered. She couldn't believe her father gave Hamid any benefit of the doubt at all. "Where would he take Ramon?"

Again, her father shook his head.

"You need to find him."

Fatemeh had no clue where Hamid would hide, but she had an idea about how to search. She pulled Alethea into the bedroom. She dressed and told Alethea to go back to bed. Fatemeh searched her dresser and smiled when she found a leather glove she'd left behind. She put it on her left arm, went out to the main room and whistled at Sah-bum. The owl obediently climbed onto the glove.

"You can't go out on the streets this late," said her father. "It's too dangerous, even with a password and even if Hamid weren't looking for you."

"Then get dressed and follow, but I'm not waiting for you." Fatemeh turned toward the door, but paused. She turned around. "Wake up my brother. Send him to the airship tethered on the north side of town. He should tell them what's happened. We'll need help. Make sure mama keeps an eye on Alethea. She's slippery that one."

Her father bristled at the orders, but nodded anyway. He disappeared into the bedroom. Without waiting, Fatemeh stormed through the door. She surprised herself by remembering the way to the bazaar. She soon reached a spot where blood stained the cobbles a darker shade of brown but hadn't been tromped away yet as people walked over it. Fatemeh lowered her arm and Sah-bum hopped off. He hopped around and screeched.

Fatemeh hooted at the owl. It bowed low and took off just as her father and brother approached. Without word, Arshad brushed past and continued through the streets.

"Did you just speak to that owl?" Kazem blinked in disbelief.

"Yes, I talk to owls, and let's hope Sah-bum finds Ramon before it's too late."

CHAPTER SEVENTEEN
OWL JUSTICE

Ramon awoke, head throbbing and with an uncomfortable crick in his shoulders and wrists. He tried to adjust his position and realized he'd been chained to a wall, standing upright. He blinked in the darkness, trying to get his bearings. No light penetrated the chamber. An outhouse tang punctuated by dust and mold made him sneeze. Reflexively, he moved to wipe his nose, but the slimy snot remained drying on his upper lip. He wriggled his nose and sneezed again.

The smell seemed little worse than the French Quarter on a hot summer day. That gave him a glimmer of hope. He was underground—perhaps near sewers. Sewers could mean a path to freedom. Then hope fell—sewers could also mask the more unpleasant odors of torture.

He backed up against the wall and tried to give himself some slack and relieve the pressure on his wrists and shoulders. It worked a little. He inched his hands upwards, to feel how the chains were joined into the wall. Before he could make much progress, a crack of light appeared in the gloom before him. A door opened and a blurry form entered. At that point, Ramon realized he no longer wore his glasses.

"Ah, I see you're awake, Mr. Morales." The voice belonged to Hamid Farzan. He closed the distance and Ramon could just discern his features. He wore a robe-like jacket over long pants with a pillbox-shaped hat perched on his head. "You should do your best to relax. You're meeting with my uncle this afternoon."

Ramon's eyebrows came together. "Your uncle?"

"He's a very important man here in Shiraz." Hamid smiled and clasped his hands behind his back. "It's very convenient that you showed up here in Shiraz. It allows us to settle this

221

business between you and me sooner than later."

"Settle this business?" Ramon would have shrugged if the chains had allowed it. "How exactly do you plan to settle it? I thought Fatemeh made it clear she has no interest in being your wife."

Hamid blew out an exasperated huff. "I am a man who gets what I want. I set my eyes on Fatemeh long ago and I intend for her to be mine."

"And what happens when she doesn't cooperate with you? Do you force yourself on her like a common rapist?" Ramon grinned when Hamid stiffened. He pressed his attack. "What happens when you grow tired of her?"

Hamid struck Ramon in the face. His head thudded on the rock wall and terrible pain blossomed. A tickle near his collar made him think blood flowed from a cut, but it could just be dust or a stray thread. With his hands bound, Ramon had no way to check.

"Shut your filthy mouth," growled Hamid. "You don't understand." He stalked away a few steps and collected his thoughts. "When I first met Fatemeh, I realized she was a remarkable girl. She had a knack for languages and medicines. Her presence couldn't help but grow my business." He shrugged, then turned around and faced Ramon. "Of course, I find her pleasurable to look upon as well, but do not presume to think that is the only thing I want. There are many pretty girls. I know of few smarter."

"At least we agree on that." Ramon pursed his lips as he considered. The more he could get Hamid to reveal, the more he could work with. "So, how exactly did you know we were here?"

Hamid gave an off-hand wave. "Your friend Captain Cisneros has been talking to a local businessman named Mazdaki. Understandably, Mr. Mazdaki has also been making inquiries, learning what he can about Cisneros and the people he associates with. He spoke to my uncle and my uncle told me. To be quite honest, I didn't think you'd be foolish enough to come here yourself despite what Fatemeh said before we were all separated. I had planned to capture Cisneros and make him confess his piracy to my uncle and we could bring him up on charges. I thought that would draw you here to Persia. You've saved me a lot of trouble and guesswork."

"So what exactly does your uncle want to talk to me about?" Ramon looked up at the chains. "You have me where you want me."

"My uncle is a very moral man and I respect that. He wants to confirm for himself that you committed adultery and that you are a murderer who consorts with pirates. He wants to look you in the eye and see what kind of man you are before he orders your death."

Ramon frowned. "Taking the law into your own hands?"

"In times of great immorality, such measures are sometimes necessary."

"You're willing to risk murder charges for revenge?" Ramon shook his head, but regretted it after a sharp pain shot up his neck.

"Murder charges? As far as anyone is concerned, you're one of many people who disappeared while walking the streets at night." Hamid reached inside his jacket and retrieved a copy of the book *Owl Riders*. "This book is getting wide distribution. I lost my first copy, but I managed to buy another from some British soldiers here in Shiraz. Seems they enjoy reading about the Russians getting their comeuppance. Either way, it's pretty damning evidence. Especially the parts that say you married Fatemeh even though she was betrothed to me and that you consort with pirates such as Captain Cisneros."

Ramon sighed. "Even if you succeed in getting me killed, Fatemeh won't return to you. She'd die before then."

"A mother kill herself before her child is grown?" Hamid's eyebrows raised in mock alarm. "She knows very well I can provide for her child." He shrugged. "She might not prefer me over you, but she's far too practical to stay away forever and to deny herself to me through the chasm of death."

Ramon slumped, letting the chains take his weight. The chains pulled on his muscles and the bruises from the earlier beating screamed a silent protest. He forced himself to stand upright.

"No matter how this plays out, I win." Hamid tipped his hat and left the chamber, pulling the door closed behind him.

Ramon gritted his teeth. He would be missed and so would Billy. Had Fatemeh gone searching yet? He still held hope that Hamid's plans could be thwarted if Fatemeh and Cisneros found him before he met this uncle. He wanted to make the sign of the cross and say a prayer. He settled for a simple request. "God, let Fatemeh find my trail, and hurry!"

Fatemeh waited in the alley facing Bazaar Vakil while Sah-bum flew over the adjoining neighborhoods. Even before sunrise, merchants entered to prepare the shops for the day's business. Sah-bum returned and perched on the roof overlooking the alley and gave two gentle hoots.

"Get down here, you silly bird." Fatemeh held out her arm and the owl descended and perched on the leather glove.

It looked at her, trilled and gave another hoot.

"Lead us to Ramon." The owl spread its wings and returned to the roof, looked into the distance and squawked its annoyance. "All right, all right." Fatemeh waved for the owl to continue. She did her best to keep the owl in sight as it led her along streets and through alleyways. Her father remained close behind.

At last, they reached a posh, residential neighborhood. The owl flew to a gate surrounding an ornate garden. It looked toward the main house beyond the garden. Fatemeh walked up to the gate and looked across at the imposing manor house. "I don't suppose we could just go in and knock."

"That is Samir Pahlavi's house," said Fatemeh's father. "He is a respected mullah, but he's often expressed his frustration with the civil courts. He's also Farzan's uncle. Somehow, I don't think we'd be welcome with open arms."

"If he's a mullah, surely that means there'll be a trial in a sharia court." Fatemeh shrugged. If there was a trial they could watch and help if the opportunity arose.

Her father shook his head. "I fear if Hamid has captured Ramon, he intends to see him dead. It is said Pahlavi has ways to make that happen if he believes the offender deserves it."

Fatemeh looked through the gate. "I see two sentries by

the door. I suspect there are more in the orchard. If they're holding Ramon in the house, going through the garden is the easiest way to get ourselves hemmed in."

"Let's go back home," said Kazem. "Hopefully your Captain Cisneros is there by now."

They returned to the Karimi's more modest home where Captain Cisneros and his first mate, Mr. Gonzalez, sat in the main room, next to Billy. "Your ... brother brought us here, but then disappeared into a back room. Billy's filled us in."

Fatemeh looked out through the front door and whistled for Sah-bum. The owl flew in through the door and landed on its perch. She then gestured for all to come into the dining room. Billy started to rise, but Fatemeh told him to lie still. He shook his head and forced himself to stand. He swayed for a moment then followed the others.

Fatemeh did her best to explain the situation as she understood it. "Hamid is obsessed with me and won't let me go. He killed his own ship's captain in his foolish quest. At this point, he's doing anything he can to get Ramon out of the way." She repeated her explanation in Persian so her father and mother would understand.

Her father considered that, then nodded. "He's too obsessed with you to hurt you."

"That's what I believe, too."

Cisneros removed his hat and scratched his head. "So why not just have Ramon and me arrested and bring us up on piracy charges?"

"If he goes through legal channels, he risks losing. Not only is there the matter of killing his own captain, there's the fact that kidnapping me initiated everything. If he went into open court, he might win, but he would still damage his own reputation."

Her father sat in silence for a long moment, then looked up. "I know men who helped build Pahlavi's compound. They bought surveying instruments from me. I believe there might be an underground passageway to get inside unobserved."

"Can you find out, for certain?" Fatemeh's eyes widened with renewed hope.

He nodded and left. Fatemeh turned to the others. "We

need to sneak in, find where they're holding Ramon and get him out as quickly and quietly as possible. Then I think it'll be time to leave."

"I had a good meeting with Mazdaki yesterday. I'd like to meet with him again, but there aren't any terms we can't conclude over wireless. If we need to leave right away, we can." Captain Cisneros folded his arms and glanced at his first mate, who nodded agreement.

Alethea emerged from the bedroom with sleep-tangled hair. "I've been listening from the other room. Is daddy in trouble?" She sat on Fatemeh's lap.

"Your daddy's been captured by some ... misguided men." She considered the best way to explain the situation to her daughter. "Misguided men can be very dangerous and twist the truth to match their own beliefs."

Billy leaned forward. "Don't you worry none, little Missy. Ol' Billy here is going to do everything he can to bring your daddy back safe and sound."

Anahita entered the room and beckoned Alethea over. Alethea sat in her grandmother's lap. The older woman began to brush out the tangles in her granddaughter's hair. Fatemeh noticed Alethea didn't fuss and squirm for her grandmother. If they made it through this, she'd have to learn that trick.

Fatemeh's father returned just then with a set of plans. He rolled them out across the table and pointed to a few locations in adjacent buildings. He then pointed to a big chamber in the basement, underneath the garden, near the big house.

Cisneros tensed. "I've seen chambers like that—under Mexico City. Those are dungeons." The raw pain in the captain's voice made Fatemeh shiver. She knew he lost property and was taken prisoner in the Mexican War of Independence, but didn't know many details.

Fatemeh looked from Billy to the captain. "Do you think we can make our way through those tunnels to get to the dungeon? I'll bet that's where Ramon is locked up. They have patrols all through the garden and could fire on us from any direction."

Billy tapped the plans.

"I see what you mean. In tunnels, the bad guys will always

be in front of us. And they probably rely on locked doors to keep people out in the first place. I imagine there will be fewer guards in the tunnels than outside the house." He shook his head as he studied the plans. "Only problem is, those tunnels are also going to hem us in."

"Someone fires a gun in there, it'll ricochet and turn it into a death trap." First mate Gonzalez grinned as though the idea amused him.

"Good thing lightning guns don't ricochet." The captain's sober assessment tempered his first mate's bravado. "They'll also blind those used to working in dark spaces."

Fatemeh considered that. She would prefer a peaceful solution to going in with guns blazing, but this plan seemed like the best way to minimize casualties. She'd gotten Ramon into this situation. She would get him out.

"How long will it take you to get ready?"

The captain consulted with Mr. Gonzalez.

"Give us an hour," said Cisneros, when he looked up.

"All right, meet back here. I'll help mom get some breakfast ready."

All seemed cheered by the prospect of breakfast. Cisneros, Billy, and Gonzalez left Fatemeh alone with her daughter, dad, and mom. She looked into her father's eyes and saw a deep sadness there.

"When this is done, will I ever see you again?"

"It depends on how all this comes out." Her answer was the honest one, but she regretted it when he looked down at the table. Her mother reached out and took his hand. Fatemeh smiled at them. "Thank you for all your help. It means everything to me that you're helping me to rescue Ramon."

He nodded. "I wish he were Mohammedan and spoke our language, but he seems a good man."

"He is." She stood and walked to the kitchen with her mother and daughter close behind.

Ramon tried to keep track of the time. The lack of reference points in the darkened chamber, though, encouraged his mind to wander and he lost focus. He considered the alien, Legion. It left Earth eight years ago. He didn't miss the alien's chatter inside his mind and he didn't miss its interference in Earth's affairs, but he sure wished he could call upon it now to let someone know where he was.

Ramon wasn't certain whether or not he still had the airship's clacker unit. He suspected Hamid's men had searched him and confiscated it, but even if he did have it, he couldn't use it with his arms chained up. Perhaps if they unchained him, he'd have an opportunity.

He feared he couldn't reason with Hamid. The man was a jealous, jilted lover with enough money to get what he wanted. Some people thought they could buy everything. Hamid didn't understand that Fatemeh would resist him no matter what. Even if he killed Ramon, even if he held her affections hostage through Alethea, Fatemeh would find ways to resist.

Again, Ramon's thoughts drifted toward Legion. If Legion were there, the alien might analyze the stone for weaknesses or tell him how he could dislocate the bones in his hand to pull them from the cuffs.

He reached back and tested the point where the chain anchored into the masonry again. Pulling had no effect, but this time he tried twisting. He thought the anchor bolt gave just a little. He turned and twisted it again.

Just as he thought he made a little progress, the door opened. A man he didn't recognize walked forward and unlocked Ramon's cuffs. Ramon slid down the wall until he slumped on the floor. He rubbed his chafed wrists. The big man grabbed him under the arm and hefted him to his feet.

The stranger shoved Ramon out into a corridor illuminated with gas lights. As he did, Ramon ran his hands along his belt. No clacker. They walked around the corner into a small room with a desk and a few chairs—a nice informal office, if not for its proximity to a room with chains on the wall. A bearded man in an elaborate, purple jacket sat at the desk. Hamid occupied one of the chairs.

The burly man pointed to an empty chair.

The man at the desk looked Ramon up and down, then spoke to Hamid in Persian. Hamid spoke the word mullah a few times. Ramon realized that must be the man's title. He didn't think that was the word for uncle, but Hamid had said his uncle was a very important man. Hamid handed over some official-looking documents and passed his uncle a copy of *Owl Riders*.

The older man scanned the documents, then opened the book to an indicated passage. Ramon wondered if he could speak and read English. If so, he wished this mullah or even Hamid would tell him what was going on. Would he even get a chance to speak in his own defense? Would it matter if he did?

The older man nodded to Hamid, then looked up at Ramon. "You're name is Ramon Morales?" he spoke in English.

"Yes, sir." Ramon swallowed. "May I know how to address you, sir?"

"I am Mullah Samir Pahlavi, an official here in Shiraz."

"Then, am I to take it this is an official proceeding, sir?"

Instead of answering, the mullah asked a question. "Mr. Morales, did you engage in … sexual relations with the woman known as Fatemeh Karimi?" Ramon wondered if the hesitance he used to speak the words "sexual relations" were the result of taboo, disgust, or just lack of English fluency.

"I have been married to her these last eight years, your honor. I have nothing to be ashamed of. We have a child."

Ramon hoped that last might move the mullah to sympathy. Instead, the old man scrunched up his face in apparent disgust. He turned and spoke in Persian to Hamid, who in turn made some placating gestures.

The mullah turned toward Ramon. "I am also told you killed many practitioners of Islam on the trading vessel called *Fatemeh*."

"Only in self-defense, sir." Ramon leaned forward. "I would be happy to make my case in open court in front of witnesses. I have witnesses here in Shiraz who will speak on my behalf. I'm willing to wait until the surviving crew of the *Fatemeh* may be called to testify."

"And yet this book—this *Owl Riders*—says you consort with pirates." The mullah shook his head. "I see no need to burden the courts with this crime. You will be duly punished at sunset."

Ramon wished he had his glasses so he could better read the mullah's face. He leaned forward. "Punished? In what way am I to be punished?"

"You are to be executed and removed as a burden to society." The mullah stood, nothing more to say.

"What about Fatemeh? Will you punish her?"

The mullah paused before leaving. "Mr. Farzan has decided to forgive her and she did not murder a ship's crew." With that, the mullah left the room.

The burly guard hauled Ramon to his feet and back around the corner to the dark cell, and chained him up. His stomach rumbled. "Don't I at least get a last meal?"

If the guard understood, he gave no indication. He left, closing the door behind him, leaving Ramon in utter darkness. Ramon hoped someone had figured out where he was and would get him out before sunset.

Billy bounced a croquet ball against a wall across from him. The wooden ball made a thud against the plaster, bounced on the ground and he swept it from the air each time. Fatemeh would have preferred more quiet, but children shouted and carts rolled through the street, making even more noise. Billy claimed the ball's rhythm helped him think. Given the beating he'd taken, she'd argued he should stay behind, but he wouldn't hear of it. Ramon needed help. Still, Fatemeh wished he wouldn't bounce the ball and risk calling attention to them.

They watched for another hour. One guard stood near the door. Every half hour, another guard strode around the perimeter and would check on the sentry by the entrance. They timed their first attack five minutes after the check-in.

Billy pocketed the croquet ball in his jacket then followed Captain Cisneros across the street where they dispatched the guard standing outside the tunnel entrance. According to Fatemeh's father, the mullah had the tunnel built as a way to discretely bring his enemies to special holding cells below, away from prying eyes.

Billy found a key on the guard's belt and they let themselves into the tunnel. They dragged the guard inside and closed the door behind them. Captain Cisneros took point as they traversed the tunnel, followed by Fatemeh. Billy, also armed with one of the captain's lightning guns, took up the rear. They walked half-way down the tunnel before they encountered any resistance. A guard stepped out from an alcove and challenged them.

Without an answer, Cisneros fired the lightning gun on its lowest setting, illuminating the corridor as a loud crack echoed through the chamber. The blast sent the guard to the ground, flopping like a fish. The captain, Billy, and Fatemeh charged ahead. Another man shouted and more guards appeared, framed by a lighted archway at the end of the tunnel.

Cisneros, Fatemeh and Billy flattened themselves against the tunnel walls as a hail of bullets flew their way. Fatemeh closed her eyes, praying they wouldn't get hit or that a bullet wouldn't ricochet into them.

Once the gunshot echoes died down, the tunnel fell quiet. A drop of water plinked against the ground. A moment later, feet shuffled and gun bolts were shoved back. Cisneros leapt into the hallway and fired the lightning gun again. The private soldiers fell back. He pressed himself against the wall as the guards unleashed another volley. Billy cursed as a bullet took his hat off.

"I'm okay," he mouthed as Fatemeh shot him a concerned glance.

Again, the soldiers needed to pause to reload. Cisneros leapt out, fired, charged forward and fired again. Two men fell back around the corner. A third stood his ground and fired. The bullet hit the captain's arm and he dropped the lightning gun's wand. Fatemeh's brow creased when she realized no blood spattered. Billy charged forward, firing his gun, charring the man who'd shot Cisneros. Fatemeh rushed up to the captain and examined his arm. Instead of blood and ragged tissue, pistons and severed control lines stood behind ripped cloth. "I'll be okay," he said through gritted teeth, then picked up the lightning gun's wand with his good hand.

The three hustled forward to a point where the tunnel widened into a circular space.

The ceiling opened to the sky above, letting natural light

fall in. Fatemeh guessed they must be below the mullah's courtyard. Several doors led away from the open chamber. The guards had spread out, so those who remained could not be taken out with a single blast from the lightning gun.

Two men strode down a staircase. One was an older man in fine clothes, who Fatemeh guessed must be the mullah. Hamid followed him.

"Stop!" cried the older man. "What is the meaning of this assault?"

"You have taken my husband." Fatemeh took a step forward and placed her hands on her hips. "You hold him outside of Persian civil authority. We demand he be returned."

"You may take his body as soon as the execution is complete," said the mullah.

Fatemeh looked from Cisneros to Billy.

"Drop your weapons and you may come and see." Hamid beckoned them forward.

"Like hell." Billy tightened his grip on his lightning gun's wand.

Fatemeh placed her hand on Billy's arm.

"Maybe we should go with them. They'll lead us right to Ramon. As it stands, we don't know where he is."

Billy sneered, but he lowered the lightning gun's power pack from his back. Fatemeh helped Cisneros do the same. As they relinquished their weapons, the guards eased closer. The mullah and Hamid led the way into a darkened chamber.

When Fatemeh's eyes adjusted, she gasped.

"You see," said Hamid, "you've arrived just in time to see justice dispensed."

Two guards held Ramon down, his head on a chopping block. An executioner stood behind and lifted an axe aloft.

"Corazón?" Ramon's glasses were gone and he tried to focus.

Fatemeh tried to rush forward, but Cisneros held her back.

CHAPTER EIGHTEEN
EXECUTED PLANS

With all eyes on the executioner, Billy slipped his hand in his pocket and produced the croquet ball he'd been playing with earlier. He hurled it straight at the executioner, knocking him backwards. The axe clattered to the ground and Ramon rolled away from the chopping block.

Before Hamid or the mullah could react, Fatemeh whistled. Sah-bum flew in through the hole that let in light from the courtyard and entered the dungeon's darkness. He swooped in at Hamid, who flailed, tripped over his own feet, and landed with a thud.

Billy rushed forward, helped Ramon to his feet, and brought him back with the others where Fatemeh untied his wrists. Sah-bum then launched himself at the mullah who ran out into the underground courtyard to escape the bird's talons. Captain Cisneros retreated after the mullah, his limp right arm flopping at his side.

Fatemeh gathered Ramon into her arms while Billy subdued the executioner, locking him into the manacles that recently held Ramon. Billy pointed his chin toward Hamid. "Shall we do the same to him?"

Fatemeh narrowed her gaze at Hamid and studied him. "Hamid, don't you realize you can't buy everything you want? Why would you think I would go with you just because Ramon had died?"

"Because you would seek to protect your child." Hamid rose to his knees and dusted off his backside. "Helping me would be the best way to assure Alethea has everything she could want."

Billy knelt low, ready to tackle him should he make any sudden moves.

233

"Everything money could buy," spat Fatemeh. "Everything but freedom. That's what I sought and it's what I'm taking back for myself and my family. Time for you to face the consequences of your actions."

"My actions are just." Hamid stood. "Just as my uncle, the scholar, agreed."

Fatemeh shook her head, then called Billy over and they locked him into a set of manacles next to the executioner.

Fatemeh, Ramon, and Billy left the dungeon and entered the underground courtyard. There, Captain Cisneros knelt next to the lightning gun's power supply, aiming the wand at the mullah with his left hand. The guards had fled, fearing the lightning gun and the owl's wrath. The bird had found a perch in the shadows and sat with its eyes closed, looking rather pleased with itself.

A clatter sounded from an adjoining stairwell and soon men in Shiraz police uniforms burst through the door and surrounded the mullah. A man in a nice jacket appeared, followed by Fatemeh's father.

"Samir Pahlavi," said the official with his hands on his hips. "You are under arrest for assault and attempted murder. You must come with us."

"I am an arbiter of sacred law, Mayor," sneered Pahlavi.

"That doesn't give you the right to order or conduct executions." The mayor shook his head. "Only the shah may do that."

"You don't have evidence that I've executed anyone!"

"Then why is there a chopping block and axe in the next room?" Fatemeh folded her arms. "And what about the man in an executioner's hood my friends subdued in the room beyond that?"

The mayor balanced a pair of pince-nez spectacles on his nose, then nodded to two of his men to check out the story. Fatemeh saw the lost expressions on Billy and Ramon's faces and relayed what was happening to them. Billy followed the police officers to help them if he could. After they left, the mayor turned to Kazem. "And who are these people?"

"My daughter and her companions," said Kazem. "I will bring a signed affidavit of what she and her friends have seen to the police tomorrow morning."

The police officers returned from the other room leading Hamid and the executioner. With a gesture from the mayor, the police officers escorted them along with the mullah up the stairs.

Billy walked up to Fatemeh and Ramon, holding a pair of glasses. "I found these near the wall where we chained Hamid. I didn't want them to get stepped on."

"Thank you, my friend." Ramon croaked out the words through a dry mouth.

Kazem eyed Captain Cisneros, then knelt down beside him. "May I?" He pointed to the hole in the captain's mechanical arm.

The captain gave a nod.

Kazem examined the arm and nodded. "That's nice work. I think I can repair it for you." He spoke in Persian, but Fatemeh translated for the captain's benefit.

"I would appreciate that." Cisneros stood and led the way back up through the tunnel and out into Shiraz's streets. From there, Fatemeh led the group back to her father's house where she tended to Ramon's injuries. Anahita Karimi prepared dinner and all but Kazem and Captain Cisneros dove in. Anahita smiled at their enthusiasm. Then she turned to her daughter and sighed.

"It will be goodbye soon, won't it?" Fatemeh's mother looked down at her granddaughter. "I have enjoyed Alethea's company. She is wise beyond her years."

"Thank you, Grandmother." Alethea spoke in clear Persian.

"We need to get home." Fatemeh reached out and took her mother's hand. "Alethea needs to get back to school."

A pained look crossed Anahita's face, but she squeezed her daughter and granddaughter's hands and nodded. "She will make you proud."

"Also, Ramon has important work to do. I've kept him too long."

"Perhaps not long enough." Anahita chuckled. "From what I've seen, you should keep him as long as you can."

Fatemeh blinked at her mother's wry remark, then chuckled

along with her before turning her attention to her father and the captain.

Kazem retrieved a tool kit and clipped away the cloth where the bullet had struck the captain's arm. He donned lenses mounted to a headband and examined the damage. Ramon winced when Mr. Karimi clipped the gutta-percha "skin" covering the mechanical arm, even though it didn't appear to bother the captain.

"What I don't get is this," said Billy, "if the mullah couldn't execute people legally, why did Farzan even take you to his uncle's house?"

"Murder me on the street in front of potential witnesses?" Ramon shook his head. "He wanted me out of the way. His uncle had the money and the means to do that quickly and out of public sight. If someone did find out, his uncle commanded enough respect in the community to talk his way out of it. He could make arguments about my faith and the actions we took rescuing Fatemeh."

Alethea shivered.

"That sounds like something Francoise told me about. She told me a story about white men who came one night, took a friend of her daddy's, and hung him. She said the white men made up stories that he'd done something bad to a white girl to convince themselves they were right, but they were just angry that he was a free black man."

Fatemeh held out her hand and invited Alethea to sit on her lap. "That's exactly what happened, Alethea joon." She looked back at her mother and spoke in Persian. "Wise beyond her years."

"She'll be trouble." Anahita winked at her daughter. "Just like you, Fatemeh joon."

"So, what happens to Hamid now?" asked Billy.

Fatemeh relayed the question to her father who shrugged.

"He is rich enough, he might bribe his way out of jail before long." Fatemeh nodded and relayed his answer.

Billy narrowed his gaze.

"We stopped him and his friends once, we can do it again!"

Ramon rubbed his neck. "We may have stopped him, but he came a little close to succeeding for my taste."

Alethea hopped off Fatemeh's lap and climbed into Ramon's. She cuddled in close and Ramon smiled.

Fatemeh looked over to her mother, then to her father who pulled the damaged ends of a control cable from the captain's mechanical arm. Once finished, he looked up and lifted the magnifying glasses. She reached out and took his hand. He gave her a sad smile.

"I wish we could stay. There is more to repair in Shiraz than the good captain's injury." Deep down, she wanted to stay and find other Bahá'ís. She yearned to hear new teachings, but left that part unspoken. She'd found peace with her father and mother. She wouldn't waste these precious last minutes breaking that peace.

Kazem didn't respond to Fatemeh's musings. He nodded to the captain and left the room.

Ramon cocked his head. "I wondered about your new-found strength. When did you get the new arm?"

The captain's fluttering smile betrayed more embarrassment than pride. "I build large machinery. Accidents happen." He shrugged his one good shoulder. "I took advantage of my resources to build a replacement."

Billy tossed his croquet ball in the air and caught it.

"Seems like everyone will want their own before long."

Again, the captain shrugged his good shoulder.

"It's a mixed blessing. Yes, I have strength, but no sense of touch. I can't caress soft skin or feel a light breeze. What's more, this new arm is still prone to injury as you've seen." The captain paused and snorted a laugh. "Fortunately, you get your healing gifts from your father."

Fatemeh almost choked on the realization as her father returned with a control cable for the captain's arm and a piece of paper. He set the cable down, then showed the paper to Fatemeh. It was the contract binding her to Hamid Farzan. "I will take this into the court and tell them I have annulled the betrothal, but Hamid has refused to return the dowry, which is the truth."

"You could have done this before."

Anahita cleared her throat. "If your father had taken this action before now, your sisters might not have found husbands.

People would have talked and said your father goes back on his word."

Kazem stepped over to his wife.

"Am I wrong to do this?"

She shook her head.

"I think you should have done it a long time ago." Fatemeh's parents kissed.

Kazem blushed then pointed to Fatemeh.

"What are you standing around for? Get paper and write. You need to give me an affidavit as well, or that villain Pahlavi and his nephew will be back home within a few days and they won't have to bother with bribes."

Fatemeh hugged her father, then released him to retrieve paper and pen. Kazem left the betrothal contract on the table and retrieved the new control cable. Fatemeh wrote out an account of what she saw in the mullah's underground lair. She translated what she wrote for Ramon.

"Anything to add?"

"A few details about being locked in a dungeon without food or water for most of the day."

"Go ahead and add them in English. Someone at the court can translate," said Fatemeh. As she passed the paper to Ramon, Kazem screwed down one end of the control cable and cleared his throat.

"I may have to go to court to testify against Pahlavi and Farzan. That may take me away from my shop for many hours. I want just one thing in return." He held the control cable along the captain's arm to measure length.

Fatemeh swallowed, her throat tight. "What is that, papa?"

"You must bring your daughter to visit again. Your mother has been allowed to spoil her rotten and I have seen very little of her." He looked over his shoulder and winked. "It's why I'm repairing the good captain's arm, so you will have a pilot who knows the way."

Fatemeh translated for Cisneros, who smiled and nodded. "Indeed. I hope to be back to sign a contract with Behzad Mazdaki."

"That crook?" Kazem apparently recognized the name. He screwed down the other end of the control cable. "I can introduce you to much better trading partners."

"Crook?" Alethea looked from Fatemeh to Ramon. "I thought he was the one who got mom..."

Ramon covered her mouth with his hand before she could break the peace and goodwill in the room. Kazem had spoken Persian and Alethea English, but Fatemeh was glad her husband didn't take chances.

The captain held out his arm and flexed his hand when Fatemeh translated. "Good as new."

Ramon passed the affidavit with his additions to Fatemeh. She placed it with the betrothal document.

Anahita placed her hand on her daughter's arm. "Are you certain you cannot stay for just a little longer?"

"I wish we could, mama. If it was just Hamid, we might." Fatemeh shook her head. "We need to get back to New Orleans and see if Ramon still has a job." She swallowed. "I also have a business to run."

"Blessed Life Apothecary," affirmed Anahita. "Yes, Alethea has told me." She pulled her daughter into a tight embrace and let the tears flow. "Go and may Allah go with you."

After dinner, Kazem, Anahita, and Arshad Karimi walked with Ramon, Fatemeh, Alethea, Captain Cisneros, and Billy back to the *Tiburón*. Ramon was glad to be on the way home with Fatemeh at his side, but as they walked through the moonlit streets, the sounds of crickets, subdued conversations through open doorways, and the scents of meals cooking made him long to explore this place and learn more about the people—the good people. He rubbed his neck. Not those who wanted him dead.

When they reached the airship, they found most of the curiosity seekers had gone home for the night. Mr. Gonzalez lowered the cargo gangplank as they stepped into the glare of the ornithopter's battery-powered lights. Pilots already sat in the ornithopters, ready to release the airship and follow it into the sky. Fatemeh hugged each member of her family in turn. Arshad gave a reluctant and hesitant hug, but both Kazem and Anahita held their daughter and granddaughter for a long time. At last, Fatemeh turned away with tears glistening on her moonlit cheeks. She took Ramon's hand and Alethea's, and walked up the gangplank.

"Are you sure you don't want to bring your owl with you?" asked Ramon "I'm sure it would be okay with Captain Cisneros."

"Sah-bum is not mom's owl," said Alethea, "only a creature who has chosen to live at grandma and grandpa's house."

Fatemeh smiled down at her daughter. "Indeed. He is old and cranky and will be happiest if he is not forced to move at this point in his life."

Ramon nodded. They waited for the captain and Billy to board, then followed the captain to the gondola. Ramon, Fatemeh, and Alethea walked to the railing while the captain gave orders for the tether lines to be released and retracted. The airship released ballast and began its slow ascent into the sky. Soon, the ornithopters followed, like an entourage for the dirigible. Ramon held out his arm and Fatemeh leaned in close to him as the gas lamps of Shiraz faded into the distance.

Once the ornithopters entered their bay, the captain shouted new orders and the engines fired up and they began their journey back to America.

Ramon turned and looked into Fatemeh's eyes. "Are you glad you had a chance to see your family again?"

Fatemeh sighed. "It wasn't what I imagined it would be. I thought they would be angry at me for leaving. I thought my father would take Hamid's side. He's a man of strong beliefs."

"The difference between your father and Hamid is that your father loves you. Hamid wanted to possess you. That's why your father could let you go and why Hamid could not."

Fatemeh looked into Ramon's eyes for a long moment, then pulled his head down and kissed him.

"That's why I let you go to Arizona in the first place to negotiate with the Apaches and the Army."

Ramon nodded. "At what cost? We may find it difficult to afford life in New Orleans if I've lost my job."

"Perhaps you can contact them and find out so we can make plans." Fatemeh shrugged. "Between Hamid's arrest and Larissa's report to her superiors you should be free of trouble."

Ramon looked from Fatemeh to Alethea. "Corazón, when I'm with you, I'm never free of trouble." He bent over and kissed his wife again.

EPILOGUE
GUMBO

A s soon as Ramon returned to New Orleans, Albert Leonard handed him a new case. According to the clerk, Jacob Darrant, Leonard had considered hiring a new assistant but drug his feet. "I think he really wanted you back," said Darrant. "But don't tell him I said that."

On the first Saturday night after their return, Ramon and Fatemeh made arrangements for Alethea to spend the night at Marie and Jacques Lalande's place.

Ramon and Fatemeh strolled through the French Quarter and explored old haunts. Ramon pulled Fatemeh into their favorite café. They sat down at an outdoor table adjoining the street. He ordered a glass of wine and she ordered water.

"It's been eight years since we last heard from Legion," said Ramon. "Do you ever think about him? Wonder what's become of him?"

"I wonder how the world would be different if not for Legion's influence."

"Clackers, ornithopters, airships, Jackalopes, battle wagons." Ramon shook his head. "They all owe their existence to Legion. I feel like he gave us these things, then left us to deal with the consequences."

The waiter approached to take their orders. They each ordered gumbo and the waiter left.

Fatemeh put her chin in her hand and considered Ramon's words. "I don't think Legion gave us those things so much as he freed us from our fears and our uncertainties. Humans built those things, but humans built them because he told them they could be built. He told those with money they were worth funding. That's all he did. Even without Legion, we humans would eventually end up in the world we're in now, or one very much like it."

"The question is, are we ready for it?"

"Would we ever be?"

Ramon didn't have an answer to that. The gumbo arrived. Ramon savored andouille sausage and crawfish in a thick roux over rice. Fatemeh had ordered gumbo z'herbes—vegetarian gumbo. "Since Legion left, I'd worried what would happen if a major crisis arose and he wasn't around to help."

"I think you found out." Fatemeh reached across the table and took Ramon's hand. "And you did fine."

Ramon closed his eyes and listened to the cicadas. Strains of piano music wafted down from Bourbon Street. "I've missed New Orleans. Do you think Hamid will leave you alone from now on? He knows where you live. I could easily imagine him coming back some day."

"We have good friends here." Fatemeh flashed him a re-assuring smile. "I know Marie and Jacques Lalande will be on watch for him."

"They didn't keep our daughter from running away." Ramon tossed back a gulp of wine.

A fluttering caught Ramon and Fatemeh's attention. The screech owl perched in a tree overlooking the table. Fatemeh looked up at it and nodded. The owl moved from one foot to the other, then flew off.

"What was that all about?"

"I suspect Alethea's checking up on us." Fatemeh squeezed Ramon's hand and returned to her gumbo. "Legion may be gone, but we have our daughter."

Ramon lifted his wine glass. "I for one think we traded up."

ABOUT THE AUTHOR

David Lee Summers became a steampunk in 1987 when he used a nineteenth century telescope on Nantucket to examine the evolution of distant pulsating stars. Since that time he has published ten novels and numerous short stories and poems spanning a wide range of the imagination. *Owl Dance, Lightning Wolves,* and *The Brazen Shark* are the first three novels of the Clockwork Legion series. His other novels include *The Astronomer's Crypt* and *Vampires of the Scarlet Order.*

David's short stories have appeared in such magazines and anthologies as *Realms of Fantasy, Cemetery Dance, Straight Outta Tombstone, Gears and Levers, Zombiefied: An Anthology of All Things Zombie,* and *These Vampires Don't Sparkle.* He's been twice nominated for the Science Fiction Poetry Association's Rhysling Award.

In addition to writing, David has edited the science fiction anthologies: *A Kepler's Dozen, Kepler's Cowboys,* and *Maximum Velocity: The Best of the Full-Throttle Space Tales.* When not working with the written word, David operates telescopes at Kitt Peak National Observatory. Learn more about David at www. davidleesummers.com.

www.ingramcontent.com/pod-product-compliance
Lightning Source LLC
Chambersburg PA
CBHW022107240626
47153CB00007B/2263